COUNT
THEIR
GRAVES

BOOKS BY JENNIFER CHASE

JENNIFER CHASE

COUNT THEIR GRAVES

bookouture

Published by Bookouture in 2024

An imprint of Storyfire Ltd.
Carmelite House
50 Victoria Embankment
London EC4Y 0DZ

www.bookouture.com

ISBN: 978-1-83525-636-7
eBook ISBN: 978-1-83525-635-0

For Barbara

ONE

Detective Katie Scott ran every morning unless weather or work prohibited it. This particular morning she was motivated to switch up her usual running routine. It was good to change a habit—at least she thought so as she climbed the steep incline to get to the Bramble Trail. Her life had returned to normal with her fiancé home safe, and the stream of cold cases she was investigating was buzzing through her mind. She preferred to clear her head in solitude, in rural settings, before beginning her demanding day.

"C'mon, Cisco," she called behind her.

The jet-black German shepherd immediately stopped sniffing the low-lying bushes and downed pine tree limbs and easily bounded up the trail behind Katie with his focus now completely on his partner.

After two Army tours in Afghanistan as a bomb K9 team, Katie was able to bring her military dog Cisco home with her to Pine Valley, California. Even though the dog was a retired veteran, he often accompanied Katie on her cases when large areas needed to be searched or when she needed extra security. Katie currently headed up the cold-case unit for the Pine Valley Sheriff's Department with her partner, Detective Sean McGaven.

The morning air was exceptionally cool and invigorating, filling her lungs as she pushed her body harder until she reached the top of the incline, where it leveled out and weaved along the ridge of the Bramble Trail. Her legs tightened and her breath became intense, but she didn't slow down. Cisco had dashed ahead and was waiting for her at the top—tongue out and ears alert, staring down.

Once at the top of the ridge, Katie paused and admired the view, feeling like she was on the top of the world. It was a place where she could take a deep breath and let whatever was bothering her fade away. There were a few houses in the surrounding area with extended acreage, but it didn't take away from the sense of being alone in nature. The towering pine trees were dense with thick branches and loomed above, producing a wonderful aroma. Down in the valley, there was a faint sound of one of the meandering creeks flowing. She enjoyed the moment as her pulse returned to normal.

Katie picked up her run again, this time at half speed, along the seldom-used trail. The path was slightly uneven, but navigable, and good for more of a workout. As she ran, she noticed that Cisco seemed agitated and not his relaxed self. The dog had tensed his body, tail lowered, and he seemed to have caught a scent in the air. Katie slowed her pace and scanned the area around them. Her senses also heightened. Nothing seemed strange to her—but Cisco still didn't relax. She took the dog's uneasiness seriously. Her hand slid up to the small holstered Beretta under her hoodie, an automatic response whenever there was a possibility of any kind of danger.

Cisco gave a low grumble and his fur prickled along his backbone.

Katie slowed.

The dog barked several times and took off in a full run.

"Cisco!"

Katie watched helplessly as her dog disappeared into the dense forest. Fearful thoughts thundered through her mind of all the potential hazards—bears, rogue hunters, loose dog packs, or armed criminals hiding out.

"Cisco!"

It was not like the dog to disobey Katie's direct commands. Her heart rate increased as she ran after him. She could feel her pulse hammering in her neck.

Dodging through the trees and climbing over a couple of low-lying branches, Katie kept moving as fast as she could, expecting to hear voices and more barking, but it was strangely quiet. She hurried from behind a grouping of pine trees and leaped back onto the trail. She saw Cisco's dark outline standing over a white bundle.

Katie slowed her pace, trying to decipher what the white object was. She moved cautiously, mesmerized by what Cisco was so adamant about alerting her to. The noble dog made several circles around the bundle, nose down, nudging it gently.

"Cisco," she whispered, as suddenly the white bundle moved and a small hand appeared. Cisco nuzzled the tiny fingers.

Katie stumbled forward onto her knees only to discover a little blonde girl with curly locks, dressed in an oversized white nightgown. The lace sleeves were longer than her tiny arms. Katie also noticed red spots splashed across the front and down the sleeves: blood.

"Good boy, Cisco," she said, petting the dog, concerned by their discovery.

Turning her full attention to the little girl, she said, "What are you doing all the way out here, sweetheart?" She looked around to see if there was someone else, but it was deserted.

There was nothing to indicate why the girl was outside. No footprints. No toys or pieces of clothing. It was as if she had been dropped here.

The sleepy-eyed girl appeared to be about four years old. "I'm cold," she barely whispered as she shivered.

"Are you hurt?" said Katie as she looked for any injuries. The girl's skin was icy, as if she had been out in the elements for a while—possibly a few hours. "What's your name, sweetheart?"

"Em... Emily," she said.

"How did you get here?"

"Mommy brought me..."

A chill ran down Katie's spine.

"Okay, Emily. Stay here with Cisco and I'll be right back. Can you do that for me?" Katie wanted to pick the girl up, hug her, and take her to safety, but she needed to assess the area first. Security was her priority and then getting the little girl to safety.

The little girl nodded. Her blue eyes stared at Katie as she pet the dog. It was a look that Katie wouldn't soon forget. The pure innocence struck her soul.

Katie stood up and unzipped her hoodie and then wrapped it around the little girl. The cool morning air hit her as she was now dressed in just a tank top. She pulled her weapon, still scanning the area. There was a farmhouse and barn down below the ridge and she assumed that was where Emily lived. There weren't any other homes within view and most were likely several acres away.

Had the little girl ventured out without anyone knowing? Did the mother really leave her here? Or was there something terribly wrong?

Katie didn't want to move Emily yet until she knew for sure that everything was safe on the property.

"Cisco, you stay."

The dog instinctively downed next to the little girl. Emily's small arms wrapped around the dog's neck as she snuggled up against him for warmth.

Katie looked around and felt that, secluded in between trees, they would be safe until she could quickly search the area. Reaching into her pocket, she made sure her cell phone had a strong signal—which it did.

"Good boy, Cisco. *Bleib... Wache...*" She told Cisco to stay and guard the little girl. Her dog's training words were in German, meaning *stay* and *watch*. Katie didn't need to repeat herself because the dog knew what to do, but somehow it made her feel better. She hated leaving them alone, but it was the best way to proceed under the circumstances. By the time help arrived, it might be too late. She needed to report to dispatch exactly what was going on so that backup wasn't blindly going into a potentially dangerous situation.

After taking one last look at Emily huddled with Cisco, Katie moved to the edge of the trail and began slowly making her way toward the backside of the house. She wondered how Emily got up the hill; there wasn't dirt or mud on her gown.

Watching for any movement, Katie carefully stepped down the incline until she was on a walkway leading to the front of a modern farmhouse. There were unusual scrolled architectural details along the rooflines and windows that made it seem to be a custom build. Katie stopped and listened. The wind had died down and she felt the temperature had risen a few degrees from when she first began her run. Even though it was still cool, her skin was warm and clammy. Adrenalin was pumping, making her arms and legs strangely prickly and a bit shaky. She maintained her focus and continued to press forward. With her gun directed out in front of her, she kept moving, expecting anything.

There was a pickup truck and a minivan parked in the semi-circle driveway, giving the impression that someone was home.

The front of the farmhouse had a large porch with white wicker chairs and colorful pillows. There was a porch swing on one end and potted plants lined up side by side at the other. A cheerful welcome mat said, "Home Sweet Home." A wind chime hung on the left side of the door and gently swayed a melody. There were several pairs of shoes carefully placed to the right side of the mat. By Katie's quick assessment, there were two adults and three children that resided in the home.

The front door was wide open. Droplets of red spattered the porch and the entrance inside. Concentrated smudges were around the doorframe as if someone had tried to steady themselves.

"Hello?" she called out, watching her surroundings.

Nothing moved. No sound came from indoors. Katie's senses were on hyper-alert. Everything seemed more vivid and louder than usual.

She cautiously stepped over the threshold and peered inside. The large open plan made it easy to see the living room, dining room, and kitchen in a quick scan. There were several photographs of the family—and she saw tiny Emily with an older boy and girl. Everything looked neat and orderly. That's what made the bloody hammer lying in the middle of the floor so horrifying.

Katie stood surveying the room for a moment, taking a deep breath. It seemed that the bloody hammer had been dropped there. There were droplets of blood marking a path to the front door. There were no obvious signs of a struggle—no broken items, chairs overturned, or shelves spilled.

Katie turned and could see that the two main doors of the barn just across the open area were standing wide open. She wasn't sure if it was instinct or fear that drove her, but she backed out of the house, careful not to disturb anything, and watchfully headed for the barn. Everything remained still and eerily quiet.

Katie kept to the sides of the barn and inched her way slowly to the opening. Her ears pounded. Her breathing shrank to shallow gasps. Staying low, she entered the building. It wasn't a livestock barn, but rather a type of workshop and storage facility. Katie scanned the interior, taking everything in. Slowly lowering her weapon, she dropped to her knees in misery, only inches from the stagnant pools of blood on the ground in front of her. Barely registering what she saw, she couldn't tear her eyes away from the four bodies of a man, a woman, and a young boy and girl neatly lined up next to each other, still dressed in their pajamas.

TWO

Katie sat with her back against the barn wall, oblivious to the cold floor beneath her. She was numb, in shock. She closed her eyes and pulled her legs up against her chest for a few seconds as she fought her emotions—grief to full-blown anger. The family murder scene wreaked havoc on her soul. She had investigated some of the grisliest crime scenes and seen what cruel acts could happen on the battlefield, but this family lying in front of her was like nothing she had witnessed before. It was the heart-shattering tragedy of senseless murder. She thought about little Emily, who had lost her entire family. Katie knew what it was like, having lost her own parents in a car accident when she was a teen. Those memories flooded back and slashed open old wounds as if it had just happened.

Katie opened her eyes. Nothing had changed except her perspective. Her heart still pounded and her vision seemed to vie with surrounding dizziness. And then... it came. Her body buzzed with a strange but familiar sensation. Returning from the Army, she'd brought home with her the nemesis of post-traumatic stress. She knew that it would never fully be cured, but she had learned to live with it, and to always move forward with her life.

"*Snap out of it*," she muttered under her breath, angry for not holding it together better to continue the search. As she stood up, feeling a bit wobbly, Katie left the barn and quickly jogged around the property, making double sure that no one else was there, while trying not to disturb any possible evidence before returning to Emily and Cisco.

Katie reached the top of the hillside and saw Cisco still huddled with Emily. The child was curled up in a ball next to the regal dog that kept watch over her. Katie continued to pull herself together and focused on what needed to be done. Retrieving her cell phone, she dialed.

"What's your emergency?" said dispatch.

"This is Detective Kathryn Scott, badge number 3692. I'm at... one... six... zero... nine Broadleaf Lane just below the Bramble Trail. Four homicide victims are located in the barn on the property. One surviving family member, approximately four years old, doesn't seem to be injured but I'd like to request medical attention and social services. Please inform patrol I'm here at the property and will meet them."

"Ten-four, Detective. Sending backup. Please stay safe."

Katie ended the call. She sat down on the ground and hugged Emily and Cisco, saying a quiet comforting prayer.

Two patrol cars rolled up to the farmhouse and parked near the truck and minivan.

Katie, holding Emily in her arms and with Cisco following, walked up to meet them.

Deputy Brandon Hansen was the first to exit his cruiser. "Detective Scott," he said, hurrying to her. "Are you hurt?" He didn't hide his expression of concern for a fellow officer. She knew him and had spoken with him a few times about his interest in becoming a detective—he was studying for the exam.

"I'm fine. We need to get this little girl checked out," she said. Emily was sleeping quietly in Katie's arms from exhaustion and cold.

"Where was she?" he asked, looking around the property.

"Up there." Katie pointed to the trail as she spoke softly. "The four bodies are in the barn. Blood inside the house. Take precaution for forensics."

"On it," he said.

"Hansen," called the other officer—Deputy Sasha Brown. Katie shifted her weight, watching the surrounding areas intently as she waited.

Deputy Hansen joined Brown and they began a systematic search of the property and started unrolling crime scene tape at the barn.

Within twenty minutes more emergency vehicles arrived—ambulance, fire truck, detective sedan, county van, and a black truck. Katie watched as each division of first responders rolled onto the property. It didn't take long before the CSU van arrived as well.

A tall man dressed in running attire jumped from the black truck and jogged toward Katie. "You okay?" He looked down at the dog obediently staying at Katie's left side.

"We're all okay." Katie was relieved to see her partner, Detective Sean McGaven. They had worked many cold cases together and he had been her rock during those investigations. They were an unstoppable team.

"What happened?" he said, towering over her.

"Out for a run. I just happened to decide to run the Bramble Trail today. Cisco suddenly took off and found Emily. She said her mother brought her there, but I'm not so sure."

"Out here? Anything could have happened to her. She could

have died if you hadn't decided to change your route today." His expression was serious as he stared at the little girl sleeping in his partner's arms. He left her to find out more information.

Katie nodded and watched him walk away. As everything unfolded around her, she realized exhaustion had begun to set in. The strenuous run and the surging adrenalin dragged at her body. Her legs and arms felt weak.

Katie walked away from the commotion as the scene began to unfold. She found a back patio area where there were two chairs and sat down, a quiet place to gather her thoughts and to keep Emily from the working area. Cisco stayed close, not only to Katie, but to Emily as well. Emily fussed a little bit, but Katie spoke softly to her, rocking her, and gave the child comfort because she knew that life was going to become difficult and forever changed. She couldn't imagine what had gone on at the house and how Emily had waited patiently for someone to return.

Emily woke up and reached for Cisco. It was obvious there was a growing bond between them.

Katie took a few more minutes to keep the calm and give comfort to Emily before she thrust herself into the investigation. She closed her eyes.

"Detective Scott?" said a woman dressed in a dark pantsuit walking up to her. "Detective Hamilton okayed me to take little Emily for medical attention."

"And you are?" said Katie.

"I'm Sandra Crane with county social services. I'm going to escort her to the hospital, until we find either a relative or a temporary foster family that can take her."

Katie nodded, not wanting to relinquish Emily, but she knew it was protocol and in the best interest of the child for protection and medical care. But something nagged at her all the same.

Detective Hamilton approached. "Scott." He nodded his greeting.

"We need protection for this little girl until we know what's going on," said Katie. "And someone needs to try to find out if she can tell us anything about what happened. My priority was to get her to safety."

"Already on it," he said. "Deputy Brown will follow the ambulance to the hospital and she will be assigned to her until further notice, which means anything she says about what happened will be documented."

Katie gave Emily to Ms. Crane. The sleepy little girl made a few whimpers and seemed to want to stay with Katie and Cisco.

"I'll keep you posted," said the social worker to Hamilton.

The detective accompanied them and walked with her to her vehicle.

McGaven approached Katie and eyed her closely. "You're not okay."

"I'm fine."

"I know you. Something really spooked you."

Katie knew she couldn't hide anything from him. They had been through too much together to brush off what she was feeling. "It's just... seeing that family lined up in the barn. It really got to me." And she couldn't stop thinking about Emily all alone.

McGaven looked around before continuing. "What do you think?"

"I honestly don't know—yet." But her mind was already running possible scenarios.

"Looks like Hamilton will be taking over the case."

"Most likely," she said as she watched the investigative scene continue around them.

Forensic supervisor John Blackburn approached the detectives. He was carrying a sheriff's department jacket. "I thought you might need this," he said, handing the coat to Katie.

"Thank you." She put it on, not realizing how cold she was until she had warmth over her arms. She zipped up the jacket and instinctively put her hands in the pockets.

"You okay?" asked John.

Katie couldn't help but smile. "I will be."

John cracked a small smile. He had helped Katie and McGaven on several cases and not just with forensics, as he was also a military veteran and a former Navy Seal. He nodded and returned to identifying and documenting the scenes.

"Unless we're needed here, I'll give you and Cisco a ride home," said McGaven still surveying the area.

"I don't know..." she said.

A white SUV drove in, which meant that Sheriff Wayne Scott wanted to see the crime scene firsthand. He exited the vehicle walking with purpose and headed straight for Hamilton. Katie was amazed how good the sheriff looked, with slightly silver-gray hair and crinkled eyes. He was fit despite his age. With the respect he commanded from all those around him, it was no wonder he was sheriff of Sequoia County. He was also her uncle.

"He looks serious," said McGaven.

"More than usual," she said.

Cisco gave a low whine.

After Sheriff Scott finished speaking with Hamilton, he headed straight for Katie and McGaven.

Katie zipped up her jacket tighter as a chill rippled through her body.

"Detectives," said the sheriff.

"Sir," said McGaven.

"Everything okay?" Katie asked. She got the feeling there was something new they didn't know.

"I just received a notice."

"What do you mean?" she said. Her curiosity kicked into high gear.

The sheriff took a breath and paused as if he was carefully preparing his words. Katie and McGaven watched him and waited. The steady work on the crime scene around the farmhouse and barn was still moving forward around them.

"It has come to my attention that the family here was in witness protection," said the sheriff.

"Witness protection?" said Katie. Her investigative mind spun.

He nodded. "When the nine-one-one call came in for this address, it triggered an alert to the US Marshals. And in turn, a call came directly into me."

"That fast?" said McGaven.

"Yes." His expression remained grim as he glanced around the property.

"What's going to happen with the investigation now?" she said.

"It gets tricky. It's my jurisdiction and I oversee the murder investigation; however, the US Marshals Service also has responsibilities."

"So it's a combined investigation—a dual jurisdiction?" she said. "Isn't that going to slow down the process? I'm sure there's information they can't share with us."

"That's where the lines can get blurry—and messy."

"It's still a homicide. An entire family was murdered. That's what should be the immediate priority," she said.

"You're right," the sheriff said. "That's why I'm assigning you and McGaven to work the case with whoever they send over from the Marshals' office in Sacramento."

Katie let out a breath. "You sure? Gav and I have tons of cold cases. Why doesn't Hamilton work with the US Marshal?"

"I'm surprised to hear you say that."

It wasn't that she didn't want to investigate the case. But she knew there were going to be political and departmental issues, which weren't something she looked forward to dealing with.

She didn't want the investigation to grind to a halt because of warring protocols.

"I can just see it's going to get messy," she said.

"Well, you're going to have to work with it. I'm not changing my mind." Sheriff Scott never minced words.

"What about the US Marshal?" she said.

"I don't know when he will arrive... something about another case first. His name is..." He reached into his pocket and pulled a small notebook. "Marshal Kyle West."

"When will he be here?"

"Don't know his ETA. But he will be in touch with you. He has both of your contact information. Hamilton will be working another homicide and burglary case near the warehouse district. So I'd suggest you both get to work on these scenes."

"Yes, sir," said McGaven.

"We're on it," said Katie.

"Oh," said the sheriff. "I know it puts your cold cases on hold, but I wanted my best detectives working this case." He cracked a small smile and walked back to the scene to speak with Hamilton before he left.

"I guess there's no time to go home to change clothes," said McGaven.

"Nope."

"You can put Cisco in my truck for now."

"Thanks."

"And you can get me up to speed. Starting with telling me step-by-step everything you saw."

Katie nodded. "Let's get to work."

THREE

Katie and McGaven began with the farmhouse since it appeared that was where the struggle began. The detectives stood on the porch planning the best way to conduct their search. They pulled on gloves and covered their shoes with protective booties. McGaven held several evidence markers ready for the interior of the house.

Through police databases and the US Marshals Service, the parents were identified as Robert and Samantha Banks, with three children: Riley, Tyler, and Emily. Now they knew who they were dealing with—at least their new identities—and could begin to piece together their last moments.

"Detectives," said Deputy Hansen. "On the other side of the house, the window in the bathroom appears to be the forced entry."

"Thank you," said Katie. She turned to McGaven. "Let's check it out."

"John and Eva are still working the barn," said the deputy.

"And haven't been to the house yet. Probably be about an hour or so." He jogged back to the barn area.

"Thanks," said McGaven after the deputy.

"He's a good officer," said Katie.

"I agree. And a cool guy." He smiled.

Katie and McGaven walked around the house checking for anything that seemed suspicious until they saw the window above the bathtub that appeared to have been pried open.

"Interesting point of entry," said McGaven scrutinizing it. Looking down along the cleared flower bed, "There doesn't seem to be any footprints. Strange."

Katie looked closely, using extra care not to disturb any potential evidence. "It was pried open, maybe with a screwdriver, and it's made some scrape marks. But... I don't think the window was actually opened, except for a crack." She peered through the window and saw a large bathroom, probably the main one. "There would be some dirt in the tub directly below, but it's clean." She gently tried to move the window, but it wouldn't budge.

"Maybe they cleaned up after themselves?"

"It's possible, but this looks more like... a diversion. No footprints. No chippings. No dirt."

"Maybe the perp decided it wasn't the right place to enter... or someone interrupted them."

"Or maybe they wanted to distract us," she said. "Mark this area for forensics just in case."

Katie thought that whoever killed the Banks family was most likely an experienced killer, so this attempt to break and enter through the bathroom window seemed too amateurish. As she contemplated about how and who, her thoughts went back to little Emily and what was going to happen to her.

McGaven retrieved his notebook. "Okay, you go first."

The detectives had a procedure they adhered to when searching a crime scene, whether it was recent or long cold. One of them would be the eyes and search slowly, making observations aloud, while the other wrote down the notes. Then they would switch positions. Sometimes one detective would pick up something the other didn't immediately see. It worked well for them, and it was a good way to be thorough.

Katie stopped at the front door. She studied the blood smear on the door trim just as she had previously. "Someone was injured and tried to get out—most likely to get help. By the height and area covered, it appeared to be an adult, either Mr. or Mrs. Banks. Unless it was the attacker," she said. "Maybe Emily is right. Maybe her mom did get her out."

She walked into the house and the bloody hammer was still in the same spot. It looked as if it had been placed carefully. It was like a scene in a movie where something jumps out at you at the most inopportune moment—for shock value.

McGaven stayed near the doorway where he could still see his partner. He remained quiet, jotting down a few notes and beginning a sketch layout of the room.

Katie stopped. "The blood smears around the door facing are on the outside, which means the person was entering the house and not leaving."

"Why is the hammer inside?" said McGaven. "Wouldn't it have been left outside or taken with the perp?"

"We can't assume anything until we have more to work with. Putting together what happened isn't going to be easy. There are assumptions, of course, but some of these puzzle pieces definitely don't make sense," she said. "And I don't think they're meant to. I think it's possible some of these things are meant to throw us off—making us spend more time on useless clues."

Katie moved in a clockwise direction beginning with the exterior of each room and then working her way through the house until she reached the middle areas. There was nothing out of the ordinary in the living room. It was tidy and well organized, which seemed a bit unusual in a house where there were three young children. The large beige sectional had several throw pillows neatly placed in each corner. The extra-large square ottoman had a multicolored blanket in browns and blues folded neatly in the middle. Katie walked slowly around the room, stopping and gazing at the few photographs and knick-knacks. There were no more traces of blood or dirt on the floor or furniture.

She moved to the kitchen, which was the only area that showed there was a family living there. A row of various kids' cereals stood on the counter, with a stack of three bowls beside it. Breakfast laid out the night before. She thought back to the family lined up together in the barn in pajamas. It made sense that they were roused out of their beds. She shuddered.

On one side of the kitchen counter was a small chalkboard with a few grocery items written on it: *milk, cottage cheese, hamburger buns*. The sink was empty, and the red light was on the dishwasher display, indicating that the last load was complete. Katie took her gloved hand and opened some of the cupboards. Dishes were neatly stacked. Glassware, cups, and various stemware were lined up orderly.

"Anything?" said McGaven.

"No. Everything seems normal."

Something caught her eye on the floor. She immediately leaned down and picked up a piece of pottery—maybe from a mug or plate. She turned over the tiny piece about half the size of a penny. She walked to the kitchen trash can and opened the lid. It was empty.

"Did you find something?" said McGaven, joining her at the trash can. "Looks like a piece from a broken dish."

"It's probably nothing," she said. "But give it an evidence marker." She carefully returned the piece to where she had found it.

Katie moved through the hallway and headed to the

bedrooms. There were three. The first one was obviously a boy's room with race cars, fun comic posters, and a bunk bed. There were toys on the floor and some clothes thrown over the desk chair. She took a moment to search the area, but everything seemed to appear normal for a boy around ten years old. Flipping back the comforter and moving the pillow, there was nothing that looked like blood.

Where were they killed?

Katie updated McGaven as he took more notes and then moved to the girls' room. It was in the same condition as their brother's. This time Katie searched through the drawers, small boxes, and closet trying to find anything to indicate any problems or if someone had been harassing or bothering them. She couldn't find anything. There were no journals or drawings. She met McGaven back in the hall.

"What's up? I don't think I've ever seen you look confused," he said.

"Not confused, but everything I've seen so far reminds me of a set. Like everything was placed in a way we would think a family of five would live. Placed, but not a reality. There should be some evidence of how they lived beyond what we visually see."

"Like?"

"Like garbage. Toys in the hallway or living room. The kitchen even feels too set up."

"Maybe they were neat and extremely particular... like obsessive-compulsive."

Katie thought about it. Of course, he could be right, but she was going to keep her suspicions and theories on hold until they searched everything on the property.

"They were in witness protection, right?" he said.

"Right."

"We're not going to get all the information unless the

Marshals Service gives it to us. We have to come to terms that there might be quite a few things we're not going to know."

Katie sighed. "Making it that much more difficult to find the killer."

McGaven's phone had an incoming text message.

"Oh good," he said.

"What?"

"John said there are security cameras covering most of the property. He's beginning to document them and will be taking the computers and cameras back to the forensic lab."

"That's a good thing."

"A place to start."

"Especially since we don't know their real names and why they ended up here in the program. There's going to be too many unknowns, making it almost impossible to get a lead."

"You're not giving up before we dig into this case, are you?"

"I said... *almost*." She looked around, trying to visualize the family's routines.

The detectives came to the main bedroom that belonged to Robert and Samantha Banks. Katie quickly assessed the bathroom, but there was no indication of anyone actually entering it. She went back into the bedroom and began checking every area —drawers, nightstands, closet, pockets of clothing.

"What are you looking for?" he said.

"I'm not sure, but something that might tell some type of story. Give us a clue about them."

Katie took extra care and time to look underneath things, including the drawer bottoms and the bed mattress. There wasn't any sign of a struggle or any traces of blood.

"This place reminds me of a motel room that has just been tidied by the maid service," said McGaven.

Katie stood in the middle of the bedroom. "That's a good description." She walked to the window and looked out. The view of the trees and the open space was beautiful. She understood why they built on the exact location. "How could this happen? Someone must've hunted them down. Watched them and their routines." She turned to her partner. "And we don't know why the family was put into witness protection. That will make things a lot clearer."

"Mob? Wrong place, wrong time witnessing a murder," he said.

Katie thought about it, but what they were discovering in the house spoke of the efficiency and planned nature of the crime. "Why was Emily left alive?"

"She's too young to know anything?"

"Let's check the trash cans to see if there's anything there before going to the barn," she said.

McGaven had turned to leave as Katie noticed a small screw lying on the carpet. On the wall above, she saw a vent, which was askew. "Wait," she said.

McGaven was at her side, scoping out the situation.

Katie got on her knees and carefully removed the heating vent. There was nothing that stood out about it or anything tucked inside.

"Anything?" he said.

"No, but..."

Katie scrutinized the drywall inside the vent and saw there was a small carved-out area. She reached inside and pulled out a letter-sized envelope—inside were Colorado IDs, not drivers' licenses, for Kent and Sharon Wagner. She laid them on the carpet and took a photo of them with her cell phone.

"Bingo. Good eye, partner," said McGaven.

"I think we got our first break."

FOUR

Katie always preferred, if at all possible, to leave the victims until last—until she had assessed and searched the entire crime scene area. Now, she and McGaven stood at the threshold of the barn just inside the crime scene tape.

Taking a moment, Katie thought it best to have McGaven go in first to make his observations and she would make notes. After first seeing the shocking scene, she wasn't sure if she could be one hundred percent objective, since it had had a strong physiological effect on her. Katie hung back with her notebook and pen ready as she observed John and his forensic technician, Eva, heading to the house.

Looking inside, it was again clear that the barn was used as more of a storage and office area than a livestock shelter or workshop. Metal containers were stacked up and lined the back walls. They were sitting on wooden pallets about five inches from the floor. Neatly typed index cards were slipped into the frame on the front to identify the contents. Several built-in desks covered the walls on the left and right. A number of chairs with padded seats and backs were folded closed and leaning against the far corner of the barn.

Katie watched her partner begin his assessment from the left and move clockwise. It always surprised her that a man who was over six foot six inches tall could move with ease and agility.

"It's very organized," said McGaven. "But in an old-school sort of way. Using filing cabinets, typed labels, and handwritten file folders."

Katie noticed that too. "Wouldn't it be more space and time effective to have everything scanned?"

"You would think." McGaven opened several drawers and pulled some of the files. "But no one can track your footprints from paper." He opened more file drawers, and then more.

"What's up?" she said.

"There's nothing but old newspaper articles."

"That's all?"

"Yep."

"What are they about?"

"Everything."

"Meaning?"

"Like everything. There are crime beat columns, home and garden, weather, everyday news..."

Katie thought a moment. "Local?"

"No, they're from... Denver... Las Vegas... Los Angeles areas... as far as I can tell."

"Current?" she said.

"That's what's weird. Nothing is current. Most are from twenty years ago, some from five years ago."

There were four large cabinets with four drawers each, which meant there were sixteen drawers full of files and newspaper articles. Katie sighed. Was it significant? Or was it nothing?

McGaven kept looking through files and searching drawers

trying to find anything else, but there was nothing. No logbooks. No accounting records. No addresses. Nothing else.

"Are there any notes or anything indicating why these particular news stories were kept?"

"Not that I can see," he said.

Katie made a few notes and entered the barn. She stepped carefully around the bodies. "Maybe there's some type of code for all this? A research project?"

"Or maybe it was what got them put into witness protection," said McGaven turning to look at his partner. "Do we know what they did for a living here in Pine Valley?"

"We haven't been given that information yet," she said. It was quickly becoming a part-sorted mess with scatters of information and not the entire story. And that bothered her.

Katie had to think long and hard about what to do with the files. At this point, she wasn't sure if the information they had was pertinent until she spoke with the marshal assigned to the case. But everything she contemplated and theorized about came back to the fact that they needed to bring them to their office to be scrutinized. She knew this case was going to be grueling and filled with long hours.

"We'll have John and Eva pull the files, document them, and load them into boxes to bring back to the lab," she said.

McGaven nodded, but his expression was sour, with a downturned mouth and crinkled eyebrows. He knew that meant time-consuming work for them.

The detectives searched the barn and found it to be clean—almost too clean, just like the house. There were no footprints. No indication there was a struggle with the family members. Again, the settings seemed strange with items appearing to be placed specifically.

Once Katie and McGaven felt that they had scoured the barn for anything to help tell the story of what had happened, they turned their attention to the bodies.

Katie held her composure. She looked at the family all lying next to each other, their arms at their sides, eyes focused on the ceiling, and their fingers slightly touching the person next to them. The display still punched Katie in the gut, but she had to push past it in order to stay objective and alert.

She kneeled next to Mr. Banks. His navy pajama top was buttoned all the way to the collar. There was excessive blood on the fabric, but it was unclear where it came from. She carefully unbuttoned the first two buttons and folded back the collar. She immediately found the source of the blood and most likely the cause of death. His chest had been slashed with a sharp object, which revealed his sternum and a portion of his ribs. It was a heinous mortal injury.

Katie took slow breaths and checked Mrs. Banks next. Her brutal slaying was almost identical to her husband's. It gave Katie pause as to how someone could have performed the same type of force and injury to two people. It was clear the Bankses had been attacked in the night sometime, but how was the killer able to kill the whole family? It indicated there might have been more than one killer to perform such a violent attack.

"It looks like a sharp instrument like a large knife did all this damage," she said. "We won't know the details until Dr. Dean does the autopsies." She gently picked up their hands to see if there were any obvious defensive wounds, but there was nothing. "Doesn't it seem strange that they didn't have any other wounds except for the slashing of their chests? And their pajamas don't have any damage from the slashing."

"The medical examiner will run a toxicology screen. Maybe they were drugged first," McGaven said.

"It's possible." She looked at the children—Emily's brother and sister. Her initial observation was that they had been strangled; there were purplish marks around their necks and petechial hemorrhaging in their eyes showing tiny red spots. Katie had seen these indicators many times in strangled murder victims. There were other injuries to their chests like their parents. No sign they had fought back. Their hands and faces were clean and blemish-free. The pajamas were neat, pressed, and buttoned to the top. Their stares were blank, focused on the ceiling.

The detectives spent a little bit more time examining the bodies, pajamas, and areas surrounding the family, including the floors, walls, and filing cabinets, before leaving the barn. McGaven briefly sketched the area and made more notes. The medical examiner's office had sent morgue technicians to remove the bodies. They waited patiently until the detectives gave the okay for them to do so.

"So what do we really have here?" said McGaven.

"For such a brutal scene, there's not much evidence. Even the garbage can was empty. The killer or killers took everything and cleaned up except for the blood around the doorway and hammer in the living room."

"Telling us what?" he said.

"I don't know yet," Katie said. "We'll have to work hard to find out the answers. But I do know no scene is perfectly sterile."

As they left the barn, Katie saw her Jeep pull onto the property and her uncle, Sheriff Scott, exit it.

"Now that's what I call car service," said McGaven watching the sheriff approach.

"What's going on?" she said.

"We need to search the rest of the property and the area where the little girl was found," said the sheriff.

"Okay," she said.

"I got your Jeep because I know you keep Cisco's gear in there and extra clothes. You up for it?" he said, but he really wasn't asking. Proficiency was a must in the investigation.

Katie was already thinking ahead to how she would have Cisco search, but she asked, "Is there a reason for searching?

Besides the obvious. I can't help but sense there's something else on your mind," she said.

"We need to push forward as fast as we can," said the sheriff.

"Otherwise..."

"Otherwise our hands may be tied. I'm not saying for sure, but I want you to do everything possible, and as fast as possible." His eyes were intense. He never wavered with his decisions, but Katie could see some concern in her uncle's reactions.

She took another look around at the barn, house, and the two vehicles. She saw the morgue technicians load the bodies and John bringing out evidence from the house. Eva was beginning a search and documentation of the cars. "I need Gav to be my spotter. There are a lot of potential hazards around the property and up on the trail."

"Whatever you need to do."

"What are we looking for specifically?" said McGaven.

"How the killer accessed the property, and if he left anything behind," said the sheriff.

"We'll get geared up and started right away." She scanned the area up around the trail. "The wind is low and the light is almost perfect," she said. "It's a good time to perform the search."

"Then I suggest you get started."

FIVE

The early afternoon weather at the farmhouse property was sunny, but there was a definite cutting chill in the air—winter wasn't too far behind. Katie had changed into her khaki pants, long-sleeved shirt, jacket, and tactical boots. She kept her long hair in a ponytail and opted for a baseball cap. Making sure she had everything she needed tucked into various pockets, she then donned a pair of polarizing sunglasses to keep her vision clear.

Cisco was excited and clearly ready to search as it was difficult for him to stay still. His high-pitched whines, wanting to go, became incessant. Katie had secured his tactical search vest and made sure his gear fit him securely with buckles and Velcro. She attached a twelve-foot lead to Cisco's vest, then turned to her partner, who had also dressed more appropriately for the rural search.

"Ready?"

"Yep," he said, grabbing several orange flags on wire to stick in the ground, making it easy to alert CSI to any potential evidence.

Katie glanced at the house and barn. John and Eva were still working the scenes and Deputy Hansen was still managing and protecting the area until further notice. Hamilton, the social worker, and the morgue technicians had all left. Sheriff Scott was talking on his cell phone in the passenger seat of a police cruiser that was going to take him back to the department.

"Everything okay?" said McGaven.

"Yes."

"What's bothering you?"

"Besides the obvious, nothing." She hated sounding stressed to her partner and had to keep her focus.

McGaven remained quiet. He seemed to match his partner's concern about the case and what they might discover.

Katie felt her arms and legs tingle, which was normal before going into a search. But today the tension and alertness felt at an all-time high. It was similar to when she and Cisco had taken point position on search missions in the military. Her senses were heightened and her reactions kicked into high gear.

She noted that the wind was mild, about five to ten miles per hour, and it was coming at them from the east. It would help Cisco to pick up any human or unnatural scents quicker.

"We need to do a perimeter search around the immediate property to see if Cisco picks up a trail," she said.

McGaven took his spotter position, staying back about ten to twelve feet and positioning himself slightly to one side or the other of the K9 team, and not directly behind Katie. He would be able to scan ahead as well as to the sides of the area.

"Hey, Detectives," said Deputy Hansen.

"What's up?" said McGaven.

"I'm here to guard the areas for John until they can release the scene. But..."

Katie stared at the deputy.

"Do you need me to canvass?"

Katie looked at McGaven. "The next neighbor is more than a few acres away and over the ridge. After we finish our search of the ground, we'll reassess."

"Got it," he said as he jogged back to his post.

"I like him," said McGaven.

Katie smiled. "Me too. He's studying for the detective exam and has asked me a few questions about it."

"I thought there was a freeze on hiring."

"There is, but I think they might get council approval for hiring another detective since we're stretched pretty thin. I understand there are new deputy recruits coming up in the next month or so."

Katie focused her attention on the yard. She wanted Cisco to begin at the farmhouse. John appeared at the doorway and nodded at Katie as she prepared to run Cisco around the house and then fan out.

Katie pulled the long leash closer so Cisco was about four feet from her and she could easily guide him through narrow areas without getting tangled up. She calmed her mind by taking a few cleansing breaths and directed her focus on reading Cisco's body language. When there was a change of behavior—like body positioning, tail actions, or various head movements—it would indicate something needed closer examination. Her stress lessened with her focus solely on Cisco and everything around her slowly faded away—that was why having a cover officer or spotter was important for her, so she could give all her attention to the dog instead of potential hazards.

The wind seemed to cease but the sun was obscured by overhead clouds casting unusual shadows around the farmhouse.

"Cisco, *such*," she said, instructing the dog to begin a search and find.

Instantly Cisco went into search mode, with his nose down,

tail down and relaxed, and ears forward. He systematically searched at a comfortable pace, weaving in and around when necessary.

Katie didn't think there would be much to investigate, but she wanted to eliminate the area for good measure. It was also a good warm-up for both her and Cisco. Her mind kept in sync with the task, but she couldn't help but think of little Emily and what was going to happen to her.

It surprised Katie that after nearly twenty minutes Cisco didn't seem interested in anything around the house except at the bathroom window and the front door. Someone had to have entered the house, although it was possible the family was lured to the barn.

"Nothing?" said McGaven, breaking their silence.

"Not yet. The house seems to be clear."

McGaven didn't respond but gave a troubled look like he had pondered how someone could murder a family and not leave any type of scent behind.

Katie directed the jet-black dog toward the barn. That was when Cisco's body stiffened, hesitated, but moved forward. It was as if he knew something bad had happened and he was entering into dangerous territory with caution. The dog immediately took them on the left side of the barn building. His nose was low and his pacing accelerated. Katie let out the leash to a longer length and kept a close watch on the dog. She could hear McGaven's footsteps move faster behind her as well.

When Cisco reached the back side of the barn, he hesitated and downed. Katie knew that reaction all too well—in the military, it meant they were close to explosives or a well-laid trap. But under these conditions, it was something else. It was something that Cisco deemed dangerous.

"Stay here," said McGaven, who had witnessed the dog's cautious behavior. He carefully searched the surrounding area.

There was nothing, which was strange. Making sure he kept off the path taken, he stepped along the vegetation area.

"Anything?" said Katie. Her voice was higher than normal and her skin tingled with anticipation, producing goose bumps down her arms.

"No. But there's a narrow trail here. And what look like fresh footprints."

"The deputies?" she said.

"No, I don't think so. The impressions have a smoother sole print than the police tactical boot." He left two flags to mark the area for forensics. He then turned to his partner. "What do you want to do?"

Katie didn't understand why Cisco had picked up on a scent of danger and she wanted to continue. "We need to search the area where little Emily was found."

"Why was she up on the trail? Did the perp leave her there on purpose?" he said looking around

"That's the million-dollar question." She stood at the start of the path leading up the hill and released Cisco from his alert position, then turned to go toward the back of the property. She had an idea. She remembered the sound of the creek flowing when she was on the Bramble Trail and thought it might be a way to bypass the regular paths to get to a parking area. Walking through the water would leave the least amount of evidence behind.

Katie and Cisco headed toward the farmhouse again and continued up the hillside where she had first entered the property. She saw John and Eva packing the CSI van with evidence along with the chain of custody as Deputy Hansen assisted them. The three looked up as they watched the detectives with Cisco head toward the upper location.

The early morning events kept rolling through Katie's thoughts. She didn't know what had possessed her to change her route this exact day, but she was extremely thankful she had. Maybe it was the luck they needed in order to get a jump on the investigation before the US Marshal changed everything.

Once at the top of the hill, the detectives looked down at the farmhouse.

"How in the world did that little girl get up here?" said McGaven. "Was she brought here or did she somehow make it up here by herself?"

"There's one other possibility."

"What's that?"

"She could have been hidden here," said Katie.

"You mean by someone in the family?"

"It's possible."

Cisco interrupted their theories and barked. Katie turned her attention to the anxious dog and gave him the command to search. The German shepherd moved in a westerly direction along the trail, keeping a brisk pace, his nose along the ground. Katie let him have a longer lead and followed. McGaven followed, making his way around obstacles and keeping a watchful eye.

Katie wondered if they would find anything useful to solving the case. The window for finding additional clues left by the killer was quickly closing. They were pressed for time due to the family being in witness protection.

Cisco led the detectives along the trail and into a heavily wooded area. Katie didn't think there was any trail left, but to her surprise there was another leading down. She could hear the moving creek clearer. The running water sounded so tranquil and relaxing, but the situation was anything but peaceful.

"Slow down," said McGaven in a gruff voice. He moved cautiously to the left and disappeared momentarily into a cluster of trees. His expression was tense.

Katie slowed the dog and kept very quiet. She waited for her partner to return and wondered what he had seen or heard. Scanning the area, Katie felt vulnerable and too exposed. It was more than just the circumstances. There was something unnatural about the area.

McGaven returned and appeared more relaxed. "Negative. Everything is okay. It looks like the trail ends at the creek."

Katie continued along the trail as they slowly zigzagged in between trees until they stood at the creek bank. Stepping carefully, scrutinizing the area, she didn't see any footprints, dropped items, drag marks, or anything of interest. Cisco seemed to have lost the scent.

Katie let out a sigh. "Nothing."

"But it's clearly how the killer moved onto the property and exited," he said. "Cisco tracked the trail and whatever he picked up on from the killer wasn't good." McGaven walked with the flow of the creek and looked around.

Katie was still disappointed. It wasn't the start to the investigation she had hoped for. They would have to wait for forensics and the autopsies to help propel them forward.

Just then she spotted something in the water hidden slightly behind some branches. "What's that?"

McGaven looked in the direction where Katie had pointed. "Looks like a plastic garbage bag."

The medium-sized dark gray plastic bag was stuck on one of the rocks. It appeared partially full as the flattened areas had caught on debris and rocks in the creek, causing it to sputter in the water. McGaven grabbed a small branch, stepped toward the bag, and kept his footing while he managed to hook it. Pulling it toward him, he grasped the sack, which was no bigger than twelve inches in diameter.

Katie watched, swallowing hard in anticipation of something potentially horrible. She watched her partner open the bag, being careful not to contaminate any potential evidence. "Anything?"

"It's just..." McGaven shook the bag. "It's just clothes.

Looks like a little girl's clothes. A blue dress with white polka dots."

Katie thought a moment. It had to do with the Banks murders, she was certain. "Bring it. We can have John examine and test it."

"So where did the killer go?"

"I would bet he went through that way." She pointed to a short trail that led to a flat gravel area that would be easy for someone to park on. "John needs to search it and see if he can find any tire impressions or anything else. I don't want to trample through here with Cisco."

McGaven made his way to Katie just as her cell phone rang. She put it on speaker. "Scott," she answered.

"Is McGaven with you?" said Sheriff Scott.

"Yes. We're both here."

"We have another one."

Katie's blood turned cold. "Another one?"

"A call came in for a location about five miles away from you. The Sanderson family has been murdered. Two adults and two children."

Her heart stuttered. "In the same way as the Banks family?" she said. Her chest felt heavy as dread filled her. *That makes four children murdered in one morning.* She felt dizzy.

"Don't have all the details yet, but Detectives Hamilton and Alvarez are there to control the area."

Katie knew they were short-staffed when the sheriff sent Detective Alvarez from missing persons to help in a homicide case.

"I need for you two to finish up there and leave John and Eva to complete the search and evidence discovery. Can you instruct them?"

"Of course," she said.

"You need to work this new crime scene in case we're

dealing with a serial case. I'll send a text with the address," said the sheriff.

"Okay." Katie's mind went into warp speed with all the possible scenarios. Were they related? It couldn't have been a coincidence. Obviously the sheriff didn't think so either. "We'll report back to you when we know more," she said.

"One more thing," he said with a pause. "Their five-year-old daughter is missing."

SIX

Katie and McGaven rode in silence all the way to the residence of the Sanderson family at 1700 Park Tree Road, lost in their own thoughts about the case. Who would want to hurt these families? As they neared the address, there were two patrol vehicles, two unmarked sedans, and the coroner. McGaven pulled his truck to the side and parked behind one of the detectives' vehicles. He didn't immediately get out, and neither did Katie.

He turned to his partner. "You okay?"

Katie nodded. Although, she wasn't so sure. A little girl was missing, and every second counted. Katie felt uncomfortable, and even vulnerable for some reason. She knew it was her imagination but couldn't overlook it.

Cisco let out a whine.

"You ready?" said McGaven.

"As I'll ever be," she said. "Cisco, you have to stay." She grabbed gloves as her thoughts wandered back to Emily. Hoping the little girl was okay and that there would be a family member to take care of her, she pushed her attention onto the next crime scene. She needed to get the job done.

The detectives got out of the truck and headed toward the house. Like the Banks residence, it was in a rural location, but this house was older and more typical of a suburban neighborhood: a plain two-story home, beige with white trim. It had been taken care of, but the slide windows were reminiscent of homes from the 1950s and 1960s. The plant beds around the house had been recently cleared and there was newly raked soil ready for winter planting.

Detective Hamilton exited the front door. His face was bleak, but his intensity was there. Pursed mouth. Still gritting his teeth. He nodded at Katie and McGaven.

"Have you heard anything about the child?" said Katie.

"No. We've reached out to friends and family—but no one knows where she might be."

"Is there an alert out for her?" she said.

"We're just getting a photograph and the alert will be out within the next hour. I've made a note of the photo we can use in the living room with minimal disruption to the scene." He looked disturbed. "Two families in one morning?"

Katie felt his pain and they hadn't even seen inside yet.

"I'll keep you updated. Anything you need. Just let Alvarez or me know."

Katie nodded. "Where are the bodies?"

"In their beds. The parents are in their room and each child in their bedroom." His face stayed grim as if the image was seared into his mind.

"How do you want to handle the scene?" said McGaven.

Hamilton took a step back. "It's yours. You two need to do what you do," he said. There wasn't the usual sarcasm to his voice but, rather, a newfound respect. "We need to get this scene processed. John is about an hour out from the other residence. If there's anything that will help find the little girl—it's imperative that if you find anything, we act right away. Time is ticking..."

Katie took a breath. "Anything we should be aware of?"

"We did a perimeter and protected the scene. I have uniforms canvassing the acreage and there's a neighbor not far from here they are talking to. We may need you and Cisco to search again. Well... if you see fit."

"Is there any indication they're in witness protection as well?" said McGaven.

"No. And I don't think they would have two families in protection in such close proximity," said Hamilton.

"Any security cameras?" she said.

"None that we've found so far."

Detective Alvarez walked over to the detectives from the back property.

"Anything?" said Hamilton.

"No. Not yet."

"Okay. There's a lot going on today and it doesn't seem to be slowing down anytime soon. You two need to get to work," said Hamilton. He moved past the detectives. "We've got a burglary scene to attend."

"Thank you, Hamilton," said McGaven.

Katie pulled on her gloves as she watched Hamilton and Alvarez walk away. Turning her attention back to the house, she readied herself for the next scene. McGaven gently touched her shoulder, letting her know that he was right behind her.

Katie eyed the entry but nothing seemed to indicate that a heinous crime had taken place. She reflected back to the bloody handprints at the Banks residence.

The detectives moved through the front door. Unlike the farmhouse, the living room, kitchen, and dining areas were cluttered. There were few windows, making it seem darker than it really was. Things seemed to be organized, but there were abundant items—photographs, knick-knacks, toys, children's backpacks, art supplies, books, and various other signs of a busy life. There were two large beige couches with a variety of colorful pillows in every size and shape. There was no clear indication of decorating, just comfort and a lived-in feel for a family of five.

Katie stopped in the middle of the room.

"What are you thinking?" said McGaven.

"How this house is so different from the Bankses' farmhouse."

McGaven remained quiet.

Katie did a walk-through around the living area and kitchen. The dishes were cleaned up and the counter was wiped clean. There were five mugs, all different, sitting on the back counter as if they were recently washed. The kitchen table had a cheerful red tablecloth and was covered with drawing tablets, crayons, and colored pens. There were children's hoodies piled on one of the chairs. Sneakers were in the corner next to a basket with various toys. It was as if the children would run into the room at any moment. Deep sadness filled Katie.

She walked toward the corner of the living room where there was a built-in desk next to the bookshelves. There were neatly stacked papers, bills, and a check register. She turned to McGaven.

"Nothing seems to be out of place. It looks like the family cleaned up for the night."

"Which means they were killed before morning too," said McGaven.

Katie then moved to the staircase. It was carpeted with wooden banisters. She imagined the kids running up and down, their voices filling the home, and the smell of cooking from the kitchen. Now, it was quiet. It was an unnatural silence that made her shiver.

Katie pushed her feelings aside. She had to keep focus. The

medical examiner's office would be arriving shortly to take the bodies.

She hurried up the stairs and paused at the landing, looking at the layout on the second level. There was a long hallway with three doors one side, and on the other was a double door, which seemed to lead to a larger room, the length of the house. All bedroom doors were closed, which seemed odd. She wondered why the detectives had closed them.

Katie decided to go into the parents' room first. Her legs felt heavy, making it difficult to walk to the double doors. It was the anticipation of what they were going to find. The memory of the Banks family lined up in the barn was still vivid. It would take a while before Katie could unsee that.

Slowly opening the dark double doors, Katie moved inside. It was a large bedroom that allowed for a sitting area with two overstuffed chairs. There were stacks of books everywhere; obviously Mr. or Mrs. Sanderson was an avid reader. She glanced around and didn't see any readers or iPads.

The curtains were open, which helped to illuminate the bedroom but it didn't lessen the horror of what Katie saw. The couple lay on their backs, side by side. The blanket and comforter had been pulled tight, leaving their arms outside the bedding and straight down at their sides. Their arms and hands were next to each other, but not touching.

"This entire room needs to be dusted for prints," she said not pulling her focus away from the couple.

McGaven nodded. "It seems the killer really took his time in here."

"I doubt they were careless, but you never know." Katie took in the posed bodies and scanned the nightstands. Then she gently moved the comforter aside. The sheets were soaked in blood.

"They were killed here, in their bed?" McGaven joined his partner and examined the bedding.

Katie looked around the bed, carpet, nightstands, and walls. There were no other traces of blood, which seemed strange. "Wouldn't there be blood spatters?" She didn't want to disturb the bodies, but both appeared to have been stabbed in the chest and neck and would have succumbed to the injuries quickly. But it would have been messy and there were no signs of struggle. It perplexed her.

McGaven leaned down and began sniffing the area. "Do you smell that?"

"What?" She leaned in close to where her partner indicated. "It's... some kind of cleaner. It almost smells like flowers. Maybe a natural cleaner?"

"Maybe," he said. He tilted his head one way then the other.

Katie realized he was looking for an indication of where cleaning had taken place. "Anything?"

"I don't know. John will have to take samples from surfaces to test if they have been wiped down recently. Maybe there's some residue."

Thinking back to the kitchen and living room, she said, "The trash cans are empty."

"Just like at the Bankses' house."

"The killer took all the garbage out again," she said.

"And I'm guessing we'll find the garbage cans outside empty as well."

Katie agreed.

"Why these two families?" said McGaven.

"It doesn't make sense. The only thing, so far, that they have in common is that they are a family with three children and they seemed to have been killed in the middle of the night with aggressive wounds." She checked Mrs. Sanderson and saw she had a significant number of defense wounds of deep scratches on her arms, wrists, and the side of her face. "Huh."

"Defense wounds?"

"Yes, but Mr. Sanderson doesn't have any. So it indicates he was attacked and killed first, without any time to react. And then Mrs. Sanderson had more time to fight back."

"Makes sense. The stronger victim—take him out first," said McGaven.

Katie agreed. She walked the room, looked in the closets, and then the bathroom. It was unclear where the attack took place. She didn't think it was the bed. Then she caught sight of something on the floor near the tub. Bending down, Katie swiped her gloved hand across the area and she stared at her fingers. It appeared to be clear liquid. It had the same cleaning smell as by the bed.

"Anything?" said McGaven.

"I'm not sure. John will have to run a test." Katie stood up.

"The entire area needs to be scrutinized for blood and anything else." He surveyed the large bathroom.

"Or, it could mean that the killer was in the bathroom. Maybe it was where he attacked them. And then cleaned it all down."

"There's something else bothering you," he said.

Katie felt that they had little to go on. "Why this elaborate scene?"

"Elaborate?"

"The cleanup, which takes extra time, and then staging the bodies—it must mean something specific to the killer. It gives us some insight into their mindset."

"You think it's someone they knew, an acquaintance or a family member?"

"It's possible, but my gut says they were chosen for another reason. Emily and the missing little girl."

McGaven frowned. "That makes everything worse." He looked at his notes. "The little girl is named Tessa—short for Theresa."

"Let's go check out the children's rooms—and especially

Tessa's room." The worst part of Katie's job was seeing murdered children. No matter how much you tried to prepare for something like this, nothing ever really prepared you for the violent death of children. It was always disturbing, causing her anger to rise, but she had to keep her head and focus on finding the killer before there was another family crime scene.

Katie took a breath and moved forward, visiting each room. Tessa's brother and sister were also in their beds with their chests slashed, but there were no other injuries or visible defense wounds. Katie examined each hand, finger, and arm. Her breath became stilted and heavy.

The attack appeared to be quick and efficient. It would have been easy to overpower such young children and they wouldn't have put up too much of a fight. She saw that each had what seemed to be a favorite stuffed toy purposely put next to the bodies. The happy faces of a bear and a dog under such horrifying circumstances was macabre. Katie felt her heart weigh heavy and at times she was close to tears, but she had a job to do and she would do everything that she could to find the killer.

Katie and McGaven searched the children's rooms thoroughly to try to find anything that might be helpful in finding out what had gone on in the week or even month before. To their disappointment, nothing seemed out of the ordinary. The rooms were typical for their ages—seven and nine years old.

Katie stood at the last door, which was Tessa's room. It was difficult for her to enter. She saw that Hamilton and Alvarez had marked a few areas with yellow evidence markers where they had searched in hope of finding a clue to where she might have gone. It made Katie's hopes of finding something new diminish even more.

McGaven remained quiet. It was clear he was not looking forward to searching the little girl's room. His usually upbeat and driven work ethic seemed to waver.

Katie entered the room and noticed it was smaller than the

others. It fit a little five-year-old girl—stuffed animal toys, pastel colors on the bedding, and the funny cartoon characters of the posters on the walls. Various toys were in plastic bins in the corners.

She immediately went to the twin bed with pretty pink colors on the comforter and saw no indications of blood or any kind of disturbance. This was some relief, but her thoughts soon turned to Emily and now wondering what happened to little Tessa. The covers were thrown back and the pillow had been pushed to the side. It was messy, hurried, making it unclear if Tessa had innocently gotten out of bed or if she was forced.

Was she taken?

Did she run away?

Did she go willingly with someone she knew?

Katie hated not having all the facts—or even most of them. It left her in a flux of anticipation but with a drive that propelled her forward.

She could hear the gentle scrape of McGaven looking through the small dresser as she opened the closet door. It was just a single-wide entry with two rows of clothing rods—an upper and lower. A couple dozen little outfits were hanging, dresses, pants, and shirts. Everything was organized by size and color. It struck her as interesting, especially for a five-year-old, that it was so organized. Perhaps Mrs. Sanderson thought it made it easier for her daughter to get dressed in the mornings. Katie moved some of the clothes and saw that the hangers were perfectly spaced.

"Anything?" said McGaven interrupting her thoughts.

"Maybe."

"There's something stirring in that mind of yours," he said with a slight smile.

"It's just… with everything downstairs. It looks like a busy family home filled with everything a family needed, but up here it seems so clean and tidy." She walked around the room looking

COUNT THEIR GRAVES   47

at each item. "If the family was attacked in their beds, why didn't someone wake up and raise the alarm? Where are the signs of struggle?"

"The killer was prepared and stealthy."

"Yes, but as you said, we're going to have to wait to see what the toxicology report says," she said. Katie thought about the five mugs lined up on the counter in a perfect line. "I think it's something we need to pursue seriously. I can't really explain it another way."

"Did you see this?" said McGaven. He picked up a framed photo of the family.

Katie looked at it. "That's..."

"Tessa looks almost exactly like Emily."

She looked at the photo of a smiling, happy family. Little five-year-old Tessa was blonde with tight curls and had a startling resemblance to Emily Banks.

"They could be sisters," said McGaven.

Katie looked at her partner. "Maybe this isn't about the Bankses' witness protection. Maybe this is all about getting to these little girls and not leaving any family member alive?"

SEVEN

Wednesday 2020 hours

It was after eight in the evening and Katie was exhausted as McGaven drove her and Cisco home. What had started out as a routine run had turned into two families massacred and one little girl who had gone missing. Her body was fatigued, but her mind spun with scenarios and flashes of the gruesome crime scenes. She had to get some rest in order to hit the ground running tomorrow.

McGaven eased his truck up the driveway and cut the engine. "Wow, I was tired, but now, I'm *really* tired."

"It was definitely a long day today," said Katie. She let out a sigh.

Cisco was dozing in the back seat, but one of his ears was still alert and forward in case anything was to happen.

"I thought Chad would be waiting for you."

"No," she said softly. "He's at a fire investigator conference in Los Angeles this week." Chad Ferguson was Katie's childhood sweetheart, and a firefighter recently promoted to arson investigator. A recent victim of kidnapping, he had immersed himself in work ever since he returned home, taking every opportunity to train. They had spent little time together. She was giving him space so he could continue to heal, but that still didn't ease her loneliness and uncertainty about their relationship.

"Oh, I'm sorry," he said.

"It's okay."

"Let me know if I'm overstepping... but are you *really* okay?"

"Yeah, I'm fine. And you know I'd tell you if it's none of your business." She smiled at her partner.

"Of course you would. What was I thinking?" He smiled back at her.

"That's okay, you weren't thinking."

"Touché," he said.

Katie opened the truck door and let Cisco out. She noticed a white sedan that drove by and down her street. She didn't recognize the car as one of her neighbors', but she realized that she was overanalyzing everything today.

McGaven joined her. "I can stay for a bit."

Katie knew he was being a good friend, caring about her well-being. "Gav, I'm okay. Really."

"C'mon," he said and headed to the front door. "Just making sure that everything is safe. It's what I do..."

Katie laughed, following her partner and Cisco. "Really? With security cameras and Cisco? And don't forget I'm a cop *and* an Army veteran."

"Yeah well, I'd still feel better." He waited patiently as Katie unlocked the front door and let them inside.

McGaven made a grand gesture, partly in fun and partly being a police officer. He checked the closets and the security of the back door. "You really should think about getting a better lock on this slider."

Katie waited patiently as her partner made a production out

of checking her home. He dramatically opened closet doors and went into each room.

"You done yet?" She smiled as she saw a single red rose lying on the counter with a simple note: *Love you.* It was from Chad and was written in his neat handwriting. It made her happy, but it also made her a bit lonely since his schedule was now taking him out of town more frequently and there was no indication of slowing down.

McGaven appeared with Cisco in tow. "Yep. Everything is safe and secure."

"Thanks, Gav. Now go home and get some rest. We have another long day tomorrow."

"Got it." He headed for the door. Turning, he said, "Don't forget to lock up behind me."

"Go!" she laughed. "See you bright and early."

He closed the door behind him and Katie locked up. She let Cisco out back and checked her security cameras. Having had troubles in the past of certain unsavory individuals accessing her property, she didn't take her privacy or security for granted.

Her thoughts were interrupted by Cisco barking. Katie stepped out the back door onto the deck and stared out. "Cisco!"

The dog was nowhere to be found.

She called again.

Walking outside, she searched for the dog's outline. Her concern was beginning to turn to fear. "Cisco!"

The black dog ran from the other side of the property. He seemed fine, but Katie was unnerved. "What's up, Cisco?" she said to the dog.

Katie walked to the other side of her house, but there was nothing. She assumed that he must've been interested in an animal or caught a scent of something in the wind.

Katie returned indoors. She was going to eat something but decided against it due to being overwhelmingly tired. She would make sure she ate something healthy in the morning. It didn't take her long to get ready for bed and she was soon fast asleep.

Katie was rattled awake. Her body jerked and she sat straight up in bed. There was a loud thumping noise.

Cisco barked and growled.

The loud banging was shaking the walls, but she took a moment to wake up. The banging was someone knocking hard at the front door.

Katie jumped out of bed and grabbed her Glock and cell phone. Quickly slipping into pants and hoodie, she crept down the hallway. Glancing at the security monitor, she saw there was a man standing at the front door. He stood to the side and seemed to be hiding his face by angling away so that the camera wouldn't capture him. He was dressed in jeans, dark jacket, and a black baseball cap.

The glowing digital clock above her stove read: 12:30 a.m. She had been asleep for barely two hours.

"Who is it?" she said moving closer to the front door.

A tall shadow moved back and forth, but they didn't answer her.

Katie flipped the outside light switch, but it flashed and the bulb burned out. Again, she said, "Who is it?"

There was a mumble in response and she couldn't make out the words.

Her first thought was that it was a drunk or lost person who'd wandered up her driveway. Even that didn't make sense. There had never been someone just knocking on her door in the middle of the night before. From the security, she didn't see that he had any type of visible weapon or seemed to want to cause harm.

Cisco had stopped barking and he was in tune with Katie's

range of emotions. He waited for her command and could sense her struggle of the best way to proceed. She could call for patrol, but she would rather take care of it herself. One man, no others she could assess.

"Cisco, *platz*." She ordered the dog to down and wait. His golden wolf eyes never deviated from her as he gently panted and waited for her next command.

Once Katie was satisfied with Cisco's position, she readied herself to open the door. Perhaps it wasn't the best choice, but it was what she felt the right thing to do. Looking down, she realized that she was barefoot but that didn't matter. She readied her weapon, prepared it with a round in the chamber, and quietly disengaged the door lock. Katie took two deep breaths before she pulled the door wide open.

A young blond man with a black baseball cap stared wide-eyed at her. He tried to reach inside his jacket.

"I don't think so. Show me your hands," she said as she eyed his hands.

"I'm sorry—"

"Get on the ground. Now!"

"If I could show you—"

"Now!"

The man decided not to argue with her as he saw the eighty-pound black German shepherd just inside waiting for any reason to attack. He slowly got down on his knees with his hands on his head.

That's when Katie saw the semiautomatic weapon tucked in his jeans' waistband. "Get down!" She lurched forward and forced him face down and pressed her knee into his back. She kept glancing around and down the driveway, making sure no one else was there.

Cisco whined and gave two quick barks, but he kept his position.

The man groaned. "I'm trying to—"

"Shut up," she said and took the gun from his belt, sliding it across the porch.

"Look in my jacket pocket. Right side," he said, winded.

Katie wasn't in the mood. Her mind raced, trying to figure out how this man might be involved in their cases—or if his presence was a random crime opportunity. Her first assumption was more likely due to the fact that something rattled Cisco earlier in the evening. It made her think he had been watching her and waiting for the right moment.

"Check it out," he pushed.

Katie retrieved a wallet and when she flipped it open there was a badge and identification: Kyle West, US Marshal. She took a good look at the photo and then the man she had face down on her porch. It was same person.

Katie took her weight from the marshal's back. "Really? What the hell are you doing at my house in the middle of the night?" She took a step back and allowed him to get to his feet. As he still kept an eye on Cisco while he slowly composed himself before he spoke, Katie still didn't fully trust him. "I'm going to ask you again. What are you doing here?"

"Let me explain."

Katie watched him and kept silent.

"This is my big break. This case here in Pine Valley is a big deal."

Katie didn't care what his excuses were at this point. "That still doesn't explain why you are at a Pine Valley detective's home in the middle of the night."

The marshal began to gain his composure and stood up straight, trying to shake off the incident. "There was supposed to be another marshal assigned to the Banks case, but he was needed elsewhere and so I jumped at the opportunity. My superiors gave me this chance to not screw things up."

"How long have you been a marshal?"

"That's beside the point."

"How long?"

He stammered for a moment. "I usually work custody transportation. Next month will be two years."

"So you're a rookie trying to make points. Does that about sum it up?" she said, trying not to sound as annoyed as she felt. "This is a multiple homicide, two families, you understand?"

"Well sorta. I wanted to work with you and Detective McGaven."

"Why?" she said as she watched the marshal's reaction. He seemed genuine about everything he had told her so far. He hadn't worked on his ability to keep his emotions in check like a more seasoned officer.

He glanced away for a moment. "There's talk."

"Talk? About what?" Katie didn't have time to care what the US Marshals Service thought. She wanted to go back to bed. She needed sleep to replenish her energy for tomorrow.

"You and McGaven are legends. By that I mean there's talk about you two working cold cases with a perfect record. You guys are the coolest... I mean, that's pretty impressive, you know."

"That still doesn't excuse you being here tonight."

"Are you going to report me?" Marshal West had a way to look completely innocent. It was most likely due to lack of experience and age, which she guessed to be in his mid-twenties.

Katie sighed. "No."

"Thank you." He let out a relieved sigh.

"But you're on notice. And next time you turn up at someone's house in the middle of the night, look at the camera and speak clearly. Got it?"

"Yes. Got it."

"So tell me, Marshal... Why are you here at this late hour?"

"I wanted to talk to you before coming in to the department tomorrow morning."

"You could have called me."

"I wanted to talk to you in person and I didn't get into town until about an hour ago." He looked nervous. "It seems I can trust you."

"You know this isn't protocol."

He nodded.

"Come in." She still had reservations.

The marshal followed Katie but kept his eye on Cisco. "Is he...?"

"Friendly? That depends." She shut the front door and headed to the kitchen to make a pot of coffee.

"On what?"

"What your intentions are. He's fully trained and a retired decorated military working dog." She released Cisco from his position.

The big dog trotted across the room and sniffed the marshal out of curiosity, but didn't seem interested at all.

West looked around and saw some framed photographs showing Katie with her Army team. "You were in the Army?"

Katie nodded.

"Thank you for your service."

Katie didn't want to regret letting the marshal in, but she was calculating in her mind how much sleep she was most likely going to get after this interruption.

Marshal West sat at the kitchen counter. "As I'm in your house, I'm thinking it probably wasn't a great way to make a first impression."

"We're past that now."

"I've been fully updated on the Banks family. They've only been in witness protection for a little over two years. I spoke with Mr. and Mrs. Banks before the trial. I just—"

"Why were they in witness protection?" she asked. Katie wanted to know their background. It may, or may not, have a direct bearing on the investigation, since there was another murdered family, but she still needed the information.

The marshal sighed and leaned back, obviously deciding whether to explain everything to her. "Wrong place, wrong time. Maybe the right time, depends how you look at it."

"That's it?" she said.

"I can't tell you everything because I'm not authorized to do so unless it pertains directly to the homicide investigation."

Katie studied the young marshal carefully, trying to get a read on him. "What *can* you tell me?"

"Mr. Banks witnessed a murder near his work, which was at a title company in Boston, one night. He was working late, past ten, and was leaving to drive home. As he was walking through the parking garage, he heard a confrontation between three men talking about murder and a huge supply of guns and drugs, so he stopped, not knowing what to do. With quick thinking, he was able to record the conversation from his phone. As things escalated, one of the men was shot." West stopped talking but stared at Katie.

Katie thought about it. "My guess is that one of the men was someone in high power that pulled strings, and the police and federal officer hadn't been able to connect anything to him. Am I on the right track?"

He nodded. "Pretty much. I was told not to disclose any of this unless it was directly related to the homicides. Need-to-know basis."

Katie got up and brought two coffee mugs to the counter. She sat down, still thinking about what he had said. She pushed sugar packets and creamer toward him. "Tell me what's on your mind. What's bothering you?" She knew there was something else and it was important enough for the marshal to come to her house in the middle of the night.

"I know you're not happy co-investigating the family's murder."

"No."

"I know the sheriff's department and a federal enforcement

agency work together with stresses. There are different motivations. Neither is wrong... but..."

"No, but it complicates things. My responsibility to the investigation and to the community is to find and arrest the killer. It's that simple."

"Of course. That's what we want too."

Katie paused and made a slightly sour face. "But you're the feds. You want to take charge and question everything we are doing. It's only going to slow down the process and give the killer more time to make the trail go cold."

Marshal West took a sip of coffee. "There's something that bothers me about this case. And, I wanted to talk to you first..."

"What's that?"

"We've found that everyone related to the case that Mr. Banks testified at are accounted for and couldn't have murdered them. That's what took me longer to get here to Pine Valley."

That comment made Katie take notice. "Doesn't mean they didn't hire someone." She realized the feds had access to more information than the sheriff's department, just as she knew that there was a second family murdered, which the feds didn't. But she wasn't going to share anything about the day right now. It would be in reports but not in the middle of the night at her home. "So what are you saying? Emily Banks was a target for something else? Kidnapping? Trafficking?"

He sighed. "It's possible that Emily might have been a target of kidnapping or trafficking; we had a team looking into missing children."

"Is that what you think or it's what the US Marshals Service thinks?"

"Right now, it's what I think."

"Huh, I see." It changed some things for Katie, which she didn't want to share with the marshal—at least not yet. She wanted to talk to McGaven. It had occurred to them that the real targets, from both families, were the little girls. The fact that the Banks family was in witness protection might have been secondary, and perhaps even unknown to the killer.

"I know I haven't made a good impression, but we're on the same side here. I want to help find the killer. That's why I came here under more informal conditions so I could explain these things. My priority is with finding the killer and working with you."

Katie wasn't going to let her guard down, but she appreciated what he had to say. "I think, Marshal West, you need to be at the Pine Valley Sheriff's Department, detective division, at 0900 tomorrow. Okay?"

The marshal was going to say something else, but he decided not to. He nodded. "Okay, Detective." He rose to leave. "I'll see you at 0900."

Katie followed the marshal to the front door and he left. Her mind was in an exhausted state, but she kept thinking about two little girls being the primary targets. The marshal's visit was unusual, but it seemed West was desperate to make a good impression to his bosses.

It took her another forty-five minutes until she fell asleep again.

EIGHT

Thursday 0745 hours

Katie finished her second cup of coffee as she worked on the murder board. The cold-case unit was located in the forensic division due to department space limitations, and she and McGaven had an office and a larger conference room that they used to lay out investigations. It worked well—at this point she never wanted to change it. The forensics area was quiet and allowed the detectives to be close to the evidence and old case files.

The board they used for the investigation was two walls, floor to ceiling, where they would affix photos of the crime scenes, autopsy reports, forensics, map locations, and lists for the behavioral profiling. After receiving a preliminary forensic report, Katie divided the investigative board into two sections— one side for each family. As she posted several photos of the Banks family, aka the Wagners, she stared at each member: Mr. and Mrs. Banks, Riley, Tyler, and little Emily. She still couldn't erase from her mind the scene in the barn.

Katie stepped back and stared at the family. It was only the beginning, but she memorized their faces.

The Banks/Wagner evidence and preliminary evidence:

Emily found at the top of the property dressed in a too large nightgown. Fresh blood on front of the gown. No injuries, no dirt or indication that the little girl climbed to her location. Someone took/hid her there? Was it her mother, as she said?

Clean/tidy rooms.

All garbage was taken away—but no waste pickup was scheduled for a few days.

Broken window at bathroom. No sign of entry.

No footprints (except those leading down a trail to creek area). No fingerprints.

Small pottery fragment/chip in kitchen—waiting testing.

Bodies found lined up on barn floor.

Blood smears around doorway.

Bloodied hammer in middle of house indicating a murder weapon, but was found that the family had been victims of some type of knife attack and not blunt force trauma. Waiting for blood on hammer to be tested.

Filing cabinets in barn filled with seemingly random newspaper articles from Denver, Las Vegas, and Los Angeles areas.

Found ID cards for Kent and Sharon Wagner of Colorado hidden in wall.

A bag with a child's blue dress with polka dots found in creek behind property.

Katie ran the entire crime scene through her mind. The big question was why was Emily up on the hillside alone? Who put her there? Her mom, like she said? Did she somehow escape by herself?

"Looks like you've been busy this morning," said McGaven as he entered the room and put his laptop on the table.

"Morning."

"Morning, partner." He looked at the board. "Somehow I thought you would have more."

"Baby steps... and lack of sleep," she said. Katie leaned against the table.

"What's up?"

"I met Marshal West last night."

"Last night?"

"He showed up at my house—late."

"What? Who is this guy?" It was clear McGaven was annoyed by the visit.

"I know, I was mad too, but it's all okay." Even though she didn't particularly agree with the marshal's behavior, she knew they had to work together.

"Katie, that's really inappropriate, not to mention unprofessional. There were probably a million protocols broken."

"It's okay. I told him I wouldn't report it, but you're my partner and we have no secrets."

McGaven let out a sigh. "Fine. So when do I get to meet this guy?"

"I told him 0900 in the detective division."

"I can't wait to meet him," he said with sarcasm.

"Just a heads up. He's a rookie but I think he could be one of the good guys. He wants to make a difference."

"What makes you say that?"

"He suggested that Emily was the target and not the family. They were collateral damage." Katie thought maybe the marshal could be someone on their side. It would make the investigation go that much smoother—and faster.

"Interesting." McGaven sat down and opened his laptop.

Katie began to organize the other side of the board with the Sanderson family when McGaven's cell rang.

"McGaven," he said. "Okay, thanks. Yeah, I know it."

"What?"

"That was Deputy Hansen. Someone has spotted Tessa Sanderson."

"Let's go."

Katie and McGaven drove to the Cedar District, which was located in the older areas of Pine Valley. It had that name because of all the cedar trees that were once abundant in that area. It was a quiet, moderately priced, and well-kept area. Crime was relatively low due to the hands-on neighborhood watch. People cared for the community, and it had been documented by the sheriff's department when a group of neighbors from that area had stopped a home invasion.

McGaven parked the detective sedan a couple of houses away from the one of interest. The street was quiet despite three patrol cars parked at the house.

Katie stepped out and her boot stuck in the mud. It had rained the night before. "Ugh." She began to wipe her boot on the lawn.

McGaven surveyed his partner's discomfort. "Sorry..."

Deputy Hansen waved the detectives over.

"So what do you have?" said McGaven.

"We received a call from one of the neighbors at 6 a.m.," he said looking at his notebook. "A Carol Ainsworth, retired, said she saw lights around 4 a.m., and saw a man and a little girl resembling Tessa later on, closer to 6 a.m., in the house, so she called the cops. We entered and searched the house, but whoever was there had already gone. There are fresh tire tracks around back. Must've been whoever had been inside. That's all we have."

"What's the status of the house?" she said. "Owner?"

"The house was foreclosed six months ago and the residents

vacated more than three months back. Mrs. Ainsworth thought it strange to see lights and didn't want any squatters in the neighborhood."

"What about the little girl?" she said.

"Mrs. Ainsworth saw her for a second, but she swore it looked like the little girl on the news." He looked back at his list. "John and Eva will be documenting the house, but it looks like they're detained at a burglary. Hamilton and Alvarez should be here anytime."

"We're going to take a look around," said Katie.

"Of course, Detective. We're going to finish our canvass of the area. I will remain to keep it protected until it's released."

"Thanks, Hansen," said McGaven.

Hansen nodded and joined the other detectives who were finishing up placing the crime scene tape protecting any potential evidence.

Katie and McGaven headed to the small two-bedroom house. It was noticeably run-down. The lawn and plants were dead—flattened brown leaves leaving way for an abundance of weeds. The paint was peeling and the windows were dirty, making it difficult to see inside.

The detectives put on their gloves and entered. The interior had been stripped of carpet and appliances, and some walls were missing drywall, exposing the frame.

"So someone killed the Sanderson family and took five-year-old Tessa to this location?" said Katie.

"We only have the eyewitness that saw something going on here. For all we know, it could have been someone else..."

"True." Katie looked around. There was a small folding table lying on the floor in what was once the kitchen. The legs had been retracted. There were several bags of fast food with only remnants of sandwiches and burgers. There were no drinks, which seemed unusual to Katie. Had the person purposely taken the drinks because of possible identification?

"Got something," said McGaven from one of the rooms.

Katie joined him. There was a small garbage bag in the corner of the room.

"That looks similar to the one we found at the creek," said Katie.

McGaven carefully opened it, leaving it on the floor. "It looks like clothing."

"A child's?" she said.

"I don't know, I want to leave it for John to properly document and collect it."

"I agree."

"It may mean nothing."

"Or... it may mean a lot," she said.

Katie continued to walk around the rooms, but she noticed nothing unusual. It was just a house that was in need of maintenance and had been sitting vacant too long.

"So the neighbor saw some light," she said, trying the light switches. Nothing happened. "So that means they had to have brought a flashlight or lantern." She exited through the back door. The lock had been pried open and was now hanging precariously. "This looks recent. Quite the flimsy lock." There were deep grooves around the doorframe.

She strode across the narrow backyard, which was only straggly weeds now. There was a small gate—left open. She found a narrow driveway just big enough for one car. There were recent tire marks, just as the deputy had described. The rain had made the area muddy, which made the tire impression clear.

Glancing down at the gate, there were several sets of bootprints from the deputies. Katie was relieved patrol hadn't trampled the tire impressions.

"Looks like they will make good impression evidence," said McGaven.

Katie nodded but she'd noticed some paper tucked at the

corner of the fence. Bending down, she pulled and found it to be a cigarette wrapper. Glancing around, she saw an area where there were three extinguished butts. "We need to mark this."

McGaven left and quickly returned with small evidence markers, placing them appropriately.

"There's not much to go on. We don't know if it was Tessa and her kidnapper. But hopefully we'll know more when the deputies finish their canvass," said Katie.

"Hey, looks like there are some good impressions," said a man from behind them.

"Hey, you can't be here," said McGaven, moving toward the man.

"Oh, but you're wrong." He reached into his jacket pocket and pulled out identification and flashed it with drama. "US Marshal West. And you must be... Detective McGaven. Wow, you're tall."

"I don't care who you are. You are contaminating this area and don't have clearance," said McGaven.

"Marshal West, what are you doing here?" said Katie. She was keeping her anger in check. Her patience was definitely waning with her encounters with the marshal.

"I was told you two were here. And if it possibly has anything to do with my case, I have every right to be here."

"You were supposed to meet us at the department at 0900." Katie didn't like the marshal's attitude. It was different than last night, which suggested he might not be someone they could trust after all. What kind of game was he playing? Now she wondered if he'd been telling her the truth—or the whole truth. "Gav is right. You need to leave," she said.

The marshal took a step forward and then decided against what he was going to say.

"We'll see you back at the department," said Katie. "We'll be about an hour."

Marshal West walked away, giving a partial wave in the process.

"What a complete jerk," said McGaven.

Katie was surprised by her partner's outburst. "Ignore him. He's got that rookie thing going on. You know, trying to prove he has all the answers."

"By acting disrespectful and contaminating a potential crime scene? That's not a great start."

Katie sighed. "I know. I'm not happy either. But it's only going to make our investigation more complicated than it already is if we don't cooperate. Let's just keep going and make things work."

McGaven stared at where the marshal had disappeared. "Fine."

"C'mon, Gav, we've got to get going. We have tons of information to sift through and people to interview."

He nodded. "We will get to the bottom of this—with or without the marshal's help."

"We definitely will," she said as she looked at the tire impression, hoping it would give them a new lead to find Tessa.

NINE

Katie and McGaven stopped at their office in the forensic division before meeting the marshal upstairs. As they entered the forensic area, they could hear voices. It wasn't just John and Eva. There were two distinct male voices—one was John but the other...

Katie paused and tried to place the other voice. "Wait," she said. "That's..."

"Who?" her partner replied.

"That voice." She hurried to the main forensic examination room and pushed the door open, interrupting John and the marshal. There was preliminary evidence lying on several tables: the Banks family's clothing. "What's going on here?"

McGaven rushed behind his partner and stood in the doorway.

"Detective," said John. He smiled. He always seemed happy to see her.

"John, I thought you would be at the house in the Cedar District," she said.

"Eva is on it. She's better than I am at impression evidence. I wanted to get back and begin working on everything we pulled from the two crime scenes."

"Marshal West, I thought we were going to meet upstairs," Katie said, turning to the other man in the room.

"Well, we did say that, but I thought it would be more prudent to get started here in forensics. And I've been chatting with John about what he's found."

"And you thought that was sensible without talking to the investigating detectives first..." said McGaven, who didn't move from the doorway. "We *were* at the crime scene and—"

"Look," said West. "I think we might've gotten off to a rough start here. That wasn't my intention." He walked toward McGaven and extended his hand. "US Marshal Kyle West."

"Nice to meet you," said McGaven, a hint of sarcasm in his voice.

"Since we'll be working on the case together, I thought I'd better get up to speed," the marshal said, glibly explaining his presence in the forensic lab. "I don't want to be the weak link."

Katie looked around at the evidence.

John stared at her with his eyebrows slightly raised. "I was told to cooperate with the feds in any way we can."

"Okay," said Katie. "Let's clear this up right now." She tried to keep her annoyance out of her voice, but as she reran the conversation she'd had with the marshal in her mind, things still bothered her.

The three men turned to stare at her.

"We're all on the same side. We all want the same thing—to find the killer, or killers. Right?"

No one said anything, but merely nodded.

"And... I say we make a game plan respectful of each other, otherwise we're just wasting time. Okay?"

"Of course," said Marshal West.

"Absolutely," said McGaven.

"We need full transparency with each other to investigate this case with the care and attention it needs," she said. She looked pointedly at West.

"Lead the way, Detective," said West as he made a slight backward movement.

"John, since we're here, do you have anything for us?"

"I'm still in the beginning of testing, but I have photos of everything if you all want to be on the same page," said John.

"Great. Let's have a look since the marshal hasn't seen anything yet," she said.

John gave a wink to Katie, and she took it to mean something along the lines of "good job for being the peacemaker."

The forensic supervisor moved to one of the computer stations and sat down on the rolling stool. He clicked on an icon with yesterday's date. The photos were in chronological order beginning with the barn and the family, then the farmhouse. As John clicked on each image for about ten seconds before moving on, no one spoke. The photos of the family were disturbing, and the detectives and marshal didn't comment.

Katie hated walking through that tragedy again, but something about the Bankses' pajamas seemed odd, as it had on site. The family members were all wearing new-looking pajamas. Was it a coincidence or was it something planned by the killer? The two children, Riley and Tyler, appeared to have been dressed in matching sets. But Riley's top was on backwards, though still completely buttoned.

"Look at Riley's pajama top," she said.

McGaven moved closer. "It's backwards?"

She nodded.

"What does that mean?" said the marshal.

"Maybe nothing — he's a kid after all. But it might mean that the family were reclothed *after* they were murdered," she said. "All the garbage has been removed—including clothes."

"I think this might help," said John. He got up from his stool and went to one of the examination tables. He donned a pair of gloves. "Notice anything?"

Katie studied the bloody clothing. "There aren't any slash marks. I wasn't a hundred percent sure at the crime scene."

"So?" said West.

"It means they were dressed in these pajamas after they were slashed."

"Is that important?"

"It's important to the mindset and motive of the killer—and the staging of the scene." Katie looked at the children's clothes as well. All were the same. There were no tears, holes, or any wear marks. She turned to John. "Is there any way to test if these were new clothes?"

"You mean like just off the rack?" said John. "Or coming in from a shipment?"

"Yes."

"Hmm... Let me see what I can do. There could be some formaldehyde resins and textile dyes that help to prevent any issues like bugs or moisture on new clothing."

"Anything about the blood on Emily's nightgown?" she said.

"Not yet. We're typing it and then we'll see if it matches her, or someone in her family."

"Thanks, John. We'll be back when you've had more time to run all the tests," she said. Katie walked to the door followed by McGaven.

"Wait. Is that it?" said West.

Katie and McGaven moved to their investigation headquarters without answering the marshal. McGaven immediately went to his laptop and keyed up some information to help with their next move. Marshal West hurried to catch up and walked into the room.

"Wow, this is great. It reminds me of a television show I used to watch." He immediately stood in front of the board reading Katie's notes. He turned. "Is this how you keep your facts straight?"

"It's where we lay out the investigation," she said.

"And where Detective Scott tries to build the killer's profile in lists," said McGaven.

"Profile? Based on?"

"Evidence from the crime scenes, criminal behavior patterns, victimology, and autopsy reports," she said, not wanting to explain everything to the marshal. She knew that some investigators didn't think much of the profiling and threshold assessments that she found useful. In Katie's opinion, it was the foundation for any investigation.

"Does that really work? I mean, can you profile the killer—to know who he or she is?" said West.

McGaven had been scrolling through searches. "If you have to ask, then you won't ever understand."

"How accurate can a profile be?"

"Pretty accurate," said McGaven.

"Profiles are used to move the investigation forward—to confirm that the investigation is going in the right direction or indicate other directions to try. Not to magically tell you what the hair and eye color of the killer is—unless it's left at the crime scene," said Katie. She gathered her jacket and notebook. "Ready, Gav?"

He shut his laptop and readied to leave.

"Where are we going?" said West.

"*We're* going to investigate," said McGaven as he picked up a file containing the Bankses' employment records. "While we wait for forensic testing and autopsy results, we're going to begin with what the Bankses were doing the week before their deaths."

"Place of work," said Katie.

The detectives left the room and headed out.

"Wait," said West. "What do I do now until results come in?"

Katie called, "Do what you normally do when your witness protection goes bad and the families are killed."

TEN

Thursday 1045 hours

Katie drove to Kensington & Associates for an appointment with the managing broker, Stevie Jackson. According to employment records and licenses, Robert Banks was a real estate agent and had worked there for two years—the entire time the family had been in witness protection. McGaven rode in silence and kept his focus out the window.

"So is this usual procedure?" said Marshal West. He sat in the back seat under obvious protest. There had been words between McGaven and West in the parking lot around who would ride shotgun. It was a childish display, but each seemed to be trying to assert their authority.

"I think it's best to observe at this point," said Katie. She wasn't looking forward to being the referee—the two men had to work out their differences professionally.

"The family that was protected by the government was murdered," said McGaven. "This has now fallen in our jurisdiction." McGaven kept his demeanor stoic but clenched his jaw. He looked at his iPad. "Robert Banks worked as a licensed real estate agent the past two years. It seems he had a few sales, but nothing that would support a family of five, or a house of that size."

West didn't take the hint to be quiet. Instead, he said, "There have been approximately nineteen thousand participants in the witness protection program. It began in 1971, and according to the government statistics, no one has ever been harmed or killed when abiding by the marshal's rules."

"Until now," said McGaven.

"Enough," said Katie. "Can we get back to the investigation? We need to find out more about the Banks family, and whether it's possible they were a target due to their testimony or if they were targeted for something else."

Her partner and the marshal fell silent. She turned the police sedan into the parking lot for Kensington & Associates. It was a small one-story house that had been converted into a business. Trimmed hedges fanned across the front of the property where two cars were parked. There was a dark hose wound around a hook. A simple welcome mat marked the entrance.

Katie pulled into a spare parking space and cut the engine. She didn't look to the men and got out of the vehicle, heading to the entrance. A glance at her watch told her it was two minutes before their appointment. She pushed open the door and immediately felt the warmth and smell of fresh coffee. A young woman with short dark hair sat at the front desk. It was a cramped area with numerous photos of properties adorning the walls.

"Hi, may I help you?" the woman said.

"Detective Katie Scott to see Stevie Jackson."

"Oh yes, of course, please wait one moment." The woman got up and disappeared into another room.

McGaven and West entered. They seemed more relaxed. The three of them crowded the front room.

A tall blonde woman dressed in a navy suit greeted them. "Hello, Detectives. I'm Stevie Jackson." She eyed McGaven.

Katie made a quick decision based on the woman's reaction and body language. "I'm Detective Scott and this is my partner Detective McGaven. My partner has a few questions for you about Robert Banks."

"Of course. Please, let's talk in my office." She waited for McGaven to follow her.

Katie gently guided West out the front door.

Once outside, West turned to Katie. "What's all that about? Aren't you going to question her?"

"No. McGaven is very capable and she seemed to like him. It helps when being questioned by the police if people are more at ease or are attracted to them."

West smiled. "And she might offer more information."

"Something like that."

"Hey," he said. "I'm not the enemy here."

"Never said you were." Katie walked away.

"What are you looking for?"

"Want to get a feel for the business. Since Mr. Banks came here every day and didn't make but a handful of sales over the past two years, I wanted to check it out."

West looked around. It was clear he didn't know what she was looking for.

Katie ignored the marshal. She noticed there were deep tire marks in the parking lot, several sets, as if a commercial truck had been there numerous times. Following the tracks, she saw the truck had stopped in the middle of the parking area. The first thing she thought was that a car had been towed. There were two cars parked. She casually walked by each four-door sedan. There were files and open house flyers on the passenger seats.

"Anything?" said West.

Katie didn't answer right away. She continued to walk

around the area. Noticing the back door, she could see a small kitchen through the window. There were several cups in the sink.

Marshal West remained quiet as he watched as Katie walked the perimeter. The real estate office sat on a large property where the closest neighbor was two hundred yards away, with a group of trees separating them. She didn't see anything to indicate something out of the ordinary. The property was clean, no garbage was strewn and there weren't any maintenance items stored in back.

"So I'm guessing you're working on your profile?" said West.

"No, I just wanted to see where Mr. Banks worked and where he spent so much time."

Marshal West frowned. "We need—"

"To be patient. We have to wait for more information from the medical examiner's office and forensics. So for now we talk to everyone we can and try to find out who the victims were and reconstruct their last days," she said. "Marshal West, have you ever conducted an investigation before? Fugitive investigations? Anything?"

"I've been involved."

"Meaning?"

"Meaning I've been a part of fugitive investigations."

"That's what I thought. Then the answer is no. Tell me, Marshal West, what is it that you have to report back to your superiors?" Katie watched him closely. She noticed he seemed nervous, fidgety, and unable to keep his hands still.

He shoved them into his pockets. "I think we're past formalities. Call me Kyle."

Before Katie could answer, a young man with short dark hair, dark slacks, and a freshly pressed white dress shirt stepped out the back door. "Hi, can I help you?" the man said.

"I'm Detective Scott," she said.

"Oh, you're investigating the Bankses?" His eyes grew wide.

"Yes. And you are?" she said.

"I'm sorry," he said moving forward with an outstretched hand. "I'm Eddie. Eddie Reynolds."

Shaking his hand, she said, "Nice to meet you, Mr. Reynolds."

"I thought there was a detective already inside. What's going on out here?" said Eddie looking around more out of curiosity than concern.

"Do most agents park back here?" she said.

"Mostly to leave spots open up front for clients."

"Did Robert Banks park back here?"

"Yeah, mostly I guess, which was weird."

"How so?"

"Well, his car tires were slashed three times."

"Anyone else's tires?"

"No."

"When was the last time?"

Reynolds thought a moment. "About two weeks ago."

"What happened?" Katie watched the man closely to determine if he was telling the truth. He seemed calm and focused. Good eye contact. She glanced up at the building and noticed there weren't any video cameras of any kind.

"The same as before... Rob came out and found one of his tires shredded so he called his road service company."

"Did they change the tire right here?"

"The first two times they did, but the last one they towed it."

"Do you remember the name of the company?"

"Um, it was Sierra Roadside."

"Thank you, Mr. Reynolds," she said. "If you remember anything that might be useful to us, please don't hesitate to call." She handed him a business card.

"Like?"

"If you see anyone suspicious around here or if there's anything unusual."

"Sure."

Katie turned to head back to the entrance to wait for McGaven.

"Is that it?" said West.

Katie nodded, not wanting to explain herself to him.

"Okay."

"You were expecting something else?"

The marshal stopped. "Well yeah."

Katie laughed. "Your inexperience in criminal investigation, specifically homicide, shows, Marshal." She turned to him. "What would you do?" Her curiosity got the better of her.

"Well, I would have pressed Mr. Reynolds harder. What kind of guy was Rob and if he saw anything back there. I don't know... questions like that." He stared at Katie.

She smiled. "I can see your thought process."

"Good."

"And if I pressed him, he'd clam up and act like he's a suspect. I wanted to make it friendly, routine. We can always requestion him at any time and he will most likely be more open to it."

"Well maybe..."

"And McGaven is questioning the manager, so we're building a rapport with this company and gaining trust. People are much more reciprocal when they feel respected and helpful."

Marshal West stared at Katie. "Well okay then." He headed to the main entrance.

Katie thought it was odd he didn't argue further. He seemed to give up easily and that made her skeptical.

. . .

Katie and the marshal waited for McGaven in the car. Katie took the opportunity to make some notes. She called the towing company, Sierra Roadside, and found out the driver, Trent Gaines, would be back in forty minutes.

McGaven left the real estate office and hurried to the car. He got in.

"Well that was interesting," he said flipping open his notebook, perusing his shorthand.

"And?" she said.

"It seems that Robert Banks had been harassed."

"By who?"

"He was getting threatening phone calls and his tires had been slashed three times."

"Did he make a report to the police?" she said.

"No. He should have to his handlers at witness protection." McGaven turned to face the marshal in the back seat. "Did you know about any of this?"

"No. I just found out about the slashed tires when you did. He never reported anything to us."

McGaven looked to Katie. "Meaning?"

"We talked with one of the real estate agents, Eddie Reynolds, and he filled us in," she said. "He didn't say anything about Mr. Banks being harassed."

"That's because he only reported it to the managing broker."

"When was the last harassing call?"

"The day before yesterday."

"Okay," she said. "So we know that someone was harassing Mr. Banks, slashing his tires, and then the entire family ends up dead, except for Emily." Katie thought about it. "We need a list of calls, both incoming and outgoing, from his cell phone and the office."

"On it," said McGaven. "Where now? The road service?"

"Yes. But I want to make another stop first."

ELEVEN

Thursday 1235 hours

Katie pulled into the hospital parking lot and found a space near the entrance.

"I thought we had a hot investigation to pursue. You know, the first forty-eight hours are the most important," said the marshal with definite sarcasm in his voice.

Katie watched McGaven tense. His jaw clenched as he remained looking straight ahead, and it was clear that he wanted to say something but was fighting the urge.

"Emily is our prime witness," she said.

"That little girl? She'll probably describe one of her stuffed animals as the killer."

Katie ignored their ride along in the back seat. She knew they needed to keep the peace between departments, so they could continue with *their* investigation. She got out of the sedan and headed straight to the main entrance. Not waiting for her partner or the marshal, she hurried to the elevator and pressed the button for the fourth floor. It was true they were taking a detour, but she needed to see the little girl and check she was okay.

Just as the elevator doors were about to close, McGaven stuck his arm in.

"Where's the fire?" her partner said.

"No fire," she said. "Just an investigation."

When all three were on board, they headed up to the fourth floor.

Katie wasn't exactly sure where Emily was located, but she turned to the left and followed the long hallway. It didn't take long to see the uniformed officer outside a door. The room was at the end, which made it easier to see who came and went.

Katie pulled her badge. "Detective Scott."

McGaven and Marshal West showed theirs.

The officer nodded, allowing them access.

The room wasn't a typical hospital room. It had a small bedroom area and then another area with round tables, including a child's play area with several baskets of toys.

Deputy Sasha Brown had been seated at a table and now stood up to greet the detectives. She was not dressed in her uniform, but rather plain clothes of jeans and sweater. "Detectives," she said, and glanced at the marshal.

"How is she?" said Katie.

"The doctors said physically she's fine, but she's confused as to where her family is," said Brown. "The child psychologist has worked with her, but it's unclear what the prognosis will be."

"Did she remember anything?" Katie asked.

"She refuses to talk about anything from that night, only things that happened before. If we push her, she completely shuts down."

It made Katie miserable that the girl was all alone. "Any family?"

"An aunt, Mrs. Banks's sister, will be here tomorrow to take her home to Arizona."

"Oh." Katie watched as the little girl played with some stuffed dolls and animals. She sat in the corner, seemingly in her own world, and hadn't looked up when the detectives entered the area. "Can I see her?"

The deputy nodded.

McGaven and West stayed with the deputy as Katie slowly approached the little girl. She was dressed in pants and hoodie. Her curled blonde hair was tousled.

"Hi, Emily," Katie said as she slowly knelt down on the floor in front of her.

Emily looked up and her eyes lit up in recognition of Katie. "Where's your dog..."

"Cisco?" Katie smiled. "He's at home."

"Can I see him?" Her blue eyes watched Katie closely.

"I don't know. Dogs aren't allowed in the hospital."

"Oh," she said and looked down at the cute doll she had been playing with.

"That's a pretty doll."

"I named her Lily."

"That's a nice name," said Katie. "Do you know a Lily?"

Emily nodded.

"Someone at school?"

She shook her head.

"Family?"

Emily didn't respond.

"I see her sometimes."

Katie wasn't sure if Emily was talking about a real person or a make-believe friend. "Where do you see her?"

"She visits me."

"At home?"

"Sometimes."

Katie treaded carefully. "Does she like to play outside?"

"Uh-huh."

Katie turned to look at McGaven. They were all listening

and watching. He gave her a slight nod as if to say that she was getting somewhere and to keep going.

Katie picked up a cute teddy bear with a big red bow. "I had a bear like this when I was about your age."

Emily looked at the bear for several seconds. "My bear had a blue bow."

Katie thought it was unusual that she said *had* instead of *has*. She also didn't recall a bear with a bow in her room. She would have to look at crime scene photos.

"Can I go home?" Emily said.

Her sad and almost soulful eyes tugged at Katie. It was as if her childhood had been taken from her.

"Not right now. But soon." That was the only thing Katie could say.

Emily went back to playing with two dolls.

"Can I visit again?"

Emily got up and hugged Katie tight. It took Katie by surprise and she fought to keep the tears from flowing.

As the detectives and the marshal rode the elevator back down to the lobby, no one said a word. Katie couldn't get the image of Emily's sweet innocent face out of her mind. The emotions welled up inside her and made it difficult to concentrate. But they did learn about someone named Lily and had to get to the bottom of it. It could be something made up or something in the child's imagination, but Katie's instinct told her that it meant something—something real.

TWELVE

Katie followed the car's GPS system and pulled up to the sign that said "Sierra Roadside Towing." Interestingly, it was part of a large junkyard with all types of wrecked compressed vehicles stacked a dozen high—and they seemed to go on for miles. The overcast day gave the area an almost sci-fi feeling.

"Whoa," said McGaven. "We've been here before, but it has grown exponentially." He surveyed the area. "I guess when the towing company bought it, they went all out to make it more modern."

"It looks more like a prison," she said.

The acres of property that stretched as far as the eye could see were enclosed with heavy metal fences and razor wire. It looked abandoned. The detectives couldn't see any employees walking around, working, or stacking more compressed vehicles.

The marshal remained quiet in the back seat.

Katie drove for another twenty-five yards until they came to a secured gate with a high-tech video speaker. Everything was painted white and red. It seemed to be trying to resemble a modern facility with several cameras, infrared and zoom, mounted—more likely found at an IT facility.

Katie rolled down the window. "Hello?" she said.

After a few moments, a man's voice said, "Detective Scott."

She frowned. "Yes."

The gate opened with a subtle consistent hum.

"That's creepy," said McGaven.

"I agree."

"I've seen those before at some software facilities in Sacramento," said Marshal West.

That gave a chill down Katie's back—her instinct had been correct.

"Pull in to the right and park in front of the office." The speaker made a click indicating that the person had turned off the microphone.

"There's still time to turn back," said McGaven as he chuckled.

"We're going in," she said.

As the voice instructed, Katie drove to the right, found the office and parked. It was another house turned into an office. She didn't see any other cars except for the tow truck bearing the mountain sky logo of Sierra Roadside Towing parked along the side.

Katie got out of the sedan and headed to the office door when it opened. A tall clean-shaven man in his fifties exited wearing tan working overalls with numerous grease stains. His intense dark eyes watched them—his stare darting from one detective to the other and then to the marshal.

"Ah, Detectives Scott and McGaven. And who is this?" the man said.

"US Marshal Kyle West." He extended his hand but the man didn't reciprocate.

"And you are?" said Katie.

"I'm Tim Denton. I own and run this place." He stood tall, proud of his accomplishments.

"It's quite the setup," said McGaven.

"I take it you're referring to the security."

"Yes."

"Well, we live in a different age now and have to keep the wrong people out and the merchandise inside. With wrecked cars there are many valuable parts—it's not just the bumpers, rims, and doors. But the GPS, catalytic converters, and tires of course."

Katie thought about all the cars and parts. "And for recycling."

"Yes, Detective, you're correct."

"Mr. Denton, you said on the phone that your driver, Trent Gaines, would be here to talk to us about a tire repair and tow for a Mr. Robert Banks at Kensington and Associates."

"Yes, he's working in the shop."

"May we speak with him?" she said.

"Of course." He gestured to an area. "Follow the path and take the second right. It'll lead you right to the shop. I have some paperwork to complete, otherwise I would accompany you."

"Thank you," said McGaven.

The detectives headed down the path that had been indicated.

"Hey, I'm going to have a look around and I'll meet up," said West.

"Okay," said Katie. She felt relieved, but questioned why he would do so.

"Just to satisfy my curiosity..." He turned and walked in the opposite direction.

McGaven shrugged and headed to the shop. They could hear what sounded like heavy machinery. It was a grinding noise.

The building was larger than Katie had imagined. There

were four large roll-up doors where cars could be dismantled. She saw car parts—doors, bumpers, and other main pieces—but also the computerized parts: GPS, motherboards, computers, and the like. The detectives paused a moment as they reached the opening of one of the industrial roll-up doors. They could see sparks flying and it was clear someone was in the middle cutting through metal with an electric grinder.

Katie surveyed the area and it didn't seem there were any other employees around. She glanced at her partner before she entered the workshop.

There was an abrupt silence. The cutting tool had stopped.

"Hello? Mr. Gaines?" she said, still moving deeper into the space.

There was only quiet in response. No tools. No footsteps. No voices.

"Mr. Trent Gaines," she said.

McGaven motioned that he would take the right. Katie nodded and proceeded in the direction of where the initial cutting noise had taken place. She quietly approached. Her senses were on high alert. Arms tingled. Breathing shallow. Everything had seemed strange the moment they had arrived. Maybe she was untrusting in places and situations they hadn't experienced before—maybe—but she trusted her gut instincts and experience as a cop more.

She saw what used to be a red Ford truck that was now in eight large sections. The doors, tailgate, and bumpers were leaning against the wall as the internal parts were grouped in sections piled on a table. She could see the cutting tool lying on a nearby rolling worktable accompanied by a wrench. She could smell the combination of electricity and chemicals produced by the torch.

Katie hovered around the area. She saw a coffee mug half full. Touching the sides of the mug, it was still warm. She felt a presence, but just as she turned, a stocky man pushed her into the rolling table, where she lost her balance, causing the table to crash into the wall, spilling the tools everywhere.

"Katie!" yelled McGaven from the other side.

She regained her composure and got up. Catching a glimpse of dark blue overalls exiting the building, she ran. "He's running. Left-hand door!" Katie was completely composed and ran out the door behind Gaines. "Stop! Police!" She knew he wasn't going to stop, but kept her wits in case he was hiding. As she fled the building and was outside in the maze of compacted cars again, she instantly realized there were many places for the man to hide and areas where she could get ambushed. The towering layers of cars blocked some of the daylight, casting shadows.

She ran faster.

Katie didn't hear any footsteps except for her own. She expected to hear McGaven's boots behind her or Gaines's heavy footsteps—but there was no sound of them. She came to the end of a row and slowed her speed. The decision to keep going or turn left or right plagued her.

Then she heard it. A soft shuffle as if someone had dragged their foot along the path. The sound was close. She slowed her breath. It was to her left, so she proceeded with caution. Glancing behind her, she expected to see her six-foot six-inch partner bounding around the corner, but he wasn't in sight.

Katie wanted to catch Gaines before he fled the premises. She inched near the noise. Deciding to lower her body, she used some of the auto graveyard pieces as her shield. She inched lower with her cheek nearly touching the ground until she could see a partial pair of well-worn steel-toed boots. They moved back and forth, indicating that the person wasn't sure what to do. Run or stay.

Katie scooted back and stood up. She retraced her steps and made her way around the stack, coming up behind Gaines. Taking a slow step at a time, she wanted to have the element of surprise. She finally saw the back of Gaines. His messy hair was wet from sweat. He ran his fingers nervously through it. He swayed back and forth, ready to bolt at a moment's notice, but his eyes were fixed on a stack of metal.

Katie retrieved her gun and directed it in front of her. "Trent Gaines. Stay right there," she said. "Don't move."

"I can't... I can't go back," he said, slowly raising his hands. There was stress in his voice.

"We just want to talk to you. I don't care about anything else right now," she said.

Heavy footsteps approached. McGaven came into view with his weapon ready.

Katie approached the tow truck driver and easily put handcuffs on him. "I'll release you when I know you won't try to run again."

McGaven lowered his weapon. "Okay, partner?"

Katie nodded.

She guided Gaines to a place where he could sit down. Watching his expression and body language, it was clear he was scared and didn't seem to pose any type of immediate threat.

"Why did you run?" she said as she returned her weapon to its holster.

"I have a couple of warrants." He couldn't make eye contact with Katie.

"For what?"

"I missed my court dates."

"What were the charges?"

"Possession and trespass."

"I see. And all misunderstandings, I assume," she said.

"Something like that." He watched the detectives looking from one to another.

McGaven remained silent and moved around in the background. His height always made people nervous, and it helped to get answers quicker if he hovered in the background but within view.

"Mr. Gaines, we wanted to know more information about your interaction with Mr. Robert Banks at the real estate office." She watched his response.

"The slashed tire?"

"Yes."

"What do you want to know?"

"You were dispatched three times, correct?"

"Yeah."

"Did anything seem strange to you?"

"No, not really. But it did seem odd that someone slashed the same back right tire... three times. He must've made someone really mad or it was some kind of payback. I dunno. The third time, I needed to tow him to the tire shop so he could get a replacement and a spare."

"What was Mr. Banks like? Was he relaxed? Mad? Upset?"

Gaines thought a moment. "He was a nice guy. But the third time I arrived he was agitated and was talking quietly on his cell phone."

"What did he say?"

"I don't remember exactly. It was kinda hard to hear. But, I did hear 'you will be sorry' and I think, 'that's never going to happen.'"

Katie thought about this. It made sense with what the manager had said about Banks being harassed. But harassed about what? Why? Did it have anything to do with what was being researched in the files in the barn?

She took the handcuffs off Gaines. "We're not going to run you in, but I strongly suggest you take care of your warrants voluntarily. Okay?"

"Yes, ma'am. I swear I will."

The detectives and Gaines walked back to the office, where Katie got copies of the paperwork for Mr. Banks's request for service. Then Katie and McGaven walked back to the car where US Marshal West waited. He was leaning against the car with his arms crossed in front of his body.

"Where did you go?" said McGaven.

"Just checked the place out."

"That all?"

"Truthfully, I got turned around, so I came back to the office to wait for you."

"Oh," said McGaven with a hint of sarcasm to his voice. He had clearly been going to say something but decided to stay quiet.

"Learn anything?" West asked.

"Some," said Katie. "We'll fill you in." She carried the paperwork. "We need to get Mr. Banks's phone records."

"Working on it," said McGaven.

Katie took another look around. Another couple of seconds passed before she got into the sedan. The high-tech equipment and surveillance, the razor wire, and the feeling that someone was watching them closely had made her uneasy.

THIRTEEN

Thursday 1630 hours

There was a tense silence in the car as Katie drove to their next destination. She glanced at her partner, who seemed lost on his iPad coordinating information. Looking in the rearview mirror, she saw that West was on his cell phone sending text messages.

"So what does your boss say?" said McGaven. He never turned to look at the marshal directly, instead he kept his intense stare straight ahead.

"They want me to stay with you guys as you trace the victimology. It seems the logical course to find out what the killer wanted to gain by killing the family."

"What about the Sanderson family? You think there's a connection?" she said.

"It would be irresponsible to speculate on that at this point in the investigation," said West.

Katie agreed with him but didn't say anything; in her mind there had to be a connection between the two families. She needed to get back to the office. "There's been no word on the Sandersons' missing little girl?"

"No," said McGaven. His expression was grim.

"We need to go to the elementary school where Mrs. Banks worked as a teacher's aide." She glanced at the time. "The kids are gone for the day and the staff should still be there."

Katie half expected to hear West say something about this, but he rode in silence sending texts on his phone every so often until the police sedan pulled into the Pine Valley Middle School parking lot. It was vacant, the last bus just leaving the area. There were no parents waiting in the pickup lines. It was easy for Katie to find a parking place near the entrance.

One of Pine Valley's deputies and a resource officer walked up to them. Katie didn't immediately recognize the officer.

Katie flashed her detective badge. "We're here to speak with the principal."

The officer nodded. "Of course, Detective. You need to use the side entrance." He escorted the detectives and marshal to gain entry to the school. "Principal Wilson is down the hallway and turn to the left. You can't miss the offices."

"Thank you," said Katie as she walked inside.

The long hallway with classroom doors was empty. The floors shined and the lockers were unusually clean. No graffiti or stickers or gouges, no names of bands or swear words. The school seemed to be well maintained and had decent security. Even so, Katie was relieved there were police officers manning a post there.

They passed a classroom where a teacher was organizing paperwork from the day. Katie paused at the doorway.

"Excuse me?" she said.

The teacher looked up and immediately stared at Katie's badge and gun, which was a typical reaction from most people.

"Yes?" the woman said.

"Hi. I'm Detective Scott and this is my partner, Detective McGaven," she said.

"I'm Gabby Rey," she said. "You're here about Sam, aren't you?" Her eyes were red from crying.

"Samantha Banks, yes," replied Katie. She saw that the woman was noticeably upset. To McGaven, she said, "Why don't you both go on and speak with the principal?"

McGaven nodded—Katie knew that her partner read her well—and continued on with the marshal. She moved into the classroom, admiring the walls with artwork and awards. The chalkboard had been wiped clean.

"Did you know Sam well?" She decided to use a more friendly address instead of being formal.

"Yes. She helped out in the classroom. We're over capacity with students and her experience was needed and we were fortunate to have had her."

"I see." Katie watched the teacher as she appeared to hold back more tears. "Did you know her only at school or also outside of the classroom?"

"We were friends. Sometimes we would get lunch together."

"Did you ever go to her home?"

"Yes, a few times. When we were getting ready for some projects," said Gabby. She took a breath. "Is it true the entire family was murdered?"

"It's an open investigation, so I really can't divulge much. But yes, it appears they were murdered." Katie wasn't going to disclose that Emily was alive. They were keeping the investigation quiet, especially the fact that the family had been in witness protection and the horrific nature of the crime.

"Oh," Gabby said, wiping her eyes. "I... can't even imagine..."

"We're trying to trace the last week or two of all their movements. Had you noticed anything different about Sam recently?"

"Well..."

"Anything you can tell me would be helpful. Did she seem different? Upset? Depressed? Scared? Was everything okay at home?"

"She was her usual self, but about two, maybe three, weeks ago, something seemed different. Well... And I guess... I guess it doesn't matter now."

Katie watched the teacher get up from her desk and walk to a storage cabinet. She opened the tall door, where inside were several drawers—each with a key lock, one with a padlock. Gabby rolled the numbers on the padlock until it snapped open. She carefully pulled out the drawer, which had a black canvas bag with a drawstring tucked inside. Katie watched and was surprised that something had been hidden in an elementary school classroom. A good hiding place, she thought. Gabby shut the classroom door and walked to her desk. She laid down the bag and pulled it open. Inside were folded papers and a cell phone.

"What is all that?" said Katie. She took a closer look.

"I'm not sure. But Sam wanted me to hide this away from the house in case she needed it. I didn't ask questions, but I know she was scared of something... or someone."

"When did she give this to you?"

"About two weeks ago."

"About the time she became stressed?"

The teacher nodded.

"Does anyone else know about this?"

"No. When I asked Sam about it, I don't even think her husband knew. I know there was something going on in her life, something big, that she wasn't telling me," said the teacher.

Katie knew it had to do with being in witness protection. But the what or why of the details was still a mystery. Was it because of the program, something in those files in the barn, or something else that got the family killed?

"Did she tell you anything?" said Katie.

"No. I didn't press her either." Gabby caught her breath as if she had said too much. "I figured if she needed to tell me she would." She hesitated as if she wanted to say something but couldn't.

Katie looked at the paperwork. There were letters from around the Colorado area and identification papers for Kent and Sharon Wagner—just like the ones they had found in the vent at the Bankses' home.

Katie looked at Gabby. "We're going to need to take this."

"Of course."

"If we need to ask you more questions..." she said and gave the teacher one of her business cards. "And if you remember something that might be important, please call me."

Gabby caught Katie's arm. "Please, Detective Scott, *please* find out who did this."

"We will do everything we can. Thank you for your time." Katie put everything back in the bag, tucked it under her arm, and left the classroom.

She looked down the hallway and didn't hear or see McGaven and West. Instead of catching up with them, she decided to take a walk around the school. It wasn't for anything specific, she just wanted to see where Samantha Banks worked, where she walked, took a break, and parked her car. Katie left the building and walked around to the back. She didn't see the resource officer. There were still several cars parked in an employee/teacher section. Katie assumed that non-teachers like maintenance and administrative personnel parked there too.

Holding the black bag tighter, she thought about why Samantha would need another phone, most likely a burner phone. These were generally used by individuals who didn't want their calls traced, particularly if they were involved in criminal activity or illicit affairs. Why would their victim need one?

Katie continued to take a reconnaissance around the property. She wanted to survey the parking locations and see if they were visible from various areas, such as the fence and trees. There was a possibility that someone had been watching Samantha and keeping track of the family. But Gabby didn't say Samantha had been harassed like her husband.

Katie moved closer to the property line. Nothing was out of the ordinary. It was just the usual old trash that had blown in and stopped by the chain-link fence. She turned and observed that someone could stay protected by a grouping of trees and watch who came and went.

Her cell phone chimed with a text message. It was McGaven: *Where are you?*

She quickly sent a text back: *Parking lot behind school.*

Within a minute the detective sedan drove around and pulled up to Katie. She got in the passenger's side.

"Learn anything?" she said as McGaven drove out of the parking lot.

"Not much. But we have Mrs. Banks's schedule and a copy of her employment file," said McGaven. He eyed the black bag. "What's that?"

"Paperwork and a burner phone that she had a teacher stash for her about two weeks ago."

McGaven raised his eyebrows. "Wow. Sounds more like a spy movie."

"What's the paperwork?" said the marshal.

"Things relating to Colorado and documents with their Wagner names. And paperwork showing that Mrs. Banks has a teaching degree."

"Sounds like she was calling people from her past on the burner phone," said West. He shook his head. "Not smart. It happens sometimes when people are homesick."

"We have a lot of things to filter through," said McGaven.

"Indeed." Katie thought about Mrs. Banks asking a teacher friend to hide the paperwork and phone for her. It seemed a bit of a desperate move and Katie was going to find out why Samantha Banks had made it.

FOURTEEN

Katie drove into her driveway and spotted Chad's large Jeep. She was glad he was there, but surprised. She thought he was working the next twenty-four hours at the fire department. At least Cisco had had company until she got home. Her uncle usually would stop by if Katie was working a big case, especially a current homicide.

Katie opened the front door. "Hello?"

No answer. Until she realized that Chad and Cisco were in the backyard. She heard the distinct play bark.

Katie opened the sliding door leading to the deck and yard. She stood for a moment watching the two of them play. Cisco would bark a couple of times waiting for the ball. Finally, Chad would throw it, to the dog's delight. This time when Cisco ran back, he raced by Chad and greeted Katie.

"Hey, Cisco," she said picking up the ball and throwing it.

"Hi, babe," said Chad walking to her. "Long day?"

Katie let out a breath. "Yes."

He wrapped his arms around her and kissed her. Holding her longer than usual, she could feel his breath against her hair.

Katie leaned back, looking at him. His intense blue eyes stared at her and seemed to read her well, like he had always. He had a scruffy short beard but his hair was still trimmed neatly, reminding her of most police officer's haircuts.

"What's wrong?" she said.

"What makes you think something is wrong?"

"Because I've known you most of our lives." She tried to force a smile, but something was definitely wrong. Katie braced for it.

Chad led her to the swing on the deck and sat down. Katie let out a quiet breath.

Chad stared at her as if he hadn't seen her in a very long time. "Katie, you have no idea how much you mean to me. Words can't describe how my heart, my soul, feels."

"I know. Our love is strong and unbreakable."

He smiled. "It's like a love story. Especially after what I went through being kidnapped and held prisoner for months, my faith in us kept me company. I never stopped thinking about you—and coming home to you."

For the first time since Katie could remember, she was scared. *Really* scared. Why was he saying all this?

"I've been thinking about this for a long time."

"About?" she said, barely able to breathe.

"You will always have my heart. That's why this is the hardest thing I've ever had to do."

"Just tell me," she said softly, bracing for the worst.

He held her hand. "I've been given the opportunity to head up a division of arson investigators in Los Angeles."

"You're leaving, aren't you?" she whispered.

Cisco dropped the ball and then he got comfortable and laid down. Chad held her hand.

"Yes. I'm going to take the job and relocate. I've been

contemplating this for a while. I love Pine Valley, but it isn't big enough for what I want to do in my career. You've always known that."

The words stung her. She couldn't breathe. Chad's love had always felt like a force that couldn't be broken.

"What about us?" she said, but she already knew the answer. She could feel it.

He took a breath.

"You could always ask me to go with you," she suggested.

"You love it here and you've got this great position. You've worked hard after the Army. You've made such a difference here. I couldn't ask you to give all that up." He watched her closely. His intensity was waning as he teared up. It was clear he had struggled with his decision—possibly the most difficult one of his life.

Katie turned away. Emotions, memories, and her entire life rushed through her mind. She would never beg him to stay—but the suffocating pain was overwhelming. It left her almost breathless.

"I would love you to come with me to LA," Chad continued. "But, I know you, and us. It would tear us apart because you have made an important contribution in Pine Valley with your cold-case work. You are amazing. Solving every case. I don't want you to start over again. You would be unhappy. Miserable. I don't want that."

"You can still ask me."

Chad leaned in, brushed his hand over her cheek. "I love you more than anyone. I want a life together but..."

"But in LA."

"Katie, honestly, would you be happy starting over at LAPD?"

She looked away. Of course not, she'd be unhappy. But she wanted Chad to be happy and thrive... even if it was without her. Remembering what he had gone through when he was held captive and what her life was like during that time, Katie began to cry.

"Katie, I couldn't ask you to leave everything here. I've been thinking about this for a while. This decision wasn't easy, but if I stay here, I will become discouraged and unhappy with my life. There's so much opportunity there for me." He hugged her tightly.

Everything in Katie's life seemed unimportant at that moment. Her cases. The farmhouse. Her friends and uncle. Everything was at a standstill. "People have survived long-distance relationships."

"True. Would you want to do that?" He looked away. "Our work makes it..."

"Almost impossible. But we can try," she said. Hating to hear her voice crack, Katie knew four hundred miles apart would eventually have them saying their goodbyes again. It would only prolong the pain and breakup.

"Do you really want to try?" he said.

Katie didn't answer. She knew the answer.

"I love you, Katie."

"I love you too." She wished there was some way to make it work out. In the back of her mind, she knew they had been drifting apart. Not with their feelings for each other, but with their plans for their lives, with what they both wanted—and needed—from them.

They remained silent and sat together on the swing for a while.

"When do you leave?" Katie couldn't imagine how she was going to get through her days without Chad.

"Monday."

"What about your house?"

"I'm renting it to one of the guys at work," he said.

There were signs Katie had ignored—she saw that now. When Chad began his arson investigator training, she knew he would need more of a challenge than just in Pine Valley—and she should have realized that would mean a bigger city or even another state.

Katie and Chad spent the night together. Katie didn't want to think about her cases, serial killers, missing children, or what she had to do. She only wanted to think about and be with Chad—even if it was only for a short while longer.

FIFTEEN

Friday 0445 hours

Katie couldn't sleep anymore, tossing and turning most of the night. She turned to watch Chad sleep. His breathing was soft and steady, and he seemed to be at peace. She wasn't quite sure how she would go on without him in her life, but she had no other choice. Even if something changed, it still didn't seem possible for them to be together. For a brief moment, she thought to wake him and tell him she would move to LA with him, that they would make it work. But she knew in her heart it wasn't in the cards for her.

She got out of bed, careful not to disturb Chad, and quickly got herself together for another long day of throwing herself into her work. She looked at Chad realizing that this was possibly going to be the last time they will be together. Bracing herself for a lasting heartache, she left the bedroom. A child was missing and two families had been brutally murdered. Her focus had to be on them.

Cisco was sad she was leaving so early—even before daylight. His whines were almost heartbreaking.

"Chad's still here and I'll have Uncle Wayne stop by later, okay?" she said to the shepherd.

Katie's drive to work was uneventful, but her emotions said otherwise. Questions—*Why? What if?* Could *we make it work?* —flooded through her mind.

The sunrise was beginning to peek through the trees and would soon give way to the morning. Katie pushed her thoughts to the case. They had a lot of information to sort through and make sense of. And the longer they didn't hear anything about Tessa, the worse the odds were that she was already dead.

Katie pulled her Jeep into the Pine Valley Sheriff's Department's employee lot. Her stomach grumbled and she realized she hadn't had her coffee yet. In a last-minute decision, she drove out of the lot and went to a drive-through restaurant, where she ordered an extra-large coffee and an egg sandwich. As she waited for her order, he mind rewound to her conversation with Chad. Her jaw tightened as she fought the urge to cry while wanting to vent her anger. Her heart was heavy and she knew she would grieve the loss as if it were a death. She was still in shock, pushing her feelings deep inside. She knew that she would have to deal with it, but for now, she focused on what she needed to do.

Katie drove back to the department and parked. The morning began to lighten and there was still a chill in the air. It was barely 6 a.m. She hurried to the back entrance of the administration building and headed down the hallway to the forensic entry. Balancing her food, she swiped her entrance badge and quickly entered.

The subtle whirring of the air system above sounded almost ominous as she walked down the hallways—not the comforting sound she had grown accustomed to. There were only energy-efficient lights, giving an otherworldly effect. She thought John might be in early, but no one was around and all the offices and labs were dark.

Katie walked to the cold-case unit's room. She opened the door and immediately saw neatly stacked boxes, which were the contents to the filing cabinets from the Bankses' barn. She put down her belongings and cup of coffee, intrigued.

On the main worktable in the middle of the room were printed-out pages of cell phone records neatly stacked and separated into paperclipped days. Denise from the records division must've completed this before she went home yesterday. Katie smiled. McGaven and Denise had been seeing each other for quite some time now. With a pang, she hoped their relationship, at least, would withstand life's trials and tribulations.

Katie looked up at the wall board, now featuring photos of each family. The driver's license images of the parents and school pictures of the children. Her breath caught in her throat. How senseless and horrifying. She stared at the photos of Emily and Tessa. Their innocence was overwhelming, as was the thought that a monster was relentlessly seeking them out.

The drive in Katie forced her to focus on the killer and motive. She looked at the location that was called in for the suspicious activity in the foreclosed house—an unidentified man with a little girl matching the description of Tessa Sanderson. What was the connection of the families? She studied the Sandersons' photographs and read their backgrounds, where the children went to school, and where the parents worked. Everything seemed normal and they appeared to be an average happy family.

Katie opened the laptop and began searching the Pine Valley area for foreclosed homes, specifically in less populated areas. She speculated that the person who took Tessa had been waiting for further instructions and that was why he was at an abandoned house.

Was the person who murdered the families and abducted Tessa the same person?

Or was it a part of something much bigger?

Katie thought about little Emily and hoped that when she got older and fully understood what happened to her parents and siblings that she would be able to recover and have a complete, happy life.

She stared at the investigation board. The faces of the victims. The injuries. The clothes. The crime scenes. The homes. The properties. The fact that it appeared that the killer or killers wanted the little girls.

She sat down and continued the arduous task of narrowing down foreclosed houses and properties. Once she was satisfied, she hit "print" and the printer in the corner slowly churned out pages. McGaven usually was the computer whiz and would dig for information that wasn't necessarily connected to the police databases. It felt good for Katie to be able to contribute to this task for a change. Her partner always made it seem easy when, in fact, it was a daunting undertaking and took skill.

The coffee had given her energy and Katie began to study the investigation with a vengeance—her unrest and sadness on the back burner. What was it that Marshal West had said at her house that night? He made mention of missing children. It didn't seem likely to her, but she had to keep all options open.

Katie keyed up organizations for missing and exploited children. She zeroed in on California, specifically the region that included Pine Valley. One of the offices was located in Mountain City and the director was Daniel Alderson. The city was about forty-five miles away, just outside of the county. She leaned back in the chair, looking at the faces of children who had gone missing. It wreaked havoc on her soul as she thought about how Emily could have easily ended up on this list.

Something caught her eye as she examined the site. There were several children connected to Colorado. The Bankses had Colorado identifications. Was that simply a coincidence?

The foreclosure list had finished printing, but Katie's attention had turned to those boxes from the Bankses' barn. She closed the laptop and got up, grabbed a box, and set it on the table. Inside were file folders with carefully handwritten labels. They captured her curiosity. She pulled out a handful of files and began sifting through them.

An hour later, the door opened and McGaven walked in.

"Morning," he said. "What in the world?" He looked around at the number of files organized and open, stacked papers, and his partner sitting on the floor. Paperwork was fanned all around her, taking up half the floor space.

"Morning," said Katie. She didn't look up.

McGaven watched his partner. He put down his jacket and laptop. "All right." He closed the door.

Katie looked up. "All right what?"

"I've known you for a while and we've been through a lot. Right?"

"I guess," she said. "What are you getting at?"

"What's going on?" he asked as he crossed his arms in front of him and leaned against the desk.

Katie stood up. "What's all this?" she said and gestured to his closed-off body language. "I'm making some headway here. And..." She watched her partner and sighed. It unnerved her that McGaven could read her so well.

He pulled up a chair and sat down. "We're not going a step further until you tell me."

Katie did the same. "I really don't want to talk about it right now."

"Tell me what's going on... before West gets here."

"I'm fine."

"That's not what I asked."

"It's..."

"Is it about Chad?"

Those words stung. And her heart felt the intense weight of the situation.

Watching his partner, he said, "I'll take that as a yes."

"Chad is taking a job in LA and moving there."

Her words hung in the room. Neither one of the detectives said anything for a minute.

"And...?"

"And so I'm staying here and we're no longer going to be..." Katie couldn't finish the sentence. "We have work to do." She went back to her boxes on the floor.

McGaven didn't say another word. It was unclear if he didn't know what to say or respected his partner's request.

The door opened and Marshal West stepped inside. He too surveyed all the paperwork. "Haven't you heard about computers?"

Katie continued with her search.

"Printing out cell phone records helps to spot numbers and fewer mistakes are made," said McGaven.

The marshal didn't say anything.

"Okay, it appears the Bankses were looking at any stories involving missing children in the Colorado area, specifically Denver," said Katie.

"Anything stand out?" said McGaven.

"There were articles printed out both from the news websites as well as actual paper articles. It seems they would track the story when a child went missing. Some were reunited with family members and a few were found murdered."

"And then their entire family was murdered except for Emily," said McGaven.

"I assume they were from Colorado originally?" she said.

"Yes," said West. "But then moved to Boston before being in witness protection."

Katie began to process that information. *Why were they*

tracking these children? Did this connect the Bankses and the Sandersons?

"Did the Bankses know someone who had a child go missing? Was there ever a family member it happened to?" she said.

"There's no indication of that. We do a strict background check on all witness protection candidates," said West. "If there was anything like that, we would have found it."

Katie stood up and studied the investigation board. It was difficult to not look at the families, to concentrate instead on the locations, behavioral evidence, and the unusual timing of the incidents. Everything, at least right now, came back to the little girls.

Katie sighed. "I've been trying to figure out what connects these families. The two little girls are a big connection and the method of death... but still..."

"What's up?" said McGaven.

"I found some interesting information on the Center for Missing and Exploited Children website."

"Okay."

"While we're waiting for the medical examiner and forensics, we need to talk to the director there. There's an office in Mountain City."

McGaven glanced at the marshal. "How do you want to work this?"

"Meaning?" she said. Although, she knew what her partner meant. Who was going to get stuck with the marshal if they split up?

McGaven didn't answer. The room became still.

"Okay, I get it," said West. "You two are trying to figure out who gets stuck with me." He smiled. "Who says that we have to partner up?"

"True," said McGaven.

"Look, I had a long talk with my boss and they have given me leeway to follow up on what I think is important." He walked closer to the investigation board and seemed to focus on the family photos, almost as if he was memorizing their faces. "The US Marshals Service doesn't take kindly to having one of their witness protection families murdered."

Katie and McGaven remained quiet for a moment.

"You mentioned at my house that you suspected the girls were the target and not the other family members. They were the collateral damage in the attempt to throw off suspicion," said Katie.

He turned. "That's right. And I still stand behind that theory."

Katie watched the marshal, seeing the determination in his eyes and body language. When he spoke of the missing children, it seemed to make him uptight and his gaze became intense.

"Okay. I have the name of the director and the location for the nearest office of the Center for Missing and Exploited Children. I want to get some background on these cases," she said.

"What about Alvarez and Hamilton? Aren't they working the missing child case?" said McGaven.

"Yes, but what I found on the site is all related to these murder cases—and these families. Anything we can find out will help with the profile of the killer."

"Fine. I can start there," said the marshal. "Text me the details and I'll report back later with my findings," he said and left the room.

"Well that was easy," said McGaven. "Now we can move forward without a fed watching our every move." He let out a sigh. "Let's get to work. I have to make several calls to relatives of the Sanderson family to see if we can get any more information. In the meantime…"

"In the meantime," Katie said, glancing at her phone for any new messages, and then sending a text to West with the details he needed, "we check out some of these foreclosures." She picked up a list where she had highlighted some properties and gave it to McGaven.

He quickly read down the list. "You think we might get lucky and pick up a trail?"

"Hiding in a foreclosed property seems like a great way to stay off the radar for a day or so."

"They could hole up and wait for further instructions," said McGaven. "No one would bother to look for them—and it would be fairly safe as long as it's in a more rural location. I'll update Alvarez and Hamilton on what we're doing."

Katie nodded. "Meet you outside." She left the office and forensic division. It felt good for her to get out and stretch her legs. Her lack of sleep, with worries and sadness, along with the intensity of these homicides, made her more stressed than usual.

She walked around the building and to the police sedan, noticing West's white vehicle. He was sitting inside and was speaking on the phone. It seemed heated and his demeanor seemed different. Katie could hear his voice but couldn't make out exactly what he was saying. She decided to move on—it wasn't her business. Hoping he would find out something useful on his mission, she concentrated on the locations they were going to visit, having narrowed the list down to four. She got in the police vehicle to wait for McGaven.

SIXTEEN

Friday 0830 hours

Katie drove to the farthest foreclosure location first, which was on the outskirts of the county in the small unincorporated town of Dwell Ravine. McGaven had checked Mr. Banks's property listings over the past two years and any new listings he went on tour to see. Nothing seemed to cross with the current foreclosures. The detectives decided to move forward based on the potential sighting of Tessa in the Cedar District.

Katie was quiet, even more than usual.

"Looks like this property has been in foreclosure for a while," said McGaven as he looked up the addresses on his iPad. "And it looks like we're out of range." He put it down and looked about him. "Wow, I don't think I've been around here in ages, even when I was on patrol."

"There are some great camping areas just east of here," she said. "I haven't been here since I was a kid though." Her thoughts went to Chad and all the fun they'd had as kids. It hitched her breath, so she concentrated intently on the road and where they were going.

"Okay, we're supposed to turn onto Branch, then left on Willow, and finally right on Pine," said McGaven.

The more Katie thought about it, the more she realized it was too rural out here. The sketchy cell signal meant it wouldn't be optimum for the kidnapper as they waited for further instructions.

She kept to the road and took the appropriate turns. It was quiet. It was extremely pastoral and untamed wilderness. They hadn't seen a house for miles. The trees became denser, blocking out sunlight, and the landscape was wild and unkempt.

"I did follow the driving instructions," she said, puzzled.

"There it is."

Katie saw what looked like three beige houses but was in fact a main house and two storage sheds. She pulled the car up to an open area where there was a bit of sunshine. She wanted to stay in the bright area and not in the shadows. "What was the population of Dwell Ravine?" she asked.

"Fifteen," he said.

"I wonder if they all moved away." She opened the car door and stepped out and went through her usual protocol of surveying the area whenever they arrived somewhere new.

McGaven got out and looked around but didn't move toward the house—or the remains of the once structured building that was a shambles now.

A pungent moldy odor hit Katie's senses. It was caused from the deep underbrush that hadn't seen sunlight in a long time. Looking up, she saw the overgrown canopy of the tall pine and oak trees. The branches had knitted themselves into an umbrella.

"No one has lived here in a very long time," she said.

The weeds and dead brush had taken over. There were no signs of footprints, tire tracks, or that anyone had been on the property in a while. Nothing had been cleared or pushed aside heading to the house.

"What do you think?" said McGaven.

"I think this is a great place to hide out, but I don't see any indication anyone has been here."

"And the next foreclosure is about twenty-five miles away," he said.

Katie took a couple of steps and studied the house. The front porch drooped forward and was hanging on by a couple of secured nails. The siding sloped in warped sections. But there was something strange about it that caught her attention. It wasn't sloped due to age, but rather seemed like it had been deliberately done.

She took a few more steps closer. There were newer two-by-four wood structures that were leaning against the sides and some of the forest brush had been carefully and purposely intertwined in between to give the illusion of abandonment. Most wouldn't suspect that there was something amiss, especially from a passing glance.

McGaven stood next to his partner. "I see it too."

There were times when the detectives were very much in tune of what the other thought. That was one of the reasons why they were so successful in solving cases—not only by going the extra mile but by reading each other well also.

Birds chirped, a group in the trees making a ruckus of leaves and shuffling branches. Some type of small animal scurried across their view from the house to the shed. The dry undergrowth made a loud crunching noise behind the critter as if made by someone walking through.

Katie decided to take a look at the improvised house, her focus on high alert. McGaven walked behind her about six feet as he scanned the surroundings for anything posing a potential danger. Their footsteps made loud noises against the brush and leaves. There was no way to stealthily sneak up on the structure.

The light seemed to dim as they neared the siding. Katie stopped. She could see there were fresh pieces of sandwich or burger wrappers on the ground nearby. "Gav," she said. "It looks like the same garbage we saw at the house in the Cedar District."

He nodded, still edgy.

Katie looked around. "But how did they get here? There's no tire tracks or footprints."

McGaven walked to the back of the house, disappearing momentarily. He returned and indicated she follow him. "Maybe this explains it."

Moving on, he pushed some dead branches out of the way and stomped some heavy weeds. Katie followed her partner. The backyard was so overgrown it was difficult to tell if it was a yard or part of some abandoned forest. But then she saw it. There was a narrow area that had been cleared haphazardly, leaving a visible path.

She hurried over, making her way through the improvised walkway. It ended at an open area where there were several boulders, as well as a back road. It was like a backwoods alley. She stopped. There were clear tire tracks and they appeared fresh.

"What do you think?" he said.

"Let's look inside. It could be anything, the old owners or squatters, and not necessarily connected to the cases."

The detectives walked back toward the house. The windows and doors had been removed and boarded up a while ago, but there was part of a wall that had a corrugated piece designed as an alternate entrance. Katie pulled it back. She was surprised it opened wide and gave her a clear view of the interior. Katie used her cell phone as a temporary flashlight. It wasn't how she expected it to be. Usually under these circumstances, she would find garbage consisting of bottles, food wrappers, and things to make chairs and tables—blocks, pallets, and other discarded items. Depending upon the type of people, there could be alcohol, drug paraphernalia, and miscellaneous articles of clothing. But here it was relatively neat—which also raised other suspicions.

Had someone been staying there for some time? Was it connected to the Bankses and Sandersons? Tessa? Were there other little girls?

Katie carefully made a quick search, but only made the same discovery as the Cedar District house. A few food and snack wrappers. Two Styrofoam cups. And a small garbage bag in the corner. She took a fresh Kleenex from her pocket and gently opened the bag. Inside, there was clothing. More specifically, little girl's clothing. A navy dress, socks, and two small T-shirts.

Katie looked at her partner at the doorway. She showed him the articles of clothing. "You know what this means?" she said.

"That we need to have John and Eva search and collect evidence."

"Those cups and the clothes most specifically," she said, backing out of the room.

"And those tire marks. Maybe they at least match the ones at the Cedar District."

The detectives made their way toward their car. McGaven called the location in to John, making the arrangements. He cautioned him on the heavily wooded and overgrown area so he and Eva could bring the right equipment.

He turned to his partner. "What's up?" That's what he usually asked when Katie seemed quiet and lost in thought.

"We don't know if Tessa was here, but..." she began.

"But, are there others?"

"It makes me sick thinking about other little girls. Can we have Denise pull up any missing young girls in the entire county to start?" she said. "And then work our way to other counties."

"On it."

Katie was uneasy. They didn't seem any closer to finding out who killed the two families and that fact didn't sit well with her. Though she was still wary of him interfering, she hoped Marshal West was finding out pertinent information that could help to shed some light on the cases.

Katie and McGaven decided they should check out the other properties on their list as due diligence; they didn't know when they would have the chance again to be in these areas of the county. It took two hours and some difficult hiking to the long-foreclosed properties, but the three other locations didn't seem to raise any red flags and were empty, showing no signs anyone had been there, so they headed back to the Pine Valley Sheriff's Department.

Katie was exhausted and starving. Her joints and stomach were vying for her attention and she needed a quick break.

"I need a burger," she said flatly.

McGaven laughed. "All that nature and abandoned houses making you hungry? Count me in."

"Maybe Marshal West has something useful for us," she said.

McGaven remained quiet. It was clear he didn't like the marshal or didn't have any confidence in him helping in the investigation.

Their cell phones pinged in unison.

McGaven read his text. "Looks like the medical examiner has some news for us. Let's hope it's good."

Katie sighed. She wasn't looking forward to seeing the families displayed on stainless gurneys, but she had to keep her mind focused on anything that would help to propel the investigation forward.

"Looks like burgers are going to have to wait," she said.

SEVENTEEN

Friday 1245 hours

Katie made it back to the sheriff's department in good time. She pulled the sedan into the parking lot and was surprised that West's white sedan was already there but didn't say anything to her partner. If they needed to speak with West, he would join them or text.

"Let's do this," said McGaven as he unhooked his seat belt and exited the sedan.

Katie followed him. She remembered the first time they both went into the ME's office and McGaven could barely look at a dead body.

As Katie entered, she expected it to be busy as usual with technicians going about their business. There were always the smells and noise that she connected with the morgue—she could still smell and hear them even after she had left. The sound of the turning wheels of the gurneys, body parts being placed in stainless containers for weighing, the low voices of technicians recording their findings. But for some reason, today she was extra sensitive to them, almost wanting to cringe every time a gurney rolled by.

The detectives moved through the morgue expecting to see Dr. Dean, the medical examiner, but he was nowhere to be found. Katie hesitated and looked at McGaven.

"You know Dr. Dean, he'll be along soon," he said.

"But I don't see the families." Katie wasn't looking forward to seeing them, but glanced in every exam room, trying to find them. The cleaning smell was overwhelming. It made her pace almost like a cornered animal.

"You okay?" said McGaven, watching his partner closely.

Katie shrugged. "Just want to get this over."

After a few more minutes, Dr. Dean emerged. He walked quickly, dressed in his usual uniform of khaki pants, Hawaiian shirt, and white socks with leather sandals. But this time he wasn't wearing the white smock that was usually spattered with blood. Today Katie almost didn't recognize him. He'd had sparse grayish hair with some missing on top of his head but had shaved it and looked as if he was starting to grow a beard. It made him look younger and maybe a bit more handsome.

"Detectives," he said with a smile. "I'm sorry for the delay. It'll be just a few moments." He disappeared into a room.

Katie looked at McGaven with a confused expression.

Dr. Dean poked his head out of an office. "C'mon."

Katie followed. It wasn't the usual office, but it was bigger and had a small lab area.

"Please sit down. I know I sent a text sooner than I should have, but I wanted you both to have enough time in between your schedules to get here."

Katie and McGaven pulled up chairs and sat down across from the medical examiner. There were two file folders on the desk.

"Okay," said Dr. Dean as he opened the files. "This is the

Banks family. Robert Banks, forty-two, Samantha Banks, forty-one, Riley, eleven, and Tyler, nine."

Chills ran down Katie's spine as she thought about Emily being the only survivor.

Dr. Dean fanned out the autopsy photos in chronological order. Katie assumed that the medical examiner thought it would be best viewing the photos and not seeing the bodies in person. Once more, she tried to erase from her mind the initial shock of seeing the family lined up in the barn as she examined the photos. Seeing the bodies cleaned up, it was clear an extremely sharp knife had been used to make such precise cuts on their chests. There were three cuts to Robert, while there were only two cuts to Samantha and the children.

"What would make this precise incision?" she said. "And they're what, three inches long?"

"These injuries weren't made by a random kitchen knife, scissors, or pocket or hunting knife," he said.

"More like a scalpel?" she said.

"Yes. Or another delicate surgical or dissecting tool."

That was a telling aspect to the killer, Katie thought.

"If I had to guess why..." continued the doctor, "and this is only my theory, the cuts are precise, not as messy, and do the job with the least amount of carnage. This was not a crazed killer swiping a knife back and forth. They wanted to keep the mess to a minimum."

Katie leaned back in her chair thinking about the hammer in the living room not making any sense, especially now knowing the surgical nature of the injuries. And how did the killer make these precise incisions without evidence of the victims fighting back?

"I'm sure you already know I'm ruling all four victims a homicide," said Dr. Dean. "Hypovolemic shock caused severe blood loss, making their hearts unable to pump enough blood to the body. Basically, complete organ failure."

"How long would it have taken for them to bleed out?" she said.

"Based on the incisions, depth and length, I would estimate minutes. Maybe three or four minutes before the body completely shut down where the heart can't pump anymore."

McGaven looked at various photos and shuffled the stack back to Samantha Banks. "Are these defense wounds?" He referred to Mrs. Banks's hands and forearms.

"Yes. But they aren't deep."

Katie thought about the bloody handprints around the front door area. "It was as if she couldn't fight back."

"The family's toxicology report indicates varying doses of benzodiazepines, which are depressants that produce different levels of sedation."

"Like a form of anesthesia?" she said.

"Not exactly, but it's sometimes used in combination. For example, with stress and depression there might be a need for a patient to relax before a procedure. Not right before, but a few hours or so," said Dr. Dean.

"How difficult is it to obtain benzodiazepines?"

"They can be prescribed by any doctor, psychiatrist, or family practitioner... brands like Valium or Xanax."

Katie's mind sped through what it said about the killer having to be skilled in scalpel precision and to know about various pharmaceutical drugs. Was the killer a doctor or nurse? Trained in these fields? Or had personal knowledge?

McGaven continued to study the photos. It was clear he was concerned at the deliberate actions of the killer. Katie looked at Dr. Dean, and he, too, seemed troubled. He wasn't his usual positive and informative self—no matter how grim or violent the homicide, he had always maintained a certain personable relationship with the detectives, making tragedies more scientific than emotional. Today he had a permanent frown and his brows seemed to knit in a distressed position.

"Dr. Dean, is there something bothering you?"

"One of the reasons I wanted to sit down with you..." he began. "I know seeing children's bodies is disturbing to say the least, but there are two things that I think will shock you both." He took a breath.

Katie sat up straight. She had never heard the medical examiner say anything like that before. It must be something unusual or horrifying. Glancing at McGaven, he had the same expression that she would expect was on her face.

Dr. Dean pulled a photo from the other file and passed it across the desk. Katie picked it up. She couldn't believe what she saw.

Looking at her partner and then to the medical examiner, she said, "Is this true?"

"Yes. Postmortem."

Katie looked at the photo again. "All the family members?"

"Yes."

The photograph showed Mr. Banks's mouth open, revealing some type of hook that had been attached to the back of his throat. "Is that a type of fishhook or lure?"

"That's what I thought at first, but it appears to be hand-made. It isn't precise, it's crudely made, but put in basically the same area of each victim."

"The children too?" she said.

"Yes."

At that exact moment, both Katie's and McGaven's phones chimed with a message. Both of them ignored it for the time being.

Katie's mind went to the hooks. What did it mean to the killer? Was it a way to silence the family? To maintain control? Or some type of branding?

"I know that it's up to you to figure why and how killers commit their crimes against certain people," said Dr. Dean. "But these deaths are a tragedy."

"You said there were two things you had to tell us," said Katie.

The medical examiner sighed and retrieved another file. "Yes. The Sandersons have almost the identical cuts, in the same places, and with the hooks in their mouths."

Katie studied the photographs. It had seemed there was nothing concrete to connect all these crimes—until now. So many questions, but so few answers.

"I've sent the findings to your emails," said Dr. Dean. "Do you have any questions?"

"I do—but not for you right now. We need to check some things," she said.

"You know where to find me when you do."

"Can we take these?" she said indicating the photographs.

"Of course."

"We will be in touch if we have more questions. Thank you, Dr. Dean."

The medical examiner stood up and nodded his goodbye. The detectives did the same. The doctor left and disappeared down the hallway, and Katie and McGaven hurried out to the parking lot. Katie breathed a sigh of relief to be away from the sounds and smells of the morgue.

McGaven stopped and read his phone. "No."

"What?" she said, watching her partner's reaction, which was pure misery.

"They've found a little girl matching Tessa Sanderson's physical description. And she's... dead."

Katie felt nauseous. Her balance wavered as she looked around the parking lot. The cars looked strangely out of focus. "Where?" she managed to say as she looked at her phone.

"Up near the foreclosed house we were just at near Dwell Ravine. The watch commander is sending the GPS coordinates."

"It's unclear who found her," she said, reading the same message.

"Anonymous person called it in."

Just as the detectives reached the car, Katie's cell phone rang. It was the sheriff.

"We just heard." Katie put her cell phone on speaker. "We're both here."

"Good," said Sheriff Scott. His voice was clear and commanding. "I want you both to take point on this since it's part of your investigation."

"Yes, sir," said McGaven.

"We're on our way," said Katie.

"I suggest you hurry," the sheriff ordered just before he hung up.

EIGHTEEN

Katie had returned home to get her Jeep, which would navigate the terrain better than a lower-riding sedan. During the entire drive, neither of them spoke about the body being Tessa Sanderson. However, it was likely that it was her given the preliminary description from the scene, but not a fact... yet. The images of those crudely handmade hooks in the family's mouths still stayed vivid in their minds.

"Katie?" said McGaven.

"Yes?"

"Are you okay?"

"Of course."

"Seriously, it's me. You handling everything okay today?"

"Do I have a choice?"

"That's not what I meant."

Katie sighed. "I had a personal upheaval that's going to take some time to work through. But, if you're wondering if I'm going to fall apart during this search and the discovery of Tessa, then the answer is no."

He smiled. "I wouldn't figure you any other way."

"Besides, I have you to lean on if I start to waver."

"Best partners," he said.

"The best." It made Katie feel validated and secure in her work. She couldn't imagine any better partner than McGaven. Sometimes, the things police officers had to deal with could be hard for the soul and heavy on the mind.

"Okay," said McGaven. "You should turn there." He pointed out a dirt road on the right that paralleled the main road.

Katie took the turn on the much narrower drive, and immediately the road turned bumpy as she navigated around the potholes. It was relatively clear of trees along the sides, but the low-growing brush was still scraping against the sides of the vehicle.

"Jeez," she said as they bobbed and weaved.

McGaven grabbed the handhold above the door. "Nice driving, partner." He laughed.

"There's no regular road maintenance out here."

"How much farther?"

"About a mile or so."

The roadway began to smooth out some, but the dirt and debris peppered the car's undercarriage in high-pitch pinging noises, making Katie slow down more. The good news was that the day was bright and the wind was minimal. With the full sun, it made the chilly air much more comfortable.

Katie was optimistic about the search but dreaded seeing the little girl's body. This particular area was on their list of foreclosed homes, but they weren't able to search everywhere. She couldn't help think they could've done something to find Tessa in time, and that was going to gnaw away at her for a long while.

"Look," said McGaven as he leaned forward in his seat looking through the window. "Up ahead."

Katie could see the police SUVs, the forensic van, and a couple of unmarked vehicles. They were parked haphazardly wherever there was level ground. They were in a type of valley where the outskirts of the mountains were all around them. Tall pine trees scattered the countryside here and there, but nothing that would make the area shaded and damp. The trunks were scarred and the gangly branches arced downward as if they were bowing. It was a strange landscape and Katie had never seen any part of Pine Valley or Sequoia County look quite like it.

"Here we go," said McGaven.

Katie knew he was just as disheartened as she was; it was one of the toughest parts of the job. She eased the Jeep to an open spot underneath one of the sparse trees and cut the engine. McGaven opened the passenger door and got out, but Katie took a few seconds, a couple of deep breaths, and then stepped out, feeling the strength in her legs steady her.

Detective Hamilton was moving around talking with officers. Both the sheriff's department and the city department were assisting in the case. It happened especially when crimes took place out in extremely rural areas—various jurisdictions would aid in the investigation. Pulling all resources in this type of case was optimum.

A white sedan pulled up and Katie immediately recognized it as Marshal West.

"I guess he was called too," said McGaven.

"I guess so," she said. Katie didn't have time to talk to the marshal. If he was there to see what was going on in the investigation, then that was fine. But as far as she was concerned, he had better stay out of their way. She walked to where Hamilton was talking with a police officer.

He saw her and nodded. "Detectives, you made good time," he said.

"That's why Katie drove," said McGaven and chuckled.

"Can you update us?" she said.

"Of course." Hamilton led the detectives toward a clearing. John and Eva were already there documenting the immediate area and sifting through the dirt and debris in a ten-foot radius of the body. They had been diverted to this crime scene before the empty house. A yellow plastic tarp covered a small area. "We've already compared her body to a recent photo from the Sandersons' house. An aunt from Santa Barbara will be flying up here to positively identify her tomorrow."

"Do we know any more about who called it in?" she said, keeping her voice even.

"It came from an anonymous tip."

"Male or female?"

"Definitely male. The call was barely nine seconds and then disconnected. No trace."

Looking around, Katie said, "And what were they doing out here, if we are to believe it was an innocent person stumbling upon a body?"

"The call came from what we assume to be a burner cell phone that was immediately turned off, so it probably came from the killer," said Hamilton.

Katie glanced around the area. It was in full view, full sun, no trees nearby, and the temperature was mild. "How long?"

Hamilton stopped. "How long has the body been here?"

She nodded.

"From the looks, maybe a few hours, but as you know, the medical examiner will pinpoint closer to the correct time of death. No one would have found her if it wasn't called in."

"Couldn't have been too long, otherwise the animals would take hold and begin to scatter the body parts," said McGaven.

Hamilton brought them to the tarp. Katie moved forward and kneeled down, took the edge of the covering, and lifted it up. The blonde hair and innocent face of the little girl stared back. Her hair was dirty, matted, and streaked with filth, which had transferred across her face, giving her features a distorted look. Her eyes, originally bright blue, were dull, nearly white, as the once vibrant life of a five-year-old had vanished well before her time. There were ligature marks on both of her wrists leaving behind purplish impressions. Even without positive identification, Katie knew the little broken body was that of Tessa Sanderson. She had now joined her family as another victim in this brutal murder spree. It was a total of nine bodies now.

Katie released a breath, realizing only then she'd been holding it. She pulled the tarp farther and saw that there were blood streaks across the girl's yellow top. There was no indication of strangulation. It seemed to be a frantic and extreme violent act. She wondered if there was a hook in her mouth as well. Not wanting to disturb any potential evidence, she was careful not to move anything.

Realizing that Tessa's injuries were reminiscent of her family's wounds made cold chills run through Katie's body and suddenly she felt like she was out in the middle of freezing winter. The sunshine didn't warm her. Looking closer, not touching the body, she saw something in Tessa's hand.

"John, be sure to bag her hands," she said over her shoulder.

"On it."

Hamilton knelt beside her. "Think it might be something from the killer?"

"We have to check everything," she said.

"What's your gut on this?" said Hamilton. He seemed genuinely interested and waited patiently for her to answer.

"It's still in the theory stage, but I believe this killer will not stop. He's playing us. Leaving specific clues. Alerting us to the body. It's a game. A power play. I also believe the entire reason for killing the families was to get to these little girls."

Hamilton barely blinked. "There will be more?"

"I don't want to believe it, but that's what I suspect." Her words were barely above a whisper. Remembering Emily hugging her teddy bear had Katie's breath catch in her throat. "We need to make sure that Emily Banks is safe. Understand?"

"Of course. I'll make sure the officer assigned at her room stays."

Katie stood up and faced McGaven. She had almost forgotten he was there. He remained quiet and stoic as he watched Katie examine Tessa. His expression was undeniably deep sadness, as it was for most of the police officers moving about the scene.

"Let's look around," she said. "We're going to lose too much daylight if we wait much longer."

"Detective?" said Hamilton.

Katie turned to look at him.

"Anything you need out there, let us know."

"Thank you. We appreciate that."

"What do you think, Detective?" said West. He had kept his distance.

"I think we have a very calculating killer," she said.

"And?"

"And, we're trying to find evidence that will lead to them," said McGaven.

"Is there anything I can do?" said the marshal.

"We're good," said Katie.

"Let me know when you have time to chat about what I found out—and vice-versa."

"West, it's going to have to be tomorrow," said McGaven. "This takes priority."

"Of course."

"And," said Katie, "it's beginning to look a lot more like your witness protection family wasn't the target. It's the girls the killer wants, which means we most likely have a serial killer on our hands."

"We'll talk tomorrow. I have to report to my supervisor anyway," said West. He gave a partial wave.

Katie slowed her pace. She felt strange, as if she should be expecting something to pop up out of the ground.

"You okay?" said McGaven. He moved closer to her and kept scanning the area. Wary also.

"Yeah," she said and stopped. She looked back and could see John and Eva working. Two police officers were moving about helping to load containers and evidence bags. Hamilton was leaning over the hood of his vehicle writing down notes. West was still in the same area where the detectives had left him.

Everything seemed normal. But it wasn't.

"Gav," said Katie. "I don't feel well."

"You sick?"

"Well no, I just don't feel like normal."

There was a low rumble that sounded like a freight train was approaching them.

"Wait... that's an earthquake," said Katie. She looked down and could see the ground moving in slow waves. There were several earthquake faults around the valley area—some were large, which would cause the underground plates to shift. Her worry was that one of the fault lines was underneath them and could open up. "Get to higher ground!"

Katie and McGaven started to run toward the tree line. Voices shouted at the crime scene. McGaven grabbed his partner and they stood together watching the pitching land play out in front of them. It wasn't a violent earthquake, rather like watching the tide roll in and out. It seemed to last for minutes, but in reality it was only seconds.

"That's a first at a crime scene," said McGaven. His voice sounded different, with a higher pitch.

"When I got out of bed this morning, I wasn't expecting

that," replied Katie. She caught her breath and her heart rate began to return to normal.

"You guys okay?" yelled John.

"We're fine!" said Katie and McGaven as they raised her hands to form a thumbs-up sign.

"What do you want to do?" said McGaven.

"Keep going."

"You sure?"

"Yes. The earth just woke us up."

"Detectives," called John.

Katie and McGaven walked back to the crime scene shaking off the reactions of the earthquake.

"Take a look," said John.

Katie looked down and saw the earthquake had partially opened Tessa's hand. It revealed a fishhook that she had tightly gripped in her rigor mortis state.

McGaven turned to his partner. "It looks like the ones in both families."

Katie stood up and scanned the area. John and Eva hadn't turned up anything sifting through the dirt, but the hook was a sign. A definite warning. The killer was taking charge like a puppeteer, but at the same time revealing more of his psychological profile. Isolation. Loneliness. Gaining control.

"Katie," said McGaven as he looked at his phone.

She studied the area to see if there was something else left by the killer.

"Katie. We've got to go."

She stood up and saw her partner's face as he read his text message.

"What's wrong?"

"It's..." He almost couldn't say it.

"What?"

"It's Emily."

It made Katie's heart skip a beat.

Emily...

NINETEEN

Katie was the first out of the hospital elevator, followed by McGaven. She moved with purpose in her heavy work boots despite the detectives being dusty and tired from Tessa's crime scene.

Katie had driven there breaking every speed limit, hoping it was all just a misunderstanding, that Emily had just wandered somewhere in the hospital. All she could think about was the lifeless body of Tessa and how Emily could end up the same if they didn't find her in time.

This wasn't about selling or trafficking these little girls—she feared it was about killing them to fulfill a twisted serial killer's fantasy.

Detective Alvarez was talking with hospital personnel. He saw the detectives and met them.

"What do we know? What about security cameras?" said Katie, looking around, trying to surmise how the abduction could have been planned and executed without anyone seeing anything.

"Are you sure she didn't wander away?" said McGaven.

"Emily Banks didn't wander away. We are still searching the hospital, but there's no indication she wandered out of her room." Alvarez remained solemn.

"Where is the officer that was posted at her door?" said Katie.

Alvarez didn't answer immediately. But then said, "He was relieved because Emily's aunt was supposed to have been here today, but she called to say that flights had been delayed and potentially cancelled."

"So *no one* was watching Emily?" said Katie raising her voice. "There should have been an officer here until she was picked up."

Alvarez ignored her comment. "Here's what we know, Detective. Emily was playing with her toys and she always stayed in her room. She had her dinner and when they came to pick up her tray she was gone."

"Security?"

"I just got done reviewing it. It showed her leaving her room at 1732 hours. She walked out to the elevator and there wasn't a sign of anyone with her. The nurses at the time were dealing with an emergency, so there wasn't anyone at the desk. No one saw her get into the elevator."

"Then where did she go?"

"We're trying to track that down. It appears..."

"It appears what?"

"There's no footage of her getting off the elevator or on any of the other floors. So we're clearing every floor, every room, every closet, we're clearing everything."

McGaven looked around. "What about the parking lot?"

"Nothing. Officers are interviewing everyone now. It's going to take some time. The hospital has been busy tonight."

Katie could feel her chest tightening and her vision blurred slightly. This was her worst fear. She should have checked on

Emily. She should have left a nanny cam in her room. She should've done something. Anything.

She went into Emily's room. It looked the same as it did when she had visited previously. There was a low table where Emily had been playing with her bear, some small figurines, and two picture books. She imagined Emily thumbing through the pages of the book, each page depicting a cute animal.

Something then caught her eye in the corner behind a table. It was difficult to see at first, but it looked like a small sphere. She moved toward it. It was plugged into the wall and seemed to be active. She didn't want to touch it in case there were fingerprints.

"Gav," she said. "Is that some kind of camera?"

"Yes."

Katie hurried out of the room to notify Alvarez. She knew she and McGaven couldn't do much until there was a solid lead. Her emotions were trying to get the best of her and she also knew she wasn't going to do the investigation any good by her emotions getting in the way.

"There's some kind of camera, like a nanny cam, in the room," she said.

"We'll get right on it."

"And," she said, "we would like the security footage, a list of who was working, and their statements and whereabouts during the time Emily was having dinner."

He nodded.

"Can you send everything over to us?" she said.

"Of course."

Alvarez hurried to the room with one of the police officers to examine the private camera.

"You okay?" said McGaven.

"You know, you're going to have to come up with a better phrasing of that question."

He studied his partner. "How are you feeling then? Positive? Negative? Feeling happy? Tell me how you're feeling today." He tried to make her smile.

"I'm fine. There's nothing more we can do here. Alvarez will handle what needs to be done and finish up with statements."

"You sure?"

"Where is she? Why did she get on the elevator alone? They aren't going to find anything about the camera. We might get lucky and find out if someone on staff here was working with the kidnapper. But it seems unlikely." She hated sounding so pessimistic, but unfortunately she had encountered such cunning abilities with killers in the past. Katie walked back toward the elevator. "Someone planned to take Emily while we were at Tessa's crime scene."

TWENTY

Friday 2200 hours

Katie couldn't get the image of Tessa's body lying in the dirt out of her mind. It kept playing over—each time with more detail. Work-related obsessive thoughts that plagued her from time to time, stemming from post-traumatic stress from her time in the Army, made for tougher investigations. Difficult situations and trauma had a way of repeating in her mind to the point of excessive fixation. The body of Tessa in combination with Emily going missing was a recipe for mental disaster. She had to break the cycle if she was going to move forward with the investigation in a clear and objective manner.

Katie pulled her Jeep into the driveway of her farmhouse. Her house was dark, which was strange, because usually the outside lights went on automatically. She knew she had been procrastinating on maintenance around the house and yard recently, but Chad usually helped her with such chores.

Chad...

Everything seemed to be bombarding her all at once. She pushed her feelings about Chad aside; she knew it was the wrong thing to do but had no other choice. She thought maybe she should make an appointment with her therapist, but of course, it would have to wait too. Her cases and Emily's disappearance took precedence over everything else—including her stressed mind. She never unloaded her personal stuff or vented to her friends or even her uncle—she still needed to learn how to accept help from others.

Katie got out of the Jeep. The neighborhood was quiet. No cars passed by her driveway and her rural neighborhood was silent. It seemed as if it were later than it was. The night was particularly dark without the moon brightly shining, making it difficult to see her front door.

Katie almost forgot she had a flashlight on her utility belt, but she quickly pulled it out and flipped it on. The beam fanned her entire porch and front door. Nothing looked unusual. She'd had some unfortunate incidents in the past and sometimes she couldn't help but think that this case was going to be like one of the other ones. Katie unlocked the front door, punched in her six-digit key code, and found the interior was the same way she had left it earlier. Her fears dismissed, she felt silly now in the lighted living room.

Cisco greeted her with his usual tail wags and whines, then made his way to his water bowl. After leaving the crime scene and hospital, she realized that exhaustion had set in. Her arms and legs felt heavy. Her mind was too tired to worry about the details of her day playing over in her mind.

Once she'd secured the house, fed Cisco, and put things away, it was time to unwind. Katie couldn't wait to get out of her dusty clothes and take a hot shower. Feeling the steamy water run over her body, and her muscles began to relax, her mind became active again. That was when it hit her like an exploding building. The force of the reality that would soon become her life came crashing down—hard.

Katie cried, which turned into deep sobs as the hot water

continued to pound her skin. She didn't know how to live without Chad. He had been there for most of her life.

Feeling a little better once her crying had stopped, Katie got out of the shower, dried off, and pulled on sweats and a loose T-shirt. With bare feet, she went to the kitchen followed closely by Cisco. The dog seemed to understand that Katie was struggling with several things and wanted to stay close to console her.

Katie prepped a few things for the next day and ate half of a leftover sandwich. She was too tired to cook. After looking at the security cameras and feeling satisfied that the night's movements were only animals and the swaying of tree branches, she went to bed. At barely past midnight, Katie fell asleep.

Just past one in the morning, there was a hard knock at the front door.

Cisco jumped up on the bed and barked. His body faced the doorway.

Katie woke and heard the knocking again. Grabbing the Glock from her nightstand, she got up and headed to the door. Peering through the peephole, she saw the blond hair and recognized Marshal West.

"What the hell?" she said annoyed.

Cisco was agitated and growled.

"Cisco, *platz... bleib*," she said.

The dog immediately sat down and stayed in place, but still faced the front door.

She disarmed her alarm and pulled the door open. "Do you not know how to use the phone or the office?"

"I'm sorry, Detective, but I wanted to talk to you."

"Now?"

"I couldn't sleep and I wanted to discuss something with you," he said. The marshal did look like he had just gotten out of bed. His hair was messed up and his clothes, now casual, were wrinkled and unkempt. He glanced around the area and peered inside.

Against her better judgment, Katie opened the door wider and let the marshal in.

"Thank you," he said and entered the house. "Is he okay with me?" referring to the dog eyeing him closely.

"Cisco is fine unless I give him a command otherwise, or if you make any fast moves."

Katie wasn't in the mood for pleasantries and wanted to go back to bed. She knew that tomorrow was going to be another intense, busy day. "Make it quick, Marshal. I don't feel comfortable talking about the case at my home and without my partner."

"I understand," he said as he took a seat at the counter. "My superiors are expecting results and that's why I'm working every angle, including observing your investigation." He sighed. "I have to find out who killed our wits and I'm afraid that we're running out of leads."

"I disagree. We seem to be under the pressure of having too much information and that is going to take time to sift through—but Gav and I have done it before and no doubt we'll do it again." She remembered previous cases that had made a stronger bond between the two detectives. It was as if they could weather anything to find the person responsible.

"Well, either way, I'm feeling the pressure."

"Welcome to the world of homicides and cold cases."

He looked away from Katie and seemed to study her photographs that were lined up in her living room. They were pictures of her and Cisco with their team in the Army, some of her and Chad when they were kids, and of her parents, that were from much happier times. Some days it was difficult to look at those photographs, but other times it gave her some peace.

Katie watched him and could tell that something had bothered him enough to come to her house. "Where are you staying?"

"At the Mountain Lodge," he said.

Katie knew the place, which was about ten minutes from her house. It was quiet and clean. She could see how the Marshals Service would put him up at a place like that.

"What's on your mind?" she said as she took a seat across from him. Not bothering to offer him coffee.

"I know your partner is annoyed having me work with you on these cases. And believe me, if it were different, I'd be out of here."

"Get to the point, Marshal."

"I went to talk to the director at the Center for Missing and Exploited Children."

"Yes?" This piqued her interest.

"At first I didn't think it was going to help or add anything to the investigation. But like you said: follow all the potential leads."

Katie made a "go on" motion with her hands, wanting him to hurry up. She watched him, trying to gauge his intent and why he chose to come to her house after midnight. He was acting like an overzealous rookie wanting to score points with his superiors.

"He explained to me that children—specifically those in foster care who have parents with mental problems and addictions, or are runaways—are exploited by many means, such as the criminal system and insidious activities as you've witnessed in your cases."

Katie listened, but it wasn't anything she hadn't heard before.

"He claimed there are more, statistically speaking, cases for missing and exploited children than we realize. And there are myths to debunk."

"What do you mean?" she said.

"Human trafficking isn't just the sex trade. It includes labor and escorts to big venues with celebrities and the rich and famous." Now he watched Katie's response. "Did you know the US is one of the worst countries for human trafficking? We're talking 1.2 million children a year. And it happens to adults too."

Katie hadn't checked statistics, but the thought of over a million children a year exposed to these types of situations made her deeply troubled. In her current emotional state, she could cry but she remained stoic in front of the marshal.

Marshal West continued, "These children are always controlled by someone, and below that there are the handlers who carry out their orders. And these handlers move around a lot, completing tasks like finding places to store the child until they receive orders."

"You mean like at the foreclosed house, for example?"

"Exactly."

"But you're forgetting that Tessa was murdered and dumped." Katie hated remembering that fact. "So she wasn't taken to be exploited in that way."

"It still doesn't change anything. There are a million reasons why she could have been murdered. Maybe the situation changed? Maybe law enforcement is getting too close and he got scared?"

Katie could clearly see his enthusiasm to solve the case, but his lack of skill was evident. She almost forgot he was still very inexperienced and that was maybe why he seemed unsure and a bit erratic in his behavior.

"I can't stop thinking about it. It makes sense to me."

"Well, making sense and having the proof can be two different things," she said.

He looked down.

"When I get back to the office, we'll see how everything adds up."

West got up. "Okay. I better let you get some sleep."

Katie showed him to the door. He left, never looking back.

Cisco followed her through the house. As Katie shut off the lights and headed back to sleep, she heard the marshal's car start up and leave. Once again, everything was quiet. Katie drifted off to sleep. This time it was restful and uneventful.

TWENTY-ONE

Saturday 0945 hours

Katie and McGaven hurried into their office the next morning.

"What's on your mind?" said McGaven.

"I just keep thinking about Emily. We haven't heard anything."

"No. But that doesn't mean we won't hear anything today," said McGaven, trying to sound upbeat.

"I guess you're right. No news doesn't necessarily mean bad news, right?"

Her partner studied her for a moment. "That's right."

Katie filled her partner in briefly about Marshal West's visit again to her house and why he thought that the killer/kidnapper was working in the circles of human trafficking.

"That's interesting, but it's more information and not necessarily the direction where the current clues and evidence are taking us." McGaven pushed his hand through his hair, which usually meant that something was bothering him. "I don't like this guy showing up at your house in the middle of the night unannounced."

"I know. I think you intimidate him. He said he thought you don't like him." Katie smiled.

"Well he's right. But I respect all law enforcement agencies, and if that means we have to work with him, then that's what we have to do."

Katie's cell phone chimed.

"Text from John. He wanted us to know about this immediately." She read it.

"What?"

"Some unexpected results are in... here's the attached file."

"What is it?" McGaven could tell something was wrong.

"John found unidentified saliva that was found on Mrs. Banks, Tyler Banks, Erin Sanderson, Emily's teddy bear at the hospital and... Tessa's clothing. He tested it and found to be the same DNA."

"That's a solid connection of proof that it was the same killer," he said.

"They couldn't find the identity of the person through AFIS but..."

"But what?"

"It's connected to two other unsolved cases in the town of Park Tree."

"Park Tree? That's in River County but it's almost on the border with us."

Katie nodded.

"How long ago?"

"Eight years ago." Katie immediately went to her investigative board. They could use maps of the areas along with the results from forensics and autopsy reports.

McGaven sat down and began going through the reports and using his laptop to coordinate database findings.

"Hey, where's the marshal?" said McGaven.

"I don't know. I thought he'd be here by now," she said. "He'll show up when he needs something."

Both detectives worked diligently for more than an hour before even speaking to one another. McGaven would occasionally add things to the wall as Katie made more lists, in between checking her phone periodically to see if anything had come in about Emily. But her phone was exceptionally quiet. It made her more anxious than usual, but she made her restless energy work for the investigation.

"Okay," she finally said. "Let's go down the list."

McGaven looked up from his paperwork and laptop. "Shoot."

"We'll start with the Bankses chronologically. The blood on Emily's nightgown was mostly Mrs. Banks, with some mixture of the rest of the family. The handprints on the front doorframe were hers as well."

"And the hammer?"

"It's strange. The hammer had Mrs. Banks's blood, but there was no indication of wounds caused by hammer blows to her body or the rest of the family," she said looking to the photograph of the wounds to the Banks family. "The excessive cleanliness of the house and the garbage being all removed seemed overly organized and well thought out."

"So what does that tell us about the killer?"

"It could mean that he prepared for every possible detail. But that doesn't explain some things: like why make it look like someone broke in when they didn't, and why leave the bloody hammer in the middle of the room?"

"And that tells us something, right?" McGaven said.

"Definitely." Katie studied the geographic locations. "It tells me a couple of things. The killer, or killers, planned, had experience in crime scenes, either by committing other crimes we don't know about or personal professional experience."

"Like a cop or someone else in law enforcement?"

"Maybe, but my gut tells me no. It could also be someone who has an academic background in forensics, or was brilliant at criminal research, or perhaps even links to law. They would know what was needed to investigate and prove a case. Or whether or not there was enough evidence to take to the district attorney's office to arrest and prosecute—if a viable suspect was found. And... we cannot dismiss how much information there is out there from the crime shows, internet, and loads of books about stories just like this."

McGaven studied the wall for the Banks family. "This does seem like something that would make a true crime bestseller."

"But that's too many maybes and not enough facts," she said. "I believe the Bankses were chosen not because they were in witness protection, but because of Emily. Being part of the witness program wasn't something on the killer's radar. They probably still don't know." She pulled Emily's school photo. The child's smiling face gave Katie a twinge in her stomach, worrying about what happened to her and if they were going to find her body like Tessa's.

Katie looked at her phone again as if it would magically give her a text message that she wanted to see. The more she looked, the more she became agitated. She pushed her emotions to become more constructive and to focus on the investigation.

McGaven read the preliminary report for the Banks family. "Looks like there was nothing unusual about the piece of pottery in the kitchen, likely just something that didn't get cleaned up... and the window area didn't indicate anything unusual—no fingerprints, footprints, no entry. It looks like you were right about it being staged to look like a break-in. Weird, if you ask me."

Katie stood staring at the Bankses' wall display. She sighed.

McGaven continued, "And... there was no biological evidence on the little girl's blue polka-dot dress we found at the creek either. It was new."

"What, nothing?"

"No, it doesn't look like it. But we can discuss more when

we meet with John. He's been sending reports to us as he gets results back to help expedite the investigation."

Katie sighed. "And of course, the cameras on the Bankses' property were blank. Obviously the killer erased them and then damaged the cameras beyond repair."

"Smart."

"Too smart." She sighed. "It seems they thought of everything, which makes me wonder if this is something that has developed over time, and maybe even practice. Or, if it's just well prepared." Katie felt as if she was talking in circles; that was the way the investigation seemed at this point. She had to take a step back and attack one thing at a time.

Katie heard McGaven shuffling papers. "It looks like the harassing calls coming in to Mr. Banks's cell phone and his work were from burner phones," he said. "And the calls to and from Sierra Roadside Towing seemed to coincide with the calls being made."

A chime came from McGaven's computer. "Oh. This is interesting."

Katie turned to her partner.

"I had Denise do some basic background on all the players around the Banks family. And Trent Gaines, the driver from the tow company, has some very interesting charges: burglary, harassment, stalking."

"I'm not surprised. We knew he had warrants, which I'm sure he hasn't taken care of yet. Why is that so interesting?"

"Well because one of his associates he was arrested with in the past is Ryan Rey."

"Who is Ryan Rey?" she said.

"Ryan Rey is married to Gabby Rey."

That surprised Katie. "The teacher that Samantha Banks worked with?"

"Exactly."

"That's not a coincidence."

"Of course not. There's no such thing as a coincidence, remember?"

"We should have a background done on Gabby," she said.

"Already done."

"Denise is so awesome."

"Yes, she is. That's my gal."

"What does it say?"

"Nothing much, but they haven't been married that long. A little over two years."

"About the same time as the Bankses have been in witness protection," said Katie. "That's interesting, to say the least."

"Well, that's not even the interesting part."

"Meaning?"

"Ryan Rey is from Colorado."

Katie began to pull together some things in her mind. She went to the files in the boxes on the floor that had come from the Bankses' barn. She pulled out two stacks that she had previously organized and selected some photocopies of articles.

"Take a look at this." She put the copies down in front of McGaven.

He quickly skimmed the articles. "This is interesting. These reports about missing girls around the Denver area. Looks like there were eight girls ranging in ages six to twelve, from three to eight years ago. Only two were found, murdered and dumped near rural industrial areas."

"Have Denise get the files for these girls. Both the missing persons and the homicide reports. This article says there were persons of interest that were cleared, but no arrests have been made since," she said.

McGaven picked up the phone and pressed an extension. "Hey, babe, can you do me a favor? Yes, it's for our investigation." He laughed. "Can you get in touch with Denver PD and get us copies of the reports for eight missing girls from three to eight years ago? Two were found murdered... and anything else you can find. I'm sending you more info. You can also pull up news articles that will give you more details." He paused. "Thanks, see you tonight." He hung up.

Katie traced the likely routes between the Banks and Sanderson homes. "Where are the residences of the Reys and Trent Gaines?"

McGaven skimmed the reports. "They live relatively close to one another in Prairie Valley, which is not far from Park Tree."

"Now we have a pattern we need to follow. See if it checks out as a new lead or not."

"You think Samantha Banks was following these murders and that's what got the family killed? She dug up something she shouldn't have?" said McGaven.

"I believe she knew something was going to happen at the house, and that's why she had some time to get Emily to safety. She and her husband just didn't have time to save the others and couldn't fight off their attacker."

Katie turned to the board and stared at the wounds that the family had endured. Samantha Banks was the only one with defense wounds, which meant she fought back.

Katie's cell phone chimed. She quickly grabbed it. The text was from John. He had some information about the wire hooks that were in all the victims' mouths.

"We need to go talk to John about the hooks," she said as another text message came in. "Oh, and Marshal West just sent a message that he had to go back to his office in Sacramento for a meeting and wouldn't be back until tomorrow."

"Fine by me," McGaven said.

TWENTY-TWO

Katie and McGaven stood at the large forensic examination table where John had laid out several types of wire. He also had the crude fishhooks that had been removed from the mouths of the two families. Katie couldn't help but feel a shiver up her spine when she saw the fishhooks lined up like the Bankses' bodies in the barn had been.

"What are we looking at here?" said McGaven.

"First, the wire that was used to create these crude versions of hooks is just any wire you can buy in the electrical area of a hardware store," he said.

Katie was surprised.

"We also excavated some wire near Tessa's body that is made from a strong version of steel, high carbon, to be exact. It's super-resilient and will last a lifetime, which is why it's mainly used for fencing and in some tools." He pointed to it.

"Okay. The wire in the hooks looks much older," said Katie.

"At first glance, it does. But it's a cheap stainless version that's made to look old and is easy to manipulate."

"So you're saying that the person who made these hooks and placed them in the mouths wanted them to look old on purpose. But why?" said McGaven.

"That seems pretty extreme," said Katie.

"And a lot of trouble."

"Nothing this monster does is random," she said as she thought about the profile she was putting together.

"Fishhooks have been made of all types of things throughout history," said John. "Bone, wood, shells, you name it. But the bottom line is that a good fishhook needs to be strong, have good surface quality, be long lasting, and inexpensive."

Katie looked over the wire samples. "So the killer chose a cheap version, which can be found in any hardware store, to make his hooks. That tells me that it's all for show and not for craftsmanship or durability. It's a symbol to him."

"Take a look at this," said John. He showed the detectives one of the hooks. "You can see with a naked eye that there are indentations of something consistent with a standard pair of pliers, most likely needle-nose pliers."

Katie studied it. "It reminds me of jewelry making."

"That's a good description." John moved to one of the computers, where there were websites up that had several pages of fishhook history from books published both recently and as far back as sixty years ago. "When I was searching for specific types of wire used to make fishhooks, I came across some interesting facts that might be useful for your profile of the killer. I sent the list to your email, but I thought it was interesting enough to bring to your attention."

Katie and McGaven read over John's shoulder.

"So in some cultures the fishhook symbolizes the relationship between humans and the ocean, according to these historical articles. Catching a fish is about hope and determination," John said.

"Hope and determination seems like an unusual pairing of words," she said.

"I agree. That's why I wanted to bring it to your attention, whether it's helpful or not."

"The hooks in the mouths of the families obviously means something significant to the killer. But we have to find out what," she said.

"Here it also refers to the hooks as representing strength, prosperity, and good luck." John turned to the detectives. "I thought it was interesting that there are several passages in these articles published through various historical fishery and outdoorsman sites that refer to 'fishing for souls.' There are also a lot of references to various religious and philosophical beliefs."

"That's creepy," said McGaven.

"Why does that sound familiar?" Katie said.

"Many famous painters through history have depicted scenes of the devil looking for souls," said John.

Katie thought more about it. It did seem to symbolize a part of the working mind of serial killers; how they fantasize and hunt for their victims. It could be the key Katie was looking for. It may have something to do with a life event or the childhood of the killer.

"I can see the wheels turning," said McGaven as he watched his partner.

"I think we have stumbled on something," she said. She looked at a diagram of a hook in one of the articles. "There's four parts," she said reading the screen. "The shank, the bend, the eye, and the barb."

"I never knew there was so much to know about a fishing hook and what it symbolizes as well as the physical qualities of the pieces," said McGaven.

"I thought the same thing," said John.

"Was there anything unusual about how the hooks were placed?" Katie asked.

"They were fastened the easiest way, to the backs of their throats postmortem. It was just enough underneath the soft tissue to keep them from falling out."

It made Katie shudder just to think about.

"A few other things," said John.

Katie could see his frown, which meant it wasn't necessarily good news.

"We tried everything we could think of, but as you know, the video security cameras at the Bankses' residence were destroyed. The dress in the bag at the creek was new and there wasn't any type of evidence left on the dress or bag."

"Okay," she said.

"Now the Sandersons' residence yielded nothing in particular. The cleaner was a combination of standard ammonia and another common cleaner with a floral scent. These are found in every store, superstore, and even grocery markets." He sighed. "The residue that was left at the house indicated that there had been a large amount used when the family was killed and it had been drying, evaporating for a while."

"That's not great news," said McGaven. "What about the foreclosed house in the Cedar District neighborhood?"

"Glad you asked. Sorry I haven't gotten the reports to you yet," said John. He moved to a computer. "Okay, the wrappers didn't indicate there was anything that could be tested and it wasn't clear how long they had been there, if they had been there for a while before the man and little girl were seen. The child's clothing in the bag was the same as the dress at the Banks' residence. It was new, like the pajamas on the victims."

"The killer bought clothes for them all as part of controlling the scenes."

"It appears so. Trying to find out which store they came from would be difficult if not impossible. Now, the tire marks and cigarette butts yielded more evidence. We retrieved DNA off the butts, but nothing has hit in the system yet. If we have someone to compare it to—that'll be another story."

Katie was thinking about the killer buying clothes and leaving behind biological evidence that couldn't be matched in their database.

"We have a great tire impression. It came from a late-model truck tire. Not a four-wheel drive but a standard issue."

"And there are probably a lot of those," she said.

John nodded. "But we will keep looking. You need to bring in a suspect and that will change everything."

Katie forced a smile. It wasn't what she had been hoping for, but they would just have to keep pushing. "Thank you, John."

"I'll update you more as the results come in. I know you two have a lot on your plate."

"Thanks," said McGaven.

When the detectives reached the hallway, Katie turned to her partner. "I think we need to talk to Gabby Rey and Trent Gaines again."

"I agree. There's no such thing as a coincidence."

"Maybe that was why Samantha was able to get a teaching aid job with Gabby—she was doing research. Her qualifications were much higher than an aide. She could have had a teaching position or been a substitute teacher."

"Makes sense. I think we're just at the brink of finding out a lot more of what the Bankses are doing with all that research."

"It's Saturday, so they'll most likely not be working. I think we need to check out their residences and maybe do a little bit of a stakeout," she said.

"Now you're talking."

Katie couldn't get the words *fishing for souls* out of her mind as they left the office.

TWENTY-THREE

Saturday 1330 hours

Katie and McGaven headed for Prairie Valley. They estimated the drive was to take about forty minutes to arrive at Trent Gaines's residence. McGaven did a quick background check. There was no indication he was married or that he'd turned himself in for the outstanding warrants.

The detectives were quiet on the ride, each lost in their own thoughts, especially after the discussion about the fishhooks. This case was just getting bigger and more perplexing by the day.

The weather was warm, but the cloud cover kept the sunlight from penetrating through the trees and along the various valleys. Katie turned off the main highway onto a single-lane road that led to Prairie Valley. There was light traffic of mostly cars, but few heavy trucks or working vehicles.

"I'm hungry," said McGaven.

"Me too." In fact, Katie was really hungry because she had been skipping meals due to the investigation and general exhaustion when she got home.

"I think there's a neighborhood grocery store with a deli up about two miles," he said.

"Sounds good."

The road twisted and turned sharply as Katie slowed the police sedan. Soon they came to an open area where the road straightened out and there was a wooden building up ahead.

"There it is," said McGaven.

The building had been added onto and was once a holding area for local fruit trees. The wooden structure had a pitched roof, open parking lot, and several signs indicating what fresh produce and deli entrees they had. There were four picnic tables with umbrellas to eat outside.

Katie pulled into the parking area where there were two cars already. The newly laid gravel crunched under the wheels. The front entrance had two large glass doors and friendly "open" and "please come in" signs were lit up. Katie got out and looked around. The area was indeed a country setting and it had a relaxed feel to it. She took a few deep breaths to lower her pulse rate.

McGaven walked ahead and entered the store followed by Katie. The inside was just as inviting. There weren't the long rows of food aisles. Everything was displayed in sections in large wooden bins and stacking racks. Besides the food, there was a deli counter and an area with local plants. Several small round metal tables and chairs were at the far corner. A few customers were shopping.

"This is nice," said Katie. "I have never been here."

"I have a few times when I was on patrol."

The detectives went up the deli counter, where a heavyset man with a thick beard met them. "What can I get you? We have a soup special with the best beef vegetable soup in the county. The beef is locally raised. And the roast beef and Swiss sandwiches can't be beat," he said and smiled.

"I'll have a cup of the soup and the roast beef sandwich," said McGaven.

"And?"

Katie smiled. "I'll have the same. Thank you." To her partner she said, "I'll grab us some drinks."

Katie and McGaven opted to sit outside in the mild weather and where it was easier to discuss case information without being overheard.

"Oh my," said Katie as she took a bite of the sandwich. "This is delicious."

McGaven had already eaten half of his soup. "Wow, the flavor is awesome."

"Is it so good because we're really hungry?" she said and laughed.

The detectives enjoyed their food, then McGaven said, "So how do you want to handle this?"

"Trent Gaines?"

He nodded. "We know he can be dodgy."

"I'm not worried about that. I want to get a look at his place and the surroundings. Maybe it might be enough for a search warrant, but we have to proceed cautiously." Katie automatically looked at her phone, still waiting for something to come in about Emily's whereabouts.

"Hey."

Katie looked at her partner.

"They'll find her."

"I hope so. Because I can't..."

McGaven reached across the table and squeezed her hand. "We will."

Katie was full of emotions with Chad leaving. She didn't know how she would get through this case without McGaven having her back. She nodded at her partner.

"Excuse me?" said a woman who had come out of the store. She slowly approached the detectives.

"Yes?" said Katie.

"You are police, right?"

"We're detectives from the Pine Valley Sheriff's Department," said McGaven. "I'm Detective McGaven and my partner Detective Scott."

"Are you looking into the stalker?" she said.

Katie studied the woman for a moment. She seemed sincere —and scared. "We're working on another case. What's your name?"

"I'm Lisa Dixon. I live just up the way on Vine Street." She was about thirty, very petite, with long dark hair, several ear piercings, and a pretty flower tattoo on her right arm.

"What is this about a stalker?" said Katie.

"There's been this truck that has been stalking the area."

"What makes you say that?" said Katie.

"At first, I thought it was someone living out of their car, you know. You see people camping up here—but this guy is different."

"How?" said McGaven.

"He watches. He waits. It seems like he's studying the area and the people. It's creepy and I feel unsafe."

"Have you ever seen him before?"

"No, that's the thing. No one I've talked to knows who he is."

"What kind of car? Color? Make?"

"It's an older truck with a camper shell. I don't know if it's a Ford, Toyota, or what. It's tan. There are some scrapes on the passenger's side. I'm sorry, I'm not good with cars."

"It's okay," said Katie. "What does he look like?"

"You can't tell," said the woman. "I mean... he seems to camouflage himself with sunglasses, baseball cap, and hoodie. I don't know if he's twenty or fifty."

Katie retrieved a business card and wrote down a phone number. "I want you to call this number. It's a direct line to one of our detectives. Tell him Detective Scott told you to call and give him all the information, including when and where you've seen this truck, okay?"

She took the card. "Thank you, Detective."

They watched as the woman walked to her car.

"What do you think?" said McGaven.

Katie was concerned. Ms. Dixon had seemed genuinely scared. "I think she's telling the truth and is obviously scared. This area of the county hasn't had a lot of exposure to crime. They'll send someone up here to make a report and hopefully patrol will make passes through here."

The detectives quickly finished their lunches and headed out to find Trent Gaines's house. McGaven had called Sierra Roadside Towing and found out that Gaines wasn't on call today.

"Heads up, Gaines is either home or out somewhere, but not at work."

"Noted," she said.

They found the short unidentified drive where there was an older manufactured home. Driving past, they saw there wasn't a truck registered to Gaines or a towing vehicle in the driveway.

Katie drove the sedan away from the drive and parked. She made sure that their vehicle wouldn't be easily spotted by anyone going by and the neighbors were too far away to notice.

There were trees lining the short road leading to the residence. Heavy brush circled around the property, which should have been scaled back to avoid being a fire hazard. It appeared that there were fences at the back of the property and some small sheds.

Katie got out and quickly changed into her hiking shoes and shed her jacket. She wanted to make sure nothing hindered her.

McGaven joined her and waited patiently.

Katie took a few steps and assessed the area. It was extremely overgrown and upon first glance there didn't seem to be any other homes. It was indeed a perfect place to stay under the radar—or hide out. She tried to connect the dots between Gaines and Gabby's husband.

As she assessed, she listened. It was difficult at first to concentrate with everything going on with the investigation and in her personal life. She noticed it was quiet—*really quiet*. No birds chirping or flying in the trees. No barking dogs. No cars. It was just her and McGaven. The only sound was their breathing.

"I checked the county clerk's office and found this property next to Gaines's. It's about two acres, so we can skirt along the side of it to take a look," said McGaven.

"Okay."

The detectives hiked onto the rural property. It wasn't easy navigating the area. There were no trails, so the ground was uneven and some of the heavy brush was immovable. They had to go over forest debris including some downed branches. Katie moved as fast as she could. There was a part of her that felt they were too exposed. McGaven kept up behind her, and he, too, seemed to move faster than necessary.

They came to a fence line of barbwire and steel posts every six feet, which was the back area to Gaines's property. The fencing looked old and was most likely used to keep farm animals in at one time. There were old paint cans, bottles, and old wooden handles from yard tools.

"Looks like a rural bone yard," said McGaven.

"What's that smell?" she said. It was overpowering, with a mixture of manure and chemicals. "It's not like any manure I've ever smelled before." She covered her nose for a moment.

"Nasty."

"What would need to be fertilized?" she said, gazing about her. "I don't see where there are farm animals or a garden of any kind." Katie's skin prickled, which made her do a three-sixty, looking in every direction.

"You feel it too?" he said.

"Maybe it's because we're sneaking around, but yeah, it feels strange."

"Let's just do a walk around the perimeter."

She nodded.

The small fabricated home Gaines lived in looked to be a two bedroom, one bath. The driveway had numerous oil spots and weeds were abundant. Outside the front door, there was nothing indicating anything unusual.

Katie kept vigilant about listening for an approaching vehicle. She didn't want to get surprised by Gaines returning home and surprising them.

As they moved farther along the property line, Katie noticed several makeshift structures resembling chicken coops but with solid walls. They were odd and out of place. She tried to get a better vantage and could see several large dog crates inside one of the coops and along the side wall stacked double high.

"What do you make of that?" said Katie. She kept her voice low.

"Not sure. Backyard dog breeding? Chickens? Other types of animals? There's no telling. He doesn't own the property, so who knows how many other people have lived here."

He was right, Katie thought.

They came to a place where there was a break in the fence. It appeared to have been left open, but it was missing a gate. Katie stopped. She saw some large plastic tubs, which looked like there was fishing gear inside.

"Katie," said her partner. "I know what you're thinking." Obviously, he had seen the gear as well.

"We need to see if there's old wire in there or if there are crudely made fishhooks in there."

"We need to get a search warrant."

"In order to do that, we need to have probable cause."

As the detectives were debating what to do next, there was a rustle near them just north of the property. Katie glanced in that direction but didn't see anything.

"We should wait until Gaines gets home and go up and knock on his door," said McGaven. "Then we can take it from there."

Katie agreed.

Just as they were about to turn around and go back to the car to wait, there was a growl. Stealthily coming out of the brush was some type of a large dog, difficult to see what breed it was, but it was huge with a big head and pointy ears.

"Gav," she said.

"I see it."

"We won't make it back to the car. I don't want to shoot it."

"We may have to," he said.

As the rogue dog came closer, its eyes were fixated on them like a wild animal stalking its prey. Katie could see a yellow-brownish stare that she had never seen before—even with all the dog training she had done. She grabbed McGaven's arm and motioned for him to follow her lead and move backward into Gaines's yard. At least there they could get cover and protect themselves.

The detectives moved slowly, as did the dog... it gave a low growl and snorting sound. Katie could see the big paws navigate easily through the thick brush as if it were nothing. They began moving faster. McGaven grabbed a short two-by-four to use as a club.

Katie glanced back and saw the main shed had a door that would help to block the dog. "Gav, here!" she said.

Katie and McGaven turned and ran to the outbuilding. Just as they made it through the opening, the rogue dog was almost on their heels.

McGaven shut the door, but there weren't any reinforced locks. He had to hold it closed with his body weight. Katie joined him and used her strength. It wasn't the best scenario, but it was the only thing that they could do under the circumstances.

The dog hit the door with such force that Katie thought the door would splinter and crack wide open.

"Having fun yet?" said McGaven as he gritted his teeth, preparing for the next dog slam.

"Just another day on the job." Katie looked inside the structure for any way the dog could enter.

Another crash pummeled the door.

"I'm going to check for any other ways in or out," she said.

"Okay!" He held firm with his body against the door, keeping it shut. "I don't know how much longer I can hold this door though."

The makeshift shed was long and narrow—and a little over six feet high. It was also very dark—in fact almost completely secured. Katie slowed her search and was amazed she wasn't able to see any cracks or open areas. There was no light shining through anywhere. No doors. No windows. No other light.

Katie kept hearing the enormous dog throw its body against the door. The door started to splinter and daylight began to peek through.

"Anything?" said McGaven. His body was growing weary and his arms were tense to their limits.

"No, we're trapped!"

"Okay, just checking!"

Katie heard the strain in her partner's voice as she ran her hands along the edges of the shed, thinking she might have missed the openings—either a window, or another door. There was nothing but that pungent smell again. It reminded Katie of some type of manure, but it wasn't anything she could recall. She didn't smell it when they had first entered, but now it was growing stronger. Then there was a burning smell like that of a fuse of some type. It began to permeate her senses. Running her hand along the upper area, she could feel some type of cord as the smell became stronger.

"Uh, Gav..." she said. "We have a problem."

"Really?"

The dog didn't seem to be giving up or tiring out anytime soon; in fact, he seemed to have gained new strength.

Katie joined McGaven again and picked up the broken two-by-four piece of lumber. She tried to find a way to jam it into the entrance and was able to wedge it into the side and crack around the bottom of the door.

The strong burning odor increased in intensity.

"Some type of fuse has been lit," she said.

The pounding on the door nearly drowned out her voice.

"What?" he said.

"There's some type of fuse that has been lit around the wall and ceiling area!" She pointed to the area.

"You kidding me?" McGaven looked around where she had directed.

There was a subtle hissing noise and they saw an ignited flame at the other end of the shed. Then it began building into a fire, along with smoke. The flames slowly crept forward.

TWENTY-FOUR

Saturday 1530 hours

Katie covered her nose. "We can't stay inside here!" She put her hand on McGaven's arm as she pulled her weapon.

They couldn't talk to one another anymore with the smoke and loud noises, but she gestured that she was going to shoot at the door in hopes of scaring away the dog and to make an exit.

McGaven nodded, moving aside. Katie took a step back, aimed, and shot at the left side of the door, hoping to scare the dog away; if needed, she would shoot the animal.

Three booms echoed inside the shed.

The detectives didn't wait any longer as they pushed the door forward, causing it to fall flat. Smoke billowed from the shed. They staggered out of the burning building and dropped to the ground.

Katie began coughing and crawling forward to get out of the way of the doorway. McGaven was right behind her, she could hear him coughing and spitting.

Catching her breath, Katie looked around but there was no sign of the dog. She kept an eye out, expecting another assault, but there was none. Moving closer to her partner, she asked, "You okay?" She quickly looked for any injuries.

"Yeah." He continued coughing. "I'm fine."

Katie noticed his hand was bleeding. She tore off a piece of her sleeve and pressed it against his hand.

"It's no big deal," he said.

"The bleeding hasn't stopped. You need this looked at and maybe a couple of stitches." She slowly got to her feet, still coughing. "Keep pressing down." She retrieved her cell phone and was relieved there was a signal. She dialed the police dispatch.

"Nine-one-one, what's your emergency?"

"This is Detective Katie Scott, badge 3692, I need assistance at the service road 211 southeast in Prairie Valley. There is a small structure fire. We need fire and police."

"Is anyone hurt?"

"Smoke exposure and my partner has several lacerations on his hand."

"Sending units with fire and rescue."

"Thank you." Katie hung up. "Let's get you moved farther away," she said.

Katie helped McGaven up and kept him steady as they walked to the front of the property to wait for assistance. She spotted a tree stump. "Sit here," she said and moved away.

"Katie, where are you going?"

"I'm going to try to slow down the fire! We can't let it jump to other structures or all the dry vegetation."

"Stop! It's too dangerous!" he said, immediately jumping to his feet to follow his partner.

Katie spotted a fire extinguisher on Gaines's porch and grabbed it. There was also a hose on the side of the house; she quickly turned it to full blast. Thankfully, the water pressure was high.

"I got it!" said McGaven.

Katie's concern was that the fire would jump to the brush and spread exponentially. She ran to the structure and began dousing the areas where flames had reached through damaged areas of the building. She kept her distance and dared to move closer as she sprayed the flames. The heat was overwhelming. The intense temperature against her face and skin felt like she was inside an oven.

"Katie!" yelled McGaven. "Move!" He began spraying the structure, causing more smoke and making it difficult to see.

Katie caught concentrated smoke in her face and lungs. She couldn't fight the fire anymore and moved away. McGaven kept watering down the areas around the structure to make it saturated and hopefully more difficult for the fire to spread.

Sirens approached.

"Katie!" McGaven urged his partner to get away from the structure and wait for the fire department. "Now!" he said.

The fire extinguisher was empty. Katie tossed it aside and that was when she saw the crate of wire that looked suspiciously familiar.

McGaven grabbed Katie's arm. "Now!"

The detective hurried to the front of the property just as the two fire trucks rolled up. Smoke was everywhere. Several firefighters hit the ground and ran straight to the area, while one secured one of the water hydrants on the service road.

The captain approached Katie and McGaven. "You hurt?"

"We're okay. Just didn't want the fire to spread," she said.

The captain frowned. "Paramedics need to check you both out." He eyed their police badges. "You on the job?"

Katie nodded. "Pine Valley Sheriff's Department. Detectives Scott and McGaven."

"Anyone else here?"

"No."

"There was a large dog that chased us to the structure," said McGaven.

"All right, putting a call in to animal control." The captain made several radio calls including the names of the detectives.

"Captain," said Katie. "The fire was started by something that was set up to ignite along the roofline."

Two paramedics hurried to the detectives.

"We'll take it under advisement and have the arson investigator examine it. He's en route," he said as he moved away.

The reference to an arson investigator hit Katie hard. Would it be Chad? She didn't think he had left for LA yet as it was the weekend. As far as she knew, he was leaving on Monday.

Katie breathed the oxygen and it made her feel better. As she relaxed, she noticed that her arm was hot and painful. She looked to her partner, who was also getting oxygen as they tended to the cuts on his hand.

A large white SUV pulled up followed by two patrol vehicles. Sheriff Scott quickly approached. Katie took the oxygen mask off and met her uncle.

"You okay? I heard about a fire up here and you and McGaven were in the middle of it. Luckily I was in a meeting not far from here," he said. The sheriff gently rubbed the smoke streaks on the side of Katie's face. "You hurt? You look like you took the fire on by yourself"

"Just some smoke and my arm was exposed to the excessive heat. It still feels hot."

"Get completely checked out. And that's an order," he said with his usual commanding tone.

At that moment, a tan truck pulled up. Trent Gaines slowly got out and stared at the spectacle going on at his house. He looked like he was going to run, but then thought better, so he walked up to the sheriff and Katie.

"What's going on?" he said. Gaining more courage, he said in a demanding tone, "I want to know what's going on here."

"Mr. Gaines," said Katie. "We're going to need you to come down to the department and answer some questions."

"Why?"

"During our investigations into recent incidents, we have come across information that refers to you," she said.

He looked around. "I can't come down now."

"Let me put it this way, you can either come down or we will take you there."

"Did you do this to my property?" said Gaines.

"You can answer questions of why you have set fire traps on your property," said Katie.

"What do you mean?" He looked spooked.

A Pine Valley deputy came up.

"Okay, Mr. Gaines, we'll give you a ride to the department," she said.

"I don't understand..."

"And you've not dealt with your warrants. I gave you a chance to take care of it," she said.

He sighed. "Fine."

The deputy escorted Gaines to the patrol car.

The sheriff walked to Katie. "I'm serious."

"I know, but we have to question a person of interest. And there are things on the property that possibly connect to the homicides we're investigating. He also had contact with Mr. Banks when he towed his vehicle. There are too many things that he's connected to in our investigation."

"I'll get a proper search warrant in place and get John out here to search and document evidence."

The firefighters had the flames extinguished and were dousing close areas with water so there wouldn't be a chance of smaller startup fires. The arson investigator had arrived, and she was relieved to see it wasn't Chad.

Katie joined McGaven. "Are you okay?" she said.

"Yeah, I'm fine. My hand doesn't need stitches. It'll be fine."

He looked at his partner. "You look like you've been in a smokestack."

"Thank you for noticing."

"Was that Gaines?"

"Yes. They're taking him back to the department, where we can question him. You up for it?" she said.

"Absolutely, you don't need to ask me twice."

"Let's go," she said.

Katie knew her uncle wouldn't be happy with her decision, but they had to talk to Gaines before he decided to run—or worse.

TWENTY-FIVE

Saturday 1810 hours

Katie cleaned up and changed into the extra clothes she had in her locker at the department. Even though it was her running clothes, she had no other choice and wasn't going to drive home and back again. It took her twenty minutes to make herself presentable. The pain on her arm from the intense heat of the fire began to subside.

When she walked out into the hallway, McGaven was already waiting for her. He too had cleaned up and changed. The only difference was that he had a bandage on his right hand.

"You look better," he said.

"I feel a lot better too."

"Ready?"

"Definitely."

"You know the sheriff is not going to be happy that we didn't go to the hospital to get completely checked out," he said.

"I know. But this is the first time I feel we're making headway."

They hurried to the detective division, where Trent Gaines was being held in interview room one. They both secured their firearms in a safe and kept their badges in view before speaking with one of the detectives.

"Trent Gaines?" she said.

"He's in room one," said the detective. "Here are the photos you asked for."

"Thanks." She took the manila file. "Did he give you any problems?"

"Nope. He's antsy though. High strung."

"Thanks," she said. Turning to McGaven, "How do you want to handle this?"

"It's your lead. Personally, I think you're scarier." He smiled.

Katie couldn't help but smile back. They were going in to question Gaines as a person of interest, using their routine of Katie questioning and McGaven lurking in the background. The arrangement had worked well in the past. Katie gave McGaven one last look of "we're going to get what we need" before she opened the door.

Trent Gaines sat at the metal table. He wasn't handcuffed, but his hands were on the table with his fingers intertwined. He stared straight ahead as if he was willing himself to sit up straight and stay strong. His thick unkempt hair was oily and a few strands lay across his forehead. His eyes were steely gray.

Katie moved farther into the room. She decided to sit across from Gaines as McGaven took up a position near a corner, crossing his arms facing them.

"Mr. Gaines. Do you know why you're here?"

He shrugged.

"C'mon now. What did I tell you at the tow yard?" she said, watching his moves.

"You told me I needed to get my warrants taken care of."

"Yes. For missing court dates for possession and trespassing." She slowly opened the file but didn't share it yet. "First, what are those sheds or chicken coops used for on your property?"

He kept staring straight ahead and kept his gaze from looking directly at her.

Katie wanted to push him, but not too much. The last thing she wanted was for him to ask for a lawyer even though he hadn't been arrested. He was just detained—for the moment.

"What do you want from me?" he said.

"The truth. All we're after is the truth."

"What? You come to my property and want to know what those structures are? Is that it?" He stared at his hands.

"To begin."

"Honestly, I don't know. They were there when I rented the place. I never even looked at them."

"How long have you lived there?"

"Two years."

"Who is your landlord?"

"I dunno. I pay to a company called Rental Inc."

"And?"

"And I've never met my landlord or the owner of the property."

"How did they show you the property?"

"They had a lock box and gave me the code."

"That seems convenient."

"You had no right to be on my property."

"You're right. We were looking for you to speak to you. But..."

Gaines now stared directly at her.

Katie wasn't going to let him intimidate her or take control of the conversation. "But, your attack dog had other ideas and cornered me and my partner." She turned her head to gesture to McGaven. He was now staring at Gaines.

"I don't have a dog." He leaned back and diverted his stare. It was clear he knew all about the dog, whether it was his or not.

"Huh, you could've fooled us."

"Prove it's mine."

Katie pushed her chair back and stood up. "I don't have to prove it. The claw marks and scrapes on the door to your shed will be proven through forensics that it came from that dog. The dog was on your property. How can you explain that?"

"I don't need to—I don't have a dog."

Katie switched gears. "How long have you had the steel wire on your property?"

"Steel wire?" Again, it was clear he knew exactly what she meant.

"We will be testing it to see if it matches items found as evidence connected to major crimes," she said.

McGaven moved from one side of the room to the other. It was a dramatic adjustment that helped to keep suspects or witnesses off balance. The process helped to make it easier to ascertain if the person was telling the truth or not. They would either keep with the same answer or flip-flop to another one. It was Katie and McGaven's own style of a lie detector.

"You're not going to find anything," he said as a last-ditch effort to make himself seem innocent.

Katie slowly pulled out two eight-by-ten photos and put them on the table. Gaines didn't look at them. He began nervously moving his leg. She slowly pushed the photos closer.

"Look at them. What do you see?" she said.

He turned his head to the side.

McGaven moved closer to him.

"Look at them!" Katie said.

Gaines gritted his teeth and looked down. He stared at the graphic photographs. They were of Mrs. Banks's autopsy and a close-up of a hook in her mouth.

"What do you see?"

He grimaced. "Why are you showing me this?"

"Do you know who that is?"

"No. Why should I know her?"

"Because we're going to find out that the wire hook in her mouth is going to match the wire on your property." Katie knew it was speculation at this point, but she wanted to gauge his reaction or see if he would give up someone else. It wasn't the best approach, but she had to do something to try to push the investigation forward.

Gaines didn't say anything.

"How many times did you meet with Mr. Banks?"

"Who?"

"The man that had the slashed tires. Mr. Banks."

"I told you before. Three times and on the third I gave him a tow to get the tire fixed and to check out the rest of the car."

"Had you ever met him before? Ever heard the name Banks?" she said, picking up the photo. "This is Mrs. Banks. And..." She pulled the autopsy photo of Mr. Banks. "This is what happened to Mr. Banks."

Gaines's eyes grew wide. "I had nothing to do with that— any of that. That's not supposed to happen."

"Not *supposed* to happen? Does that mean you knew something was going to happen to the Banks family? Did you know the entire family was murdered?"

Gaines appeared to shrink slightly in his chair. "No, no, no..." He slammed his fists on the table. "You're not going to pin this on me. I may be a lot of things, but I'm no killer."

"What about your partner, Ryan Rey? Would he murder this family?"

Gaines blinked in surprise.

"Who else do you work with? Or who do you work for?" she said.

"It's not like that," he said.

Katie could feel her anger escalating, but she didn't want to jeopardize the ground she had gained talking with Gaines. "Enlighten me, what is it like?"

"I'm no killer..."

"What is it like?" Katie went a step further and pulled out a photograph of Emily Banks. It was a cute picture of a smiling, sweet, innocent little girl. It hurt Katie to the core wondering where Emily was, what she was feeling, and what was going to happen to the girl if they didn't find her in time. Katie pushed the photo in front of Gaines. "Look at her."

He paused and then looked down, staring at the smiling face. He didn't move or seem to show a physical recognition, but there was something there in the way he kept his eyes on the girl. There was a conscious recognition.

Katie wanted to lunge across the table and pull Gaines from his chair. She wanted to make him tell her where Emily was—and why she had been targeted.

"What exactly are you involved in?" she said, remembering the things that Marshal West had explained to her. "You kidnap little girls for profit?"

Gaines hung his head and mumbled something that Katie couldn't understand.

"What?"

"I'm done talking."

"Tell me what you know about this little girl."

"I'm done talking..."

Katie tried several other questions, but Gaines kept to his word and didn't say anything more. Soon after, Katie and McGaven watched as an officer took Gaines away to a holding cell until his warrants were sorted out and a judge heard his case for bail.

"What do you think?" said McGaven.

"I don't know if he did it, but he knows something."

McGaven nodded. "I agree. I thought you were going to beat it out of him."

"Trust me. I thought about it."

TWENTY-SIX

Saturday 2200 hours

When things slowed down it was the most difficult for Katie; when the leads ran dry and the adrenalin of a case subsided she had to face her emotions, and her life. It wasn't the same as when she was running, which helped to clear her mind. Katie couldn't sleep. She couldn't eat. She didn't want to talk to anyone. She didn't answer text messages from her uncle, McGaven, or John. They were checking in on her, which made her feel good. But she didn't want to talk about Chad or how she felt about the case. They were family. That was how she explained the people in her life that she worked with—family.

Every time she closed her eyes, she saw Tessa or Emily, hugging her teddy bear. Both equally heart-wrenching to Katie —she felt helpless. She wasn't sure she could take it if Emily ended up like Tessa.

As she sipped at another cup of hot tea, she curled up on the couch dressed in pajamas with Cisco fast asleep next to her. Her breathing felt strange due to the smoke but her arm felt much better. She was exhausted, mentally and physically.

Rerunning everything that had happened that day was only making her body and mind weaken.

The tea felt soothing and she was about to have another. Then it hit her. She hadn't heard from Chad. She knew he was moving and it was a big upheaval for him, but she was upset he hadn't been in touch. She had to come to terms that she wasn't a priority to him anymore. It wasn't as if they were never going to talk again—but at the moment it felt like a part of her had died.

Katie got up and headed to the kitchen. Cisco grumbled at the movement and then resituated himself before falling back to sleep.

Suddenly her Jeep alarm went off. Blaring in between honks and a siren, it shattered the silence.

Katie immediately grabbed her keys to try and disarm it, but the signal wouldn't work through the walls. Cisco stood on the couch barking.

Katie grabbed her Glock and headed to the front door. She peered through the peephole. There wasn't anyone outside, but her car kept blaring.

Barefoot with her gun guiding her way, Katie cleared the porch and the front yard before moving toward the Jeep. She tried her fob key again, and suddenly it shut off the alarm abruptly.

Katie breathed a sigh of relief.

Silence filled the night.

Cisco's rapid barks then filled the silence.

Katie could feel the cold driveway beneath her bare feet, making her shudder. Her pajamas weren't warm enough for the chilly evening. Thinking the alarm was a malfunction of sorts, she neared her car. On the passenger's side window were words written in some type of grease marker.

You'll never find her.

Katie stood motionless, staring at the words. She wasn't sure what disturbed her more—the fact that the person who had written the message was obviously talking about Emily, or why her house security system didn't alert her to the motion in her driveway.

TWENTY-SEVEN

Sunday 1015 hours

Katie left her house early even though she'd only had three hours of sleep. Police officers came out and searched the area surrounding her house, including the driveway, but didn't find anything. They documented the message on the window and dusted for prints, but there was nothing. She wasn't hopeful of anything concrete, but the good news about the incident, at least in Katie's mind, was that it was clear they were making someone nervous.

Strangely, her security cameras didn't pick up anything. There had been intermittent disruptions to the video when it didn't pick up motion. That made her uncomfortable. John said he would do a complete maintenance of her security system and update the computer software to troubleshoot everything in the next few days.

Katie needed to get out of her house, so she and Cisco went for a hike. The fresh air and quiet time helped her to relax. It didn't stop her from thinking about the case, but it did give her a break. She wasn't going to be able to keep going at this pace if she didn't take care of herself.

After forty-five minutes, Katie found herself at a spot that she hadn't visited in a while. It was as if an unseen force was pulling her. She needed advice, to let her vulnerability show, and to feel closeness without any judgment. She knew she would never feel one hundred percent closure, but she also knew she would feel better and maybe she would see everything with better clarity.

Katie and Cisco walked down the path and then slowly down the grassy aisle. The two headstones of a loving mother and father were waiting for her. Putting down a bouquet of flowers, she looked up as a few birds flew from a nearby tree, followed by a gentle breeze.

She sat down next to the graves of her parents. Cisco took his place next to Katie as he had done so many times before. The dog remained at attention with his senses on high alert as his partner took her time. He was on watch.

Katie didn't immediately speak. She sat in her quiet solitude and softly said a prayer that meant the most to her.

Finally, after about ten minutes, she said, "I love you both so much. I miss you and think about you every day." Katie took a moment to fight back the tears. "I don't know what to do without Chad. I'm not sure if I can continue to do this anymore. I cannot let a child die because I can't figure out who took her or where she is... I just can't..." Katie choked up as tears rolled down her face. She took a few more moments to catch her breath and to try to relax. She didn't realize how much of a burden she carried—it wasn't just one thing but many things she carried twenty-four hours a day. Something had to give. She needed comfort but also needed a healthy direction to head in.

"I couldn't save Tessa," she whispered, shaking her head in shame. "I don't know if I can live with that... I need your advice... I've never felt so completely broken up about victims before... not like this... sweet, innocent Emily has no one. I have to save her..."

Cisco nudged his long body closer to Katie. It was usual for the dog to sense her pain and want to comfort her in the only way he knew how. This was his quiet moment and he would stay with her for as long as she needed.

Katie couldn't hold back any longer. The tears came full force. When it finally seemed as if they would stop, she wiped her face. "I know you would know what to say right now. How to make me feel better and how to put things in perspective." She smiled. "You would tell me that not only can I do this, but that I've always been able to solve the case. You both didn't raise a quitter." She laughed. "I couldn't have asked for such wonderful, loving parents. Our time together was too short... so short..." Katie looked up at the sky. It was serene with a few passing clouds casting down morning sunlight through the trees. Looking around her, she was alone at the cemetery. But there was a peace that she could feel all around her. It washed over her, like the wonderful rays of sunshine, and she couldn't help but feel her parents were wrapping their arms around her.

Katie pet Cisco and stayed in front of the headstones for another fifteen minutes until she felt better.

She stood up. "I love you both," she said. And then Katie and Cisco walked back home.

TWENTY-EIGHT

Monday 0745 hours

Katie had been in the cold-case office for almost an hour. She spent most of her time staring at the boards, studying the families, the locations, and the injuries. Why them? How were they connected besides the two little girls? How were they chosen? Who was calling all the shots? Gaines didn't seem like the mastermind to her. From everything they had gathered and the crime scenes, it wouldn't be a reach to suggest that these families had been targeted for some time. The killer would have wanted to make sure they fit "his" ideological perfect victims. Therefore, planning was key.

Katie went back through the articles found at the Bankses' barn, the phone records, the crime scenes, the hospital, and Gaines's property.

"What am I missing?" she said.

She moved to the report from Gaines's house and property. There was old wire consistent with the hooks, but they couldn't find any evidence that he was the one who had constructed them. There was other fishing paraphernalia, but since Gaines rented the property, it couldn't be automatically connected to him. At best, it was circumstantial. And there were no indications Emily had been in the house.

Gaines would be in lockup for a couple of months due to his warrants, so it was good news he wouldn't be able to continue whatever he was involved in—at least for now. And it gave Katie and McGaven a little leeway to continued moving ahead.

You'll never find her...

Katie was going to do everything she could to find Emily.

She sent another message to Detective Alvarez asking about any new information on the girl's disappearance. The answer was always the same: *Nothing new, but we're tracking down every lead. Didn't find anything on the nanny cam at hospital.*

Katie dialed a number into her phone.

"Pine Valley Elementary, how can I help you?" said a cheerful woman.

"This is Detective Katie Scott from the Pine Valley Sheriff's Department. I want to know if I could speak to Gabby Rey?"

"I'm sorry, Detective, but she didn't come in for her early class this morning. Would you like to leave a message?"

Katie paused. "No, no thank you."

Katie sat for a moment taking everything in. She looked at Gaines's background check where it showed that he had been arrested with Ryan Rey in the past. It had been a couple of years, but it was still a connection. She looked up the property where Gabby and Ryan owned a house and found a local phone number. She dialed it. The phone range six times and went to voicemail where Gabby's voice had been recorded. Katie hung up and didn't leave a message.

They needed to get to the Rey residence. She stood up just as McGaven entered.

"Whoa, where are you going, partner?" he said.

"We're going to the Rey residence in Prairie Valley," she said. "Gabby hasn't shown up for work."

"There could be a million reasons why," he said.

"Let's go check it out."

"After you," he said.

Katie was careful not to exceed the speed limit. Monday morning traffic wasn't as hectic as other mornings—either most people couldn't get out early enough or had the Monday morning flu. She turned off the main highway once again and traveled the single lane road.

"When were you going to tell me about Saturday night and your Jeep?" said McGaven.

"It's nothing."

McGaven studied his partner. She drove with purpose, like the devil was chasing them. "Nothing? I don't think so. Having the message 'you'll never find her' is a big deal."

"You know what it means."

"What?"

"It simply means that whoever is part of all this... we have them scared. That's all."

"Oh, that's all. I was worried there for a moment."

Katie took the corner a bit fast and the sedan slid slightly into the oncoming lane. "Someone is trying to throw us off our game. It could be anyone. It's not difficult to figure out we're investigating these homicides and looking for Emily."

"Do you really believe it could be anyone—and not the killer or someone who is an accomplice to the killer?"

"It's possible." She glanced at her partner. "We don't know enough yet."

"And yet a lot has happened." He studied her closely. "Katie, you feeling okay?"

She sighed, giving him a stern look.

"I didn't say, 'Are you okay?' I changed it up a little bit."

Katie couldn't help but smile. McGaven had a way about

him, a good-natured, kind way. It was clear that he meant what he said. She sighed again. "I'm doing okay. That's the best I can say right now until we catch this killer."

Katie's cell phone rang.

"Detective Scott," she answered.

"Detective. I assume I'm on the speaker."

"Yes. McGaven is here as well." Katie recognized Marshal West's voice. "What can we do for you, Marshal?"

"I'm in your office and you aren't," he said.

"We're on our way to conduct an interview."

"Okay. Anything you want me to check on?"

Katie thought a moment. "How are your paper skills?"

"Excuse me?"

McGaven smiled.

"Your paper skills," she said.

"Oh, I get it. You want me to make some sense out of all this paperwork."

"Just the boxes in the corner." She waited.

There was silence from the other end of the phone.

"Marshal West, are you still there?" she said.

"I hear you loud and clear. I guess... I can track that down."

"Thanks. We'll see you soon." Katie ended the phone call.

"Do you think he's going to do it?" said McGaven.

"I don't know why not. He's a rookie. It'll be good for him to gain some experience until his supervisors tell him to go back," she said.

Katie continued on Raven Canyon Road, which was in the opposite direction to where Trent Gaines lived. The roads were wider, some with double lanes, which made their driving time faster.

"It's just up ahead," said McGaven looking at his phone GPS. "Take Fern Way."

Katie turned right on the road and continued. It was a nice housing area. There were several homes, but it appeared each house was on about five acres. The homes were various wood structures and not modular or manufactured residences. Every house they passed had a maintained yard and home. A large black-and-tan dog with floppy ears ran up beside the car giving two barks.

"Great. Another dog," said McGaven.

Katie laughed. "It looks like a nice dog. Probably got out from a neighbor's yard. Nothing to worry about."

They found the Rey residence. Two cars were in the driveway—a small blue compact and a black SUV.

"Looks like they're home," said McGaven. "Maybe they took a day off and aren't answering the phone?"

Katie wasn't so sure. She parked a few car lengths after the driveway. Taking notice that the closest neighbors didn't have a vantage of the Rey home, it gave them more privacy and it also meant that if something happened no one was likely to see it from their house.

The detectives got out of the car, surveying the area. The homes were mostly one-story medium-sized residences. Katie noticed that it was really quiet, especially after the wind died down. Even the dog had disappeared. She looked at the Rey residence and observed that the curtains were open, which, along with the two cars in the driveway, suggested someone was home.

Katie wanted to proceed with caution. She turned to McGaven and nodded, then gestured that she would approach on the right, meaning the left side was for him. When they were going into an unknown situation, even when things seemed calm and quiet, they still needed to be on high alert. There were countless situations across the US when police officers were killed when approaching a residence under suspicious circumstances, victims of an ambush. The detectives took precautions and had each other's back until the situation was under control.

Katie walked up the driveway on the right and stopped

briefly to look inside the SUV and then the small car. Nothing looked out of place. There was nothing inside the cars and she saw the red flashing light indicating the alarms were set. Maybe her mind was working overtime. Maybe her judgment was skewed by the fact that Emily was still missing. The longer they didn't find the little girl, the more likely that she could ultimately end up like Tessa.

Katie pushed the awful images from her mind. She kept moving and she could see in her peripheral that McGaven was keeping her pace.

Once at the front door, Katie pushed the doorbell. They could hear it chime inside. Waiting, they kept watch around them, and of the street. It still stayed quiet. Katie pressed the doorbell again. The chime echoed but there was no sound of movement or any bark from a dog.

Katie nodded to her partner as she moved to the right and looked in the windows. Both the curtains and blinds were wide open. She couldn't see anything at first except for living room furniture, but then she saw a pair of boots from the other side of a large gray sofa. She stood up on her tiptoes and verified it was indeed someone on the floor—not moving.

Katie told Gav and retrieved her gun as she hurried to the front door. McGaven pulled his weapon, took a step back on the porch, and used a stomp-kick tactic, which thrust in the front door. It slammed against the inside wall.

McGaven entered first, sweeping left and right. "Sheriff's department!"

No answer. But they could hear low voices coming from the kitchen.

Katie entered behind her partner, going low and covering him. She went left and looked in the bedrooms. "Clear!" Her heart was racing and she could barely breathe.

McGaven replied from the main area, "Clear."

Katie joined her partner where they saw Ryan Rey lying on

the floor. There were two gunshot wounds in his chest. Based on his decomposition and the rigor mortis that had set in, he had been dead for several hours.

Katie turned her attention toward the kitchen, where she found Gabby Rey lying face down on the floor with a bullet wound in her back. She kneeled and touched Gabby's wrist, which was cold.

"In here," she called. "It's Gabby. She's dead."

TWENTY-NINE

Katie was careful not to disturb anything, but still looked around the Reys' home. "Looks like Ryan Rey was shot first and Gabby tried to run before she was hit. Looks like nine-millimeter rounds, but I don't see any casings."

"The killer was quick, efficient, and had the presence of mind to pick up after himself," McGaven said.

Katie looked around. "It doesn't appear to be any type of robbery or home invasion. Nothing looks tossed or taken." She didn't like the scene. Everything seemed to give the indication that it was more of a hit than anything else.

McGaven had left and then returned with gloves. Both detectives quickly slipped them on. They took a quick look around the living room, dining, and kitchen areas. Everything seemed as normal as any living space. The scenario was casual, evening time. It appeared that Gabby had been fixing dinner and was watching television on the iPad—the voices they could hear. Ryan had been having a drink and must have been sitting in the living room. It seemed likely the killer was someone they knew and had let inside their home.

The detectives couldn't locate cell phones or any other personal items like a scheduler, phone list, or any calendars. There wasn't any sign of another glass and all the garbage was gone. That fact raised suspicion. It was similar to the lack of trash found at the other two crime scenes. It was circumstantial but the modus operandi seemed to be the same.

Katie looked through cabinets and drawers. Opening one of the drawers, which initially looked like an overflow of miscellaneous items, she found a small navy zippered bag. Inside were several bundles of hundred-dollar bills—at least ten thousand dollars.

"Found motive," she said.

McGaven entered and saw the money. "It's certainly a motivating factor."

"It seems that Mr. Rey could have been involved with Gaines."

"Then things went bad. Why didn't the killer take the money?" he said.

"Probably didn't know about it. The house doesn't look tossed."

"Mrs. Rey probably went along with the plans for a while, taking children, and then something caused her to change her mind." Katie remembered seeing something in one of the bedrooms she had previously cleared. She returned to the small, tidy space, which was most likely a guest room. There was nothing personal on the dresser or nightstand. But the single-door closet had several items hanging—a coat, a long-sleeved orange sweater, and a small child's dress.

The dress caught Katie's eye. It made her think of the dress found in the garbage bag at the creek along the Bankses' property. She turned and went through the drawers, but everything else in the room was empty. Searching the pockets of the adult coat, she found some papers that were folded in quarters. Carefully opening them, she found they were photocopies of articles dating back several years. They were about children being targeted for kidnapping then ultimately murdered by specific features, area, and situation. The articles weren't in depth, but they gave some alarming statistics.

Katie wondered how Mrs. Banks and Mrs. Rey met each other. Was it by chance? Were they part of some organization? It was unclear, but they seemed to have joined together as an alliance.

Gazing outside, she saw two small sheds reminiscent of what was found at Gaines's rural rental property. The backside of the Reys' acreage was vast but was also extremely dense with trees and undeveloped areas. It was essentially a thick dark forest.

"Hey," said McGaven at the doorway. "Looks like Eva will be processing the house. John is more than busy." He looked in the room. "Anything?"

"There's a child's dress hanging in the closet. Did the Reys have children?"

"No. At least from the background check, it stated no children."

"Huh, Gabby taught at the elementary school." She frowned.

"Maybe she couldn't have children and working with kids helped to fill that void for her."

"Maybe," she said and looked around. "Something seems out of place here. It's too clean and empty. As the only other bedroom, there should be more." Katie continued to study the area, as well as what she could see outside. It was difficult to not think about Emily, and if anything, being in the Reys' house had made her feel even more uncomfortable.

The detectives returned to the living room and kitchen. Katie leaned close to the kitchen counters and smelled them.

There was the definite hint of a recent cleaning solution. She opened the cabinet beneath the sink and found dish soap, dishwasher crystals, window cleaner, and extra sponges. There were none of the usual disinfecting cleaners nor anything like the lingering smell from the countertop.

Katie could hear McGaven on the phone coordinating with the sheriff's department, forensics, and the medical examiner's office. He gave explicit instructions of what to expect and wanted to maintain the integrity of the scene, so any extra and unnecessary personnel was discouraged.

There was a cookbook on the counter, written by one of those celebrity chefs that had their own television show. Katie picked it up and thumbed the pages. She wasn't exactly sure why the book drew her. Maybe it was because the counters were so neat, especially if Gabby was preparing dinner, which indicated the killer might have cleaned more than the trash cans. She put the cookbook back where she had found it and noticed a corner of a piece of paper poking out of it. With her gloved hand, she carefully opened the book to the page, revealing a small slip of paper with nine digits written in blue ink: 1 7 3 9 2 1 5 4 7.

At first, Katie thought the numbers were a phone number missing a digit. Though the first two digits didn't represent any area codes in California. She looked at the paper closely to see if there were any other indentations—like if the pen didn't fully write a number—but there was none.

"Nine digits?" she said.

"Nine digits?" repeated McGaven entering the kitchen.

"I found this piece of paper in Gabby's cookbook," she said. "There are just nine digits: one, seven, three, nine, two, one, five, four, seven."

"Maybe it's just a bookmark? It looks like it was torn from something else."

"No, I don't think so."

"Nine digits... Social Security number... tax ID numbers... I'm not sure, but maybe a property ID... or an IP address?"

Katie thought about all the things McGaven mentioned. She took out her cell phone and took a photograph before returning the slip of paper to the book. "Eva will have to dust everything for prints."

The detectives walked out to the driveway just as a police cruiser showed up. Which was also when Katie's phone rang.

"Detective Scott."

"Is Cisco at the police kennels?" said Sheriff Scott.

"No, he's at home," she said.

McGaven turned to his partner, listening.

"I pulled up the Rey residence location on the internet as soon as the call came in. If anything is possibly connected to the homicides and missing girl, you must let me know immediately."

Katie listened to her uncle and looked to her partner.

"I saw there's a large area of woods behind the house," the sheriff continued.

"Yes. They're really dense and it's definitely undeveloped."

"You and McGaven need to gear up... and you need to pick up Cisco and conduct a thorough search," said the sheriff.

Katie glanced at her watch. "It'll be about an hour and half. That's if we hurry."

"Then I suggest you get going. And Katie?" he said.

"Yes."

"Be careful." The sheriff ended the call.

Katie looked at McGaven. Another patrol rolled up behind the first one.

"Let me guess. We've got another search to do," he said.

"You got it."

"Let me talk to patrol first before we go."

McGaven spoke with the two officers while Katie took a last walk around the house, doing a quick inventory of everything they would need to conduct a search. She made a special note that they would need something to cut through the heavy brush and low branches. It was going to be a grueling search. And the densely grouped trees would block out proper light.

She walked back to the car.

McGaven approached. "Let's roll."

THIRTY

Katie and McGaven arrived back at the Rey residence with Cisco. They were all ready for the arduous search and had prepared accordingly. They knew it would be just as challenging as other searches in the past, but since there was a connection between Mr. Banks, Gaines, and the Reys, they had to take every possible direction they could in order to find the killer—and find Emily alive.

Katie parked her Jeep on the street. There were more first responders present and the forensic services SUV, which meant that Eva was there.

Katie and McGaven got out and began securing their gear. Katie felt like she was going into battle and those anxious physical symptoms along with vivid memories began to surface. She wore heavier gear, tactical pants, boots, long-sleeved shirt and jacket, in addition to her utility belt with her gun, flashlight, and a useful tactical knife. All that gear would be hot, but she had to make sure she protected her body. She ignored her lightheadedness and tingly arms and legs as she made sure Cisco was protected. She put on his cool goggles because it would help protect his eyes from the wild sticks and brush. After double-checking the dog's vest and collar, he was ready to go.

Cisco knew there was something big going on and he responded with whines and a couple of high-pitch barks.

"So I'm glad I don't always have to dress like this... I'm going sweat," said McGaven.

"That's the whole point," she said. "C'mon, isn't it manly to sweat instead of perspiring?" She laughed, trying to lighten the mood and help with her own uncomfortable feelings.

"If you say so," he grumbled.

Katie and McGaven fitted their mini listening devices in their ears and microphones on their clothes so that they could talk quietly but still be able to hear one another.

A patrol sergeant joined them. "You ready to search the back area?"

"Yep," said McGaven. "Katie and Cisco are leading and I'm their cover."

"Do you need another spotter?" said the sergeant.

McGaven looked at Katie and shrugged.

"Actually, a spotter would be great if you can spare the body," said Katie.

"Deputy Hansen is here," he said and left the detectives. They heard him call the officer and explain the situation.

"Cool, I like Hansen," said McGaven.

"He's going to have to grab one of those department jackets to protect his arms and torso."

"Where's Hamilton?" said Katie.

"Don't know. They'll keep the integrity of the crime scene until he arrives."

"I'm just surprised he's not here yet," she said.

McGaven unfolded a regular map of the area. "How do you want to approach this area?"

"If we think about what our killer would do... if they were

going to hide something or dispose of something," she said, studying the map.

"I would go here." McGaven pointed to the left side of the property. "There are two large grouping of trees, but I bet there are some nice open areas in between."

Katie nodded. "We'll be able to see if the area has been trampled recently or if soil has been moved around."

"You mean Cisco will know."

Cisco gave a bark.

Deputy Hansen joined the detectives. "Okay, where do you need me to be?"

Katie showed the deputy on the map where they would enter and explained how they needed him to fan out to the left about twenty feet behind McGaven.

"Ready?" said McGaven.

Katie and Deputy Hansen nodded. Katie, with Cisco leading, moved in point position as they made their way to the backyard.

Katie noticed she was a little bit nervous, which didn't make sense. She was fidgety and found her breathing was shallow. She had done hundreds of searches and this wasn't any different, except there weren't insurgents setting traps and shooting at them. It should have been easy to conduct this particular search—but it wasn't.

Katie and McGaven stopped at the two cages, which were large chicken coops. They looked as if they had been out in the elements and unused for years. The old wood had splintered vertically, the chicken wire had turned to rust, and the roofs showed signs of holes and weather damage. Katie took a closer look, but they were empty and didn't seem to have had anything in them in a very long time. The two coops had a smell of mold, but no signs of anything else. She turned to

McGaven and shook her head. Even Cisco didn't seem interested in them.

As Katie exited the patio area and the chicken coops of the Reys' backyard and headed left in the north direction, the sun disappeared behind cloud cover. That meant her visual was going to be slightly impaired in the darker areas of the forest cover. She glanced behind her and saw McGaven in his vantage position and Hansen taking up the rear but keeping watch. McGaven's height was an advantage where he could see quite a distance.

After a few steadying breaths, Katie gave Cisco the search command and the dog instantly pushed forward. With his body taut while moving in a systematic motion, ears alert and forward, and his tail relaxed, Cisco was set. His light footsteps and agile movement were perfect for the terrain ahead.

Katie's thoughts were always on the investigation but when she had Cisco her attention was on reading the dog's body language. There were subtle movements that acted like cues to what he was sensing and smelling—even well before he alerted. She let out the leash to about six feet but was prepared to shorten it at any moment.

The footsteps from McGaven seemed to echo all around them. As they entered the first closed area, where trees appeared to grow in circles, the surrounding sounds became muffled.

Katie listened to the various footsteps, her breathing, and watched the dog's movement through the brush. Her body and focus became more relaxed, but extremely aware of everything. She had learned to hone her skills of identifying sounds, smells, and movement around her in such a way that it made her become one with the environment.

"Anything?" said McGaven quietly in her ear.

"Negative."

"Clear areas so far."

Katie was glad to hear there weren't any types of holes, ravines, or impassable parts of the forest.

The pungent smell of the pine was something that made Katie think about when she was a kid and her parents were alive. It reminded her of picnics, hikes, and camping. Sitting out under the stars at night in the summer made her miss those days.

As they moved through the forest, the walking area began to narrow. Katie had to almost stop to get over a limb and keep her face away from the dried brush. It was different walking the terrain as opposed to looking at an aerial version of where they were going. At one point, Katie had to climb around an area to get to the other side. It was a tight fit and she wondered how McGaven and Hansen would manage it.

"It's getting narrower," she said softly.

"Affirmative."

As Katie clambered over another limb, she thought they should head back in another direction. The feeling of chasing your tail hit her. If they had a difficult time getting to the area in their protective gear, how could anyone else? It wasn't far from the patio and backyard—approximately fifty yards—but seemed miles away from the police activity.

The ground's surface began to change. The soil was looser and seemed to have more clay mixed in it. There was also loose shale around, which was usually found in wetter areas such as creeks and rivers. The surrounding area became greener and the leaves were larger as if they were in a more tropical location. It seemed strange to Katie because she hadn't seen any indication of a creek on the map that would explain the greener plants.

"Is there water nearby?" she said.

"Not that I know of, but we did have record rains last season."

Katie took the rain into consideration as they cautiously moved forward.

Soon Cisco slowed his easygoing pace... his body stiffened and his tail rose and pointed straight. Katie didn't move the leash, rather she let Cisco decide when he was going to move.

There was a dark area where the soil had been disturbed. She reeled in the lead to where Cisco was two feet from her. The dog didn't alert, but it was clear he didn't like what he was sensing. There was a complete change of body movement.

"We have something," she said. Pulling Cisco close to her, Katie edged forward taking one careful footstep at a time. "I'm taking a closer look."

It looked like a big pile of fresh dirt, like something you see in a garden just before it was added to an area. There wasn't any obvious odor coming from the pile; it looked moist and would most likely have some type of moldy or dense forest smell. As she inched forward, the mound of dirt appeared like it had been tunneled upward from an animal burrowing into the ground.

"Anything?" said McGaven. "Be careful. I'm right behind you."

Katie glanced back and could hear her partner's footsteps but didn't see him yet. She knew she shouldn't move any farther without him. But the area intrigued her. She needed to know what it was and why it was there. Cisco was curious as well, but he wasn't tense and he seemed to be back to a calmer demeanor.

Katie kept looking closer, almost hypnotized by her surroundings. She noticed there was a ravine, a slight crevice, close by and she wondered if the recent earthquakes they had been having had caused the ground disturbance.

"Katie?"

"Nothing yet. Where are you?" She was concerned McGaven wasn't in position to be their spotter.

"We need a chainsaw," he grumbled.

Katie took a step back, looking around her. There was an area where the brush was cleared back and it seemed recently. That seemed odd. Looking down, it was more packed than the area they had come through. Walking behind the tree, she saw another path that paralleled the property line. Of course, she thought. They should have inspected the area better.

"I've found a better route," she said.

"Affirmative."

"Go toward the property line."

Katie waited for McGaven to respond. She stepped back and her boot sunk, burying her ankle and foot. Moving her foot back and forth, Katie tried to loosen it, so she stepped with her other foot. And that's when the soil gave way from the small ravine and she began sliding downward. Grabbing at the sides, brush, and empty air, she tried to catch her balance.

Katie had let go of Cisco's leash and could hear him barking above her. Clawing the ground, wanting to get to her, the dog kept barking.

The fall felt like it was in slow motion... strangely dizzy... weirdly quiet... the soil turned muddy and it slowed her descent. Large chunks of sticky mud stuck to her body and face. When Katie finally stopped, lying on her back, she had only fallen about ten feet, but it seemed like she had been falling for an eternity. Her right foot caught on a tree root.

Katie sat up with difficulty with her foot in a precarious position. "Ugh..." Mud had infiltrated everything. Her clothes, shoes, coat sleeves, her belt, and her face. She wiped mud chunks from her ears and from her hair. Inspecting her weapon, she hoped it was okay and with some cleaning would be good to fire.

"Katie! Katie!" said McGaven as the radio cut in and out intermittently.

"I'm fine," she said as she slowly moved, making sure that she didn't have any injuries. "I think I ate a chunk of mud." She spit several times. Removing her knife, she sawed at the root, releasing her foot.

Cisco's barking ceased.

"Hey," said McGaven from above with Cisco at his side. "What are you doing down there? What's with all the mud?"

Deputy Hansen appeared. To McGaven he said, "I'll got get some rope."

McGaven nodded. The deputy took off.

Katie saw Cisco trying to inch toward the edge, pushing with his large front paws.

"Cisco, no! *Bleib*," she commanded, telling him to stay.

"What is this place?" said McGaven looking around.

"I don't know, I was thinking the same thing before I fell."

"It looks like the rain had disturbed everything."

"That's when I found the other way in. An easier way," she said.

"All this water must've been from the rain we've had the past couple of months. It must've drained to this spot, and since it's so dark here, the sunshine couldn't dry it up," he said.

"Sounds about right." Katie decided to try and climb out, but every time she stepped up the mud wouldn't allow her to get any traction. "This sucks."

McGaven laughed. "I've never seen you so frustrated and... muddy..."

"Come down here and tell me that." Her footing was slippery and she found it difficult to stay standing. She slipped and landed on her knees. She attempted a few more times before admitting defeat and waiting for Hansen to return.

THIRTY-ONE

Monday 1645 hours

Katie and Cisco with McGaven as their spotter continued to search the back property of the Reys, but nothing indicated anything that might be of the criminal nature.

Detective Hamilton had arrived to assist with the two homicides. The house and property were buzzing with activity, which had now attracted neighbors. Patrol officers were keeping everyone out that didn't belong at the scene. Official vehicles had jammed up the quiet street and there were sheriff's department personnel walking in and out of the Reys' house. Gabby and Ryan had already been taken back to the medical examiner's office.

Katie was a mess. The only place where she could try to clean up was at the outdoor hose. She didn't want to get inside her Jeep and drive all the way back to the department or her house in her condition. Luckily, she had some extra clothes in the car along with several towels.

"You okay?" said McGaven. He carried a heavy jacket for her.

"I think so." Her teeth chattered as she dried off. "I need to change out of these clothes."

John walked up. "You can change in the forensic van."

"Thanks," she said. She took the jacket from McGaven. "I'll be right back." Katie checked on Cisco, and then grabbed some clothes from her gym bag. She couldn't stop shaking.

You'll never find her...

The stress was overwhelming and for the first time since she took over the cold-case unit, Katie wasn't sure if she could catch the killer to make the killings stop. It was torture. The image of Tessa's body kept running on an endless loop in her mind. *The longer time goes by and there's no word about Emily—the worse it's going to be.* The little girl could already be dead and it was just a matter of time until they found the body.

Katie quickly shed her wet clothes and shoes. She pulled on a pair of black running pants, T-shirt, hoodie, dry socks, and running shoes. She instantly felt better but decided to put on the coat that McGaven had brought her too. The bulky fabric helped her warm up. She combed her hair with her fingers and pulled it back into a fresh ponytail.

There was a small mirror on one of the shelves. She looked at her image staring back. Her face was drawn and pale. At least the mud was gone, but it was the look in her eyes that scared her. It was the gaze of someone after a traumatic incident. She knew it well. The first time she had witnessed what war could do to the soldiers who were fighting for a cause—no matter the side—it had stuck with her. And that's how she felt now. War-impacted.

Katie quickly gathered her wet dirty clothes and put them in a trash bag to take back to her car. She opened the back doors of the forensic van and stepped out. It was warmer than she thought, but the light and temperature were fading. She dropped the bag into the back of her Jeep.

A few more vehicles were at the scene.

"Excuse me," said a woman with dark long hair. She was dressed in jeans and a sweater, but still seemed to be cold with her arms crossed in front of her.

Katie turned to her. "Yes?"

"Are you a detective?"

"Yes. Detective Scott."

"Are they dead?" she said as her eyes darted to the Rey house and back to Katie.

Katie didn't want to talk about it and she was bound by the legalities of an open homicide investigation. She knew patrol was canvassing the area and speaking with neighbors. Ignoring the question for now, she said, "What's your name?"

"I'm Sara Engles. I live across the street," she pointed.

"How long have you lived here?"

"About three years."

"Did you know the Reys?"

"Yes. Well, Gabby I knew. We would have coffee together and my daughter went to her school—not in her class though."

Katie glanced at the Reys' house and saw that everyone involved was now outside in the back area. "Had you noticed anything unusual lately?"

"What do you mean?"

"Did you notice any changes to Gabby's behavior? Or anyone at their house recently?" said Katie. She watched Sara and could gauge the woman was being truthful by her mannerisms, eye contact, and answering the questions directly.

"No. But she had been hurried lately, not having much time to socialize."

"Did she ever confide in you about any problems she was having?"

"We talked about the usual stuff. She complained about not having enough school budget for her class. And my daughter

Faith, I was worried about saving enough for her college. Just stuff like that."

"I see."

"Why? Do you think that—"

"Ms. Engles, this is an open investigation, so we really can't talk about it. We're trying to get some background on the Reys and anything that happened in the last couple of weeks."

The woman nodded.

Katie took her cell phone, which miraculously still functioned. She pulled up a photo of Nick Gaines and showed it to the neighbor.

She looked at it. "Yes, I've seen him. It's Ryan's brother."

That shocked Katie, but she didn't let it show. "When was the last time you saw him?"

"I'm not sure. It was a couple of weeks ago... I think. I had just come home from work and I saw him drive by." She paused. "I've only seen him and an older man."

"Older man? What did he look like?"

"Uh, tall, thin, light brown hair, glasses, fifties or sixties..."

Katie pulled up another photo, this one of Emily Banks. "Have you ever seen this little girl before?"

"I don't think so. The Reys didn't have children, but Gabby has a sister with kids. I've only seen them on occasion."

"What about last night?"

Ms. Engles took a moment, clearly scanning her memory. "It was Sunday night and it's usually very quiet around here. I didn't see or hear anything out of the ordinary."

"Did you see any other cars?"

"No, I'm sorry."

"I don't have any cards on me, but if you think of anything or see anything out of the ordinary, please call the Pine Valley Sheriff's Department," said Katie.

"I will. Thank you, Detective." The neighbor walked back to her house.

Katie watched Ms. Engles walk away, thinking about what she had told her.

"Hey," said McGaven.

"Hi."

"You look better."

"I feel better now I'm warm again." Katie looked at police officers coming and going through the front door. "I just spoke with a neighbor."

"What did she say?" he said.

"Basically, we're on the right track. Trent Gaines has been seen coming over many times. It seems Gabby told the neighbor that Gaines was her husband's brother."

"Makes sense."

"And, there was an older man... fifties or sixties..."

"Okay," he said. "We'll have to go over our lists to see if we can identify him."

"The neighbor, Ms. Engles, hadn't seen any children except for Gabby's sister's kids."

"Hmm."

"What's wrong?" she said.

"Do we know for sure Gabby even has a sister?" he said. "She said Gaines was her husband's brother and we know that's not true."

"It's easy to find out."

"I'm on it," he said as he began walking to the house. She soon lost sight of him.

"Katie." John approached her. "I have a little bit of time this evening to run some maintenance on your security system."

"You don't have to do that now. I think we all have full plates," she said.

"Well normally I would agree with you, but I have strict orders from Sheriff Scott."

Katie laughed. "Of course."

"Can you blame him?"

"I guess not."

"Don't worry about the investigation slowing down. Eva can take care of anything necessary once the evidence gets back to the lab. Dr. Dean will need detailed photos."

Katie nodded.

"Eight p.m.?"

"That should be fine. Thanks, John."

"No problem." He walked back to the crime scene.

McGaven emerged from the house.

"Where did you disappear to?" said Katie.

"Just doing my due diligence," he said with a big smile on his face.

"Tell me."

"I ran down some interesting information from police databases. It seems that the older man Ms. Engles was referring to is Tim Denton."

"The owner of Sierra Roadside Towing?"

"The same. I tried to call him at the business. No answer. I'm trying another number with the same results."

The more Katie thought about it, the more she realized the puzzle pieces were falling into place. There was a common thread woven throughout, but they didn't have the exact answers they needed yet.

"We need to talk to Gaines tomorrow," McGaven said.

Katie nodded. "He needs to answer some serious questions. But we don't know whether or not he's the killer. My gut says yes and no. He'd most likely do whatever he's told, but he's not the mastermind."

"Not that guy," he said. "Hamilton is going to talk to Gabby's school tomorrow to see what other information he can find. Deputies are still canvassing—maybe they might find something."

"We're covered for now. I'm exhausted. We have a big day

tomorrow," she said. Her body was tired; she felt as if she was walking through drying cement. Her head ached. She longed for a nice hot shower. "C'mon, we have everything we need right now. Tomorrow is another day."

THIRTY-TWO

Katie managed to feed Cisco and take a shower before John was scheduled to arrive. She thought a couple of times that she should cancel, but knew her uncle would give her an earful if she did. It was better to have diagnostics run on the security system. Truthfully, it did bother her that the cameras didn't pick up the motion of someone at her Jeep writing the message on the window.

You'll never find her...

The scrawled message stayed with her. Even though it was disturbing, it was also telling. It meant that Emily was still alive. The killer was taunting her and the police.

Was it a challenge? Or was it going to be another heartache that she would have to live with?

Katie was combing her wet hair when the doorbell rang. Cisco immediately rushed to the front door barking. He sniffed around the frame and seemed somewhat satisfied. He stopped barking and excitedly ran from one end of the living room to the other.

Katie gazed through the peephole and saw John patiently standing there carrying a brown paper bag. It was clear he had showered and changed into fresh jeans and a T-shirt. She noticed he had shaved. She had remembered the first time she had met him—there had definitely been a spark between them that she chose to ignore.

Katie opened the door. "Hi."

Cisco ran up and sniffed the guest.

"Hey, Cisco," he said. Looking at Katie, "You look like you're feeling better."

"Please, come in." She opened the door wider. "Yes. That hose bath wasn't going to do it." She laughed.

John walked into the living room. He glanced up at the corners of the room and around the front door.

"You looking for indoor cameras?" she said.

"No, but I think you should have motion sensors."

Katie frowned.

"What?" he said and smiled.

"Do I have to remind you, and I say this to Gav all the time, I'm a police officer, Army veteran, and I have a military working dog. I think interior cameras or sensors are unnecessary—at least at this point."

"Okay. But you may have to take it up with the sheriff."

"Don't remind me," she said. "So what's in the bag?"

"I figure you hadn't had time to eat, so I brought some sandwiches and deli salads."

"That's very thoughtful. Thank you." Katie was hungry, but she probably would have just gone to bed without eating if John hadn't been coming over.

John went into the kitchen to unload the bag. "So I wasn't sure which kind of sandwich you wanted, so I got three different kinds. Turkey? Ham? Roast beef?"

"Turkey is great." Katie was touched John was so thoughtful. Honestly, she wondered why he didn't have a girlfriend.

Eva his technician gave him a difficult time about it, but it was his choice. She didn't know much about his past—maybe that would answer a lot.

"I also have potato salad, macaroni salad, and a fruit salad," he said.

"If I wasn't hungry before, I am now. I'll take a taste of each."

"Ah, a woman who's not afraid to eat." John prepared plates and joined Katie at the counter.

They made light conversation as they ate. It was nice for Katie to take her mind momentarily off work.

After, John ran some diagnostics on the laptop computer, which had the main software that ran the security system. He took the time to check all the cameras, making sure they were secured and properly in place. There were two cameras that seemed to have been loosened and weren't as secure as they were at installation.

"How's it going?" said Katie.

"It's fine. I've updated the software and it should be more efficient. But... I've gone over the time in which your Jeep's alarm went off. And..."

"And what?"

"Well, there are some weird irregularities."

"Irregularities?" she said.

"Check this out." He ran the video from the disturbance—before, during, and after.

Katie watched. Everything seemed normal, until the time of the incident when there were two quick flashes. It was difficult to see unless you were looking for it. "Is that a flash of light?"

John nodded. "I think it was from one of those laser pointers."

"Or a scope sight."

He nodded. "Just like that. Your archived video goes into a cloud file, so we can check it from that time."

"But why didn't the software know that there was something like a laser light?"

"My guess, it was a quick flash just long enough to cause the system to reboot. If a laser, like a laser pointer, hits the camera, too close or too long, it can damage it. Laser beams have a very high energy density. My guess would be that the individual knew that a quick exposure to the laser would damage the footage just for a few minutes."

"That would be long enough for someone to write that message on my car," she said, sighing. "Now the real question is... was it a prank or a real warning?"

"'You'll never find her' could be generic. I mean it is possible." He kept her stare.

"I see what you're saying. If someone knew I was working cold cases, they could just be stating that in a way that would seem like any case I'm working on... they could hate cops or whatever. I'm sorry, I'm not making sense." Katie laughed nervously.

"Katie, it's okay," he said and gently touched her arm. "I'm not going to say that I know how you feel or I've experienced what you have, but I do understand difficulties and hardships, both personal and professional. And I'm here if you need to talk or vent or whatever. One veteran to another."

He waited for Katie to regain her composure. She didn't know how to answer him at first, but she often forgot that John was a veteran, an ex-Navy Seal, and it was obvious that he had seen combat. Combat veterans could definitely relate to one another. There was a silence between them, but it wasn't awkward.

She finally said, "Thanks, John. I appreciate that." She didn't want to discuss anything at the moment, partly due to the fact that she didn't know if she could have a serious conversation without crying.

"I'm going to check each camera and make sure they are registering motion," said John.

"There's a ladder on the side of the patio," she said.

John went outside through the sliding door and was gone for about fifteen minutes before he returned. He then sat down in front of the laptop and spent another ten minutes to make sure everything was working correctly by running tests and installing monitoring software to alert when something had interfered with the camera lenses.

Katie cleaned up the kitchen while waiting. Cisco was already asleep on the couch after such a long and exciting day.

"Okay. I think we're secure now," said John. He got up to face Katie. "I know it's been a long day and I'm up early tomorrow."

"Thank you, John. I really appreciate you taking the time."

"Safety is important. Besides, I don't want to get on the bad side of the sheriff," he said, smiling.

"I don't think you will. In fact, I don't know what the department would do without you running the forensic division."

Cisco made puppy noises in his sleep.

Katie and John laughed.

"Cisco has the right idea. I'll see you tomorrow," he said.

Katie walked him to the door. "Thank you for dinner."

"Goodnight," he said.

After John had left, it was completely quiet again. That was when all the thoughts began to surface, reminding her that life was different now—and she was alone.

THIRTY-THREE

Tuesday 0830 hours

Katie drove to the sheriff's department as soon as she was up. She took the quiet time driving to reflect on the Reys' murders. Someone had come to their house, they let him in, and he murdered them. Her first thought was Gaines, but he was in jail. The next possible person was Tim Denton, but there was no evidence to indicate that he was the likely regular visitor to the house. Katie thought back to when she had spoken to Gabby in her classroom. She'd put her edginess and sadness down to the fact that Samantha Banks and her family were murdered, but now, she wasn't so sure. There was something else and she couldn't pinpoint what it was.

The black bag that Katie retrieved from the locked cabinet in the classroom hadn't revealed much about what Samantha was researching. It led back to Colorado, but that was where they were from. And it was easy to dismiss it as something of a go-bag in case the family needed to leave in a hurry, but there weren't any identifications or passports for the children. That was concerning.

Katie arrived at the sheriff's department and parked. She'd had a good night's sleep, but sitting in her Jeep, she felt exhausted even before her workday began. It was obvious that her tiredness was due to mental stress. She pushed her woes aside and replayed yesterday's events.

There was a knock on her window and she startled at the interruption.

John stood there. "You okay?" He held a couple of files.

Katie got out of the car. "Morning. I'm fine. Just thinking about the Rey crime scene."

"We're making some progress."

"You must've arrived early," she said.

They walked to the administration building together.

"I don't sleep much. I came in around 4 a.m."

"Lucky you. I turn into a bear if I don't get enough sleep."

John laughed.

They entered the forensic division and Katie went to the investigation office. Before she opened the door, she heard voices inside. It was McGaven and Marshal West. It seemed to be cordial; they were discussing the events of yesterday. Katie heard the words *Rey residence* and *the bodies*. That was a good sign. They needed to figure out how the marshal could help the investigation—since they had the federal office behind them.

She pushed open the door. "Good morning."

"Good morning. Finally..." said McGaven.

"I needed some extra beauty sleep," she said, putting her things down.

McGaven was on the computer and West seemed to be adding the details of the Rey crime scene to the wall.

"You two seem productive," she said eyeing several colorful sticky notes spread across the table. Each indicated the different crime scenes. Katie had never seen McGaven do that before—he usually preferred to keep everything on his iPad or phone.

"We have a busy day. Not sure how we're going to get to everything," said McGaven.

"We need to go back to Gabby's school and look around her classroom and see if we can get anyone to talk about her," she said. Looking at the wall, she continued, "Have you been able to contact Tim Denton or anyone at Sierra Roadside Towing?"

"Negative."

"We need to go check it out. I'll go," she said, grabbing her jacket again.

"Wait a minute," said McGaven. "You can't go alone. That's not a good idea."

"Gav, it's not like I haven't done it before."

"That's what I'm afraid of," he said with sarcasm.

"Fine, let's go."

"I'm waiting for the background reports on employees at Gabby's school. We need them before we can make a visit and talk to staff about Gabby and Mrs. Banks."

Katie sighed. He was right.

"I'll go with Detective Scott," said Marshal West.

Katie looked at McGaven with an annoyed expression.

"C'mon, make me useful around here until my superiors pull me out of Pine Valley."

"Fine," she said. "Let's go, Marshal."

"Have fun," said McGaven.

Katie left the police sedan for McGaven since he was going to the elementary school, and she thought taking her Jeep would help to blend in easier. She quickly reviewed with West the security system they had experienced before at Sierra Roadside Towing, but she had also noticed another way inside the yard.

She glanced at the marshal and made sure he had his badge and gun. He seemed ready. Katie knew he was inexperienced, but she needed backup in case something went sideways. He appeared to be ready for anything—obviously wanting to impress his supervisor and to move up. She got that.

"Can I ask you something, Detective?" he said.

"Call me Katie."

"Okay, Katie. Why do you do this?"

"What do you mean? Why I'm a cop?"

"Why do you work cold cases? I've heard that you and McGaven have solved every case you've investigated," he said.

"Maybe there's your answer." She felt he was taking this opportunity to study her. Maybe more information for his reports?

He chuckled. "Good answer. You know what I mean. Obviously you could work at any department, but you stay in this area and the sheriff is your uncle."

Katie neared the tow yard. "Is there a question?"

"I just mean—"

"You're trying to say that I'm wasting my experience here in Pine Valley."

"Something like that. I don't mean any disrespect. This town is great too, but..."

"But you think I should be working for a big department where there are more homicides and cold cases. Maybe even a state or federal position?" She eyed the marshal.

West shrugged. "I was just curious. That's all."

"Don't sweat it, Marshal. I love this area and I want everyone to be safe—most importantly feel safe. I like the fact it's one of the most beautiful places where you can still be out in the wilderness in minutes. Where the air is clean and where... and... it feels like home."

"Pine Valley is lucky to have you," he said. West then watched the scenery go by and didn't ask any other questions or offer any personal information until, "Huh..."

"What?" she said.

"I'm just wondering."

"What?" The comment from West had raised her interest.

"Have you noticed this area?"

"What do you mean?"

"I mean, it's away from any other large buildings and it sits isolated. It appears that this location was picked for a reason," he said. His expression remained neutral as he gazed out the window.

Katie thought about it. "I can see your point. Isolated. Where no one could spy on what you're doing. And you could see anyone coming from some distance, especially with all the technology. Tow trucks bringing in wrecked cars wouldn't have any reason to cause suspicion."

"There's your answer."

"So what you're saying is that the technology is isolated as well—there's strong signals along the valley area. And who would suspect the wrecking yard is doing anything nefarious?"

He nodded.

Katie maneuvered the Jeep down a back service road. The county had quite a few of them, but you had to know where they were located. This one was narrow, but the Jeep handled it easily.

"Where are you going?" said West.

"I wanted to have a look at the yard from another vantage point," she said. "We've already entered from the main gate, but that's not going to do us any good right now since no one seems to be here."

The view was from the east side, where you could see the acres of property, and the heavy metal fences and razor wire. It still looked deserted; there were no employees moving about and no equipment working. It was quiet. In fact, it looked like a high-tech ghost town.

Katie didn't want to drive near the secured gate entrance with the videos, cameras, and other technology. She knew there were cameras all around the property, but she didn't feel there were as many eyes watching from back here.

"What's that?" said West.

Katie looked at what he had mentioned. It was part of the property where there were still remnant fence panels from the old yard. "Good eye."

She pulled the Jeep to the side and just off the roadway under a tree.

"What are you thinking?" he said, unhooking the seat belt.

"Since we can't get a hold of Mr. Denton at home or work, and his employee Trent Gaines is in jail, we can consider this to be an emergency."

The marshal smiled. "Lead the way."

Katie took a quick walk along the fence line. There was an old gate that was covered with wood. It appeared that this fence hadn't been retrofitted with the new enclosure.

"What is it you want to look for?" he said.

"Anything that might indicate what they're up to here. Specifically, a connection with the Reys and Gaines."

"How do we stay away from security?"

"Since it falls under exigent circumstances, we can enter."

"Interesting."

As she walked back to the old gate, West snapped something in it and the wood pieces dropped to the ground.

"Got it."

"How did you do that without tools?" she said.

"I used to help my dad with his house remodeling projects growing up. And I learned a few things."

"Great work," she said. "Do you still help him?"

West looked down. "No. He passed five years ago."

"I'm sorry."

"He never got to see me get my marshal's badge."

Katie could see the anguish and pain on the marshal's face. She knew all too well what it was like to lose a parent. "I'm sure he would have been proud of you." She didn't know what else to say in the awkward moment.

West gave a slight smile and then pushed the gate open. Katie stood for a moment in case there was some type of blaring alarm that they didn't anticipate. There was nothing. She breathed a sigh of relief.

"Let's go," she said. "I want to head to the office to see if Denton is around and just not answering his phone."

The long aisles of the yard impressed Katie as it did on her last visit. She had never seen anything quite like it. It was amazing how they could stack compressed cars, parts, and miscellaneous portions of automobiles in almost perfect formation. The sunlight reflected off bumpers and trim pieces as quick flashes of light.

Katie moved with purpose as West stayed close. She would have preferred McGaven be at the location, but they covered more investigative area this way.

Each aisle was long, with a main walkway area crossway to it. Before moving around a corner, Katie took precautions, slowed, listened, and then continued.

They finally made their way near the office.

Katie abruptly stopped.

She looked around the garage area. It wasn't like it had been when they were there a few days ago. The tables and cabinets had been rearranged, cleaned, and moved along the back wall. The tow truck was parked outside at the end of the garage stalls.

"Was it like this when we were here before?" said West.

"No. It's been cleaned," she said, looking down. "Recently. I can still smell the disinfectant."

"Why?"

"I don't know. It appears that Mr. Denton wanted to totally clean the area."

"To get rid of evidence?" he said.

"Possibly." She looked around, deciding if they should

vacate and come back later with reinforcements. She examined the floor closer and could see that it had been washed. The flow of water would move toward the drainage system; there was a slight change of floor level making it easier to channel. She leaned down and put her fingers around the area. It was still wet, but when she looked at her fingers there was a slight red hue.

"West," she said.

He leaned over and saw what she referred to. Quickly grabbing a long metal tool from the workbench, he inserted it into the culvert and pushed up a piece of the grate, and then another. He dropped the tool and stood up.

Katie and West peered down.

Stuffed inside the culvert was a man. His oddly broken body, legs, and arms, smashed to fit the space, looked more like a disassembled mannequin. He wore a set of mechanic's overalls with grease stains smeared across the front pockets. He was without shoes and his face had been stove in. By the appearance of the body, the man was older than Tim Denton.

Katie went to the wall where there were certificates and pictures of employees. It showed a photo of Tim Denton, the owner, smiling—but it wasn't the man they had met a few days ago who had identified himself as Tim Denton. It was the man stuffed underneath the garage.

THIRTY-FOUR

Tuesday 0945 hours

McGaven drove to the Pine Valley Elementary School. When he arrived there were several signs with photos and teddy bears in remembrance of Gabby Rey. There were also a few adults and children paying their respects.

He drove into the parking lot and around the main building. There were several cars parked and he assumed it was teachers, admins, and security. He decided to park and check out the school.

It felt strange not having Katie with him, but she was right that they needed to cover as much ground as possible. He too felt that Emily's time was running out. His personal opinion was that the little girl was still alive, especially since Katie had that message on her car, but they needed to find her as soon as they could.

McGaven walked through the parking lot and glanced at each vehicle. He didn't know precisely what he was looking for here, but he wanted to casually look inside the school building in case something stood out.

The back and side of the building had a colorful mural painted on it. It was uplifting and cheerful with depictions of children playing, studying, and living. He hadn't really noticed it the last time they were here.

There was a side door that was for maintenance, security, and any deliveries. There was a camera two feet above the top of the doorway. McGaven stood there, waved, and showed his badge. He then knocked several times on the metal door. It echoed and the high-pitched sound was in contrast of the quiet surrounds with the occasional chirping birds.

The door opened. A tall man in his forties wearing a brown janitor's uniform answered. He poked his head out, "Can I help you?"

"Detective McGaven," he said. "I need to speak with the principal or whoever is in charge today."

The man hesitated but opened the door wider.

"Thank you," said McGaven. He moved quickly through the door and followed the maintenance man through the long areas where there were refrigeration units, pipes, and storage rooms. The temperature was warm, making it uncomfortable. The equipment made a loud hum.

They stopped at another door, which didn't have any identification on it. The maintenance man opened it. "Here you go."

McGaven looked at the man. "I didn't catch your name."

"Ron. Ron Harris."

"Thanks, Ron."

The man nodded and waited for McGaven to leave.

McGaven walked down the hallway past student lockers. It was vacant, there were no children around. It was clear they had closed school for the day in remembrance of Gabby Rey.

The detective's footsteps were the only sound being made. He expected to see a teacher or administrative personnel, but he didn't run into anyone. Remembering where the principal's office was, he headed in that direction.

McGaven came to a classroom with cards, pictures, and stuffed animals at the entrance. He stopped and studied some of the condolences and "miss you" sentiments. He could determine the difference between students, teachers, and parents. One card stood out to him. The writing... the wording... the red ink pen. It said: *You will never be forgotten.* It struck him as familiar, but there was no name or signature. It was a white piece of generic cardstock and not a greeting card.

McGaven pulled his phone from his pocket and took a photo of it. He scanned the rest of the items on and around the doorway, but nothing else caught his attention. Putting his hand on the doorknob, he turned it. The door was unlocked. He walked in and quietly shut the door behind him, then retrieved a pair of gloves in his pocket.

He hadn't seen Gabby's classroom the last time he was here, but Katie had spoken to her teacher. The room was typical of a school with student desks, a teacher's desk, and papers and artwork creatively presented on the walls. McGaven saw the cabinet where they had retrieved Samantha Banks's hidden paperwork. He went to it and noticed now that the drawers were all unlocked. He opened all of them—but they were empty. He systematically checked all the shelves and drawers, but there was nothing besides student supplies.

He sat down at Gabby's desk, looking around the classroom. Opening the drawers, he was surprised they were all empty, but he ran his hands around inside anyway. It seemed strange that Gabby had been dead for barely twenty-four hours and yet her classroom had been sanitized of all her personal effects.

He was disappointed.

Looking back at the cabinet, it seemed odd to him. If Samantha Banks had been conducting some type of research, why would she trust that cabinet to privately store important documents like the ones they had found at Banks's home behind the vent? They had found out that Samantha had a teaching degree and could have been a full-time teacher or substitute with her own class. Why would she take a step down unless she wanted to stay close to Gabby?

McGaven stood up and walked toward the cabinet. It was a cheap particle board cabinet that could be found at any office supply or discount superstore. The detective reached for the top and ran his hand along the surface, but there was nothing there. He continued to run his hand down the sides and then the back. There was something rough, an area that wasn't flush with the rest of the rear panel.

McGaven pulled the cabinet forward a few inches and then a bit more. He turned it to view the backside. There was a thin piece of wood that had been attached to the back—purposely added. After taking a photo, McGaven took a small utility knife from his pocket and carefully pried it away. It was just large enough to allow a piece of paper to fit. He carefully slid in the knife, not damaging what was there, and a photo appeared. He took some tissues from the teacher's desk and used them to delicately pinch the photo and slide it out of its hiding place.

It was an old photograph and was approximately three inches by five inches in size. The quality was faded, but it showed a couple with two children. It appeared to be from several years ago. The man wasn't smiling—his expression stern. The woman was smiling with a hand on each of the children's shoulders. There was a little girl, blonde and smiling, about seven years old. There was a little boy, much younger, leaning against Mom. There was nothing written on the back of the photo identifying the subjects or the year it was taken.

McGaven quickly took a photo of the picture. He then slipped it into an evidence bag he had retrieved from his pocket and pushed the cabinet back against the wall. Taking a slow look around the classroom, he checked items attached to the wall, desks, chairs, and a small bookshelf with binders and papers.

Nothing.

He wondered who the people were in the photo that Samantha Banks hid behind an elementary school cabinet. Were they her family? Were they the people she was tracking down or researching?

A text came in from Denise letting him know the reports of the eight missing girls in Colorado were in his office. He looked at the photo again. Could the family in the photo be connected to the Bankses' Colorado research? Maybe they were key to working out what the Bankses had been doing.

McGaven left the classroom. There still wasn't anyone around, so he walked toward the principal's office. He heard voices, so he moved toward a room that appeared to be the teachers' lounge. A couple of the people inside seemed to be on the borderline of a heated argument. He listened for a moment.

The door was slightly open, so McGaven pushed it and saw there were four people, two men and two women. He assumed they were teachers.

"Is there a problem here?" said McGaven. His height, gun, and badge made his presence known.

Everyone stopped and stared at him.

Finally, a man spoke up. "No, everything is fine."

McGaven watched the group carefully. "Do any of you know if Principal Wilson is here?"

"Uh, no, she was here and then left for a meeting," said a woman.

"Officer, is something wrong?" said the man.

"Detective McGaven from the Pine Valley Sheriff's Department. I was following up about Gabby Rey," he said.

Two of the people looked away and couldn't meet his gaze.

"Are you all teachers here?" said McGaven.

They nodded.

"Can you tell me anything about Gabby Rey?" he said.

"What do you want to know?" said one of the women.

"Was she liked? Did she have any problems with anyone at the school? Did she act any differently lately?" he said. "Things like that."

"I really didn't know her," said the other woman. "I only saw her at meetings and some school events. She was always helpful and nice."

"Were Gabby and Samantha good friends?" said McGaven.

"They seemed close and were always talking quietly, but when someone entered the classroom they stopped. Thinking now, I just thought it was about the classroom, but it did seem like they had some serious things they were discussing and didn't want anyone else to hear them," the first woman said.

McGaven made notes.

"Gabby was one of the good ones," said the man who hadn't spoken yet.

"What do you mean by that?" said McGaven.

"It's just that she would always stay late, offer to help for any events, and managed to stay positive about anything."

McGaven thought about that for a moment as he remembered her sprawled-out body with a gunshot wound on the kitchen floor.

"Detective, did her death have anything to do with Samantha's..." The man couldn't finish his sentence.

"It's an ongoing investigation and I'm afraid I can't answer that question. But know we're doing everything we can to find the killer." McGaven reached in his pocket and gave the four teachers his card. "Please call me if you think of anything that might be helpful—no matter how small." He wrote down their names in his notebook.

They nodded. The men put the card in their pockets, but the women stared at it longer than necessary.

"Thank you for your help," said McGaven. He left the teachers' lounge and retraced his steps. He had planned to leave by the front where the security officer was stationed, but decided he would leave by the way he had come in.

The maintenance door was unlocked. Looking around, he didn't see the maintenance guy, so he headed in. The area was instantly warm and the machinery must've kicked on, if the loud noise was anything to go by. It was a jarring and mechanical sound that was difficult to ignore.

McGaven kept walking through toward the back door and the parking lot. The backup maintenance lights flickered, went dark and then lit again. Something was up. He hurried to the exit.

Suddenly a strong hand grabbed his shoulder, causing him to slightly turn off balance; then a fist punched his face, knocking him to the ground. He felt two kicks to his side. Pain shot up through his torso. His breathing wavered.

Then everything went black.

THIRTY-FIVE

Tuesday 1050 hours

Katie maintained the crime scene at Sierra Roadside Towing, waiting for Detectives Hamilton and Alvarez to arrive. Both she and Marshal West did a quick search of the immediate area, making sure the killer or killers weren't on the premises—nor were any other surprises.

Katie's cell phone rang. She looked at the caller ID and it was police dispatch, so she quickly answered it.

"Detective Scott."

"We have two deputies on their way. ETA is twenty minutes."

"Okay."

"A security issue came up from that address. Can you open the front gate for the deputies?"

"I don't know." Katie looked at the office. "I have access to the office, so I'll report back about the gate."

"Ten-four."

The call ended.

Katie waited a moment.

"What's up?" said West.

"Dispatch said there's an issue with the security at the front gate."

"It is impressive. And probably hard to open without having access to the controls. What do you want to do?"

"Get into the office."

"Okay, let's go," he said.

Katie left the garage stalls and walked to the office. She remembered the man calling himself Tim Denton had come out the front door when they'd first visited. Walking up the steps, she tried the door. It was locked, but that wasn't surprising. Katie walked back down and went around the building. She wanted to keep the damage to a minimum if she could. There were two cameras aiming down at the area, but it didn't matter now with the owner murdered and stuffed underneath the auto bay.

Katie came back around the front. West was standing there waiting for her to make a decision.

"You don't have any suggestions?" she said.

"This is the sheriff's department's gig."

"But you can still have an opinion."

"True, but I have to be careful. I'm here in Pine Valley as a marshal, because of the Banks family being murdered on the feds' watch. So I can't intervene on some things that aren't directly related."

"I get it."

Katie went back to the front door. It had three vertical panes of glass and a steel frame. She knew it would be tricky, but she went to search for something that could smash the double-pane windows and an item that could be used to pry the lock if needed.

She hurried down one of the wreckage aisles where she remembered seeing some tools used for auto dismantling. Katie began rummaging around to find what she needed. West didn't come with her. She assumed he was waiting for her at the office.

Katie looked around. There were all types of tools, some needed to be plugged in and others were manual. She scanned the area and spotted a long type of steel wedge that would do the trick. Reaching up, she couldn't quite touch it even on her tiptoes.

Pushing on the stacked exterior vehicle doors, they seemed secure and not about to go anywhere. The car parts, interior and exterior, were organized and piled with expertise. Katie began to climb up, one foot at a time; it felt secure and immobile, so she continued her scale. It was almost like climbing a rock wall.

Katie had almost reached the metal bar when she heard a scraping sound. She froze, trying to decipher where it was coming from. Then her climbing area began to vibrate. Instantly she began to backtrack as something from the top fell, hitting every other piece on the way down. It barely missed her head.

She felt hands grab her waist and tug her toward the ground, and she scrambled using her legs, trying to get away from the falling metal. West had plucked her away from the pile. The noise was deafening as the metal hit the ground, bouncing and then landing to the left and right of her. West had used his body to cover her as they waited for the noise to stop. Katie was pressed against him and she could smell a slight scent of soap.

When it seemed safe, Katie got to her feet and examined the carnage. "Thank you, I think," she said breathless.

"You think?" he said and smiled.

"How'd you know?"

"I could hear a weird scraping sound. Thought I better check on it."

She nodded. "I did too. But I don't think it's because of this pile." Katie pulled her weapon.

West looked surprised.

"There's someone here," she said.

The marshal pulled his weapon as well.

They stood quietly.

Katie could still feel her heart pounding as she caught her breath. Now, she was focused on the intruder. She indicated that she was going down the aisle to search in a strip grid pattern. She stealthily moved, aware of her surroundings, specifically the towering masses of cars, trucks, buses, and various parts.

She glanced behind her and saw West bringing up the rear in correct formation. Keeping a steady pace, Katie went down the rows until they were back at where they had entered. The gate was wide open, but she knew they had shut it. Someone had recently gone through it. The big question was... who?

Katie lowered her weapon. She was frustrated and still shaken by what could have happened if West hadn't been there to help her avoid the falling metal.

"You okay?" said West.

"Yeah," she sighed. "I'm fine."

"So who was here? Did someone follow us or were they already inside?"

"Good question. But what concerns me is that I didn't see any cars or hear anything. How did they make their escape?"

West looked around and appeared to be thinking about the possible scenarios.

"C'mon, let's get that office open," she said. Her frustration was bordering on anger, which meant she was going to get that office open no matter what.

Katie hurried back to the office with West close behind her. He didn't question her decisions. Good. She definitely wasn't in the mood to be doubted at this point. She grabbed the large metal probe and returned to the office door.

The metal tool was heavier than it looked. West grabbed the other end to help balance the weight as Katie readied herself to ram the window. The first blow didn't do much except push them back harder. After the third and fourth strike, the window began to give with a crackling noise.

They took a brief break and then they attacked again. This time, one of the vertical windows let go and splintered inward.

"We got it," she said. Standing for a moment, listening, there were no alarms. There could have been a silent alarm, but police dispatch already knew they were there. Reaching her hand inside, Katie released the two double dead bolt locks and opened the door.

Katie was immediately inside. She was shocked. The interior of the office was like something out of sci-fi movie with not one, but three, computer workstations. It wasn't the type of setup a towing and auto-wrecking business would need. It was more what someone would use for surveillance and investigations.

She moved slowly into the room, not touching anything. There was paperwork piled on one of the desks that looked like invoices but didn't have the billing party listed. They also didn't seem to be for the usual goods or services; it seemed the services were initials. It didn't make sense.

West came in and began checking stuff out.

"Stop," said Katie. "This entire office needs to be dusted for prints and thoroughly searched."

West immediately pulled his hand back. He seemed to be confused by everything—at least that was what Katie thought as he looked around.

"What is all this?" he said.

"I'm not sure. But whoever was impersonating Tim Denton used this place as some kind of command center." She looked around. "Obviously, this property is a perfect cover and location for whatever someone wanted it to be." Katie spotted a computer that was labeled "security and gate entrance." She took a small hand towel and used it to press the keyboard and use the mouse until she found how to open the gate. Looking at the computer, she could see the video camera feed and watched the gate swing open.

"Hey, check this out," said West. He stared at another screen.

Katie joined the marshal. The screen showed a collage of photos of children.

Katie gasped. One of the photographs was definitely Emily Banks with her curly blonde hair—and she was holding the teddy bear from the hospital.

THIRTY-SIX

Tuesday 1115 hours

McGaven heard a set of footsteps, quick and purposeful, walk away and then the outside door opened and closed. Opening his eyes, he tried to sit up, but it was slow and painful. He tried to recall who slugged him but hadn't seen who it was. His first thought was the maintenance guy, but the footsteps didn't sync.

Some of the maintenance equipment cycled off and it became much quieter.

"What are you doing?" said the maintenance guy standing over him holding a wrench.

"Someone knocked me down."

"You?"

"Yeah, someone came up behind me and got the drop," he said and finally stood up straight. "Please drop that wrench." His head pounded, making his vision blurry, and his ribs were painful every time he took a breath.

Harris did what he was told and put the tool down nearby. "They'd have to have had the element of surprise due to your size."

"Where were you?" said McGaven. He knew he didn't do it but was curious as to what he would say.

"Me? I was taking a look at the sink in the boys' bathroom."

"Did you see anyone that shouldn't be here?"

"No. I haven't seen anyone except you."

McGaven went to the exit door and looked around. There were the same cars parked and no sign of anyone. He looked down but it was mostly asphalt with some fine gravel mixed in, and there were no identifying footsteps. It was cooler outside than in the maintenance area, which felt good.

McGaven wiped his head, finding blood on his hand. His injuries began to increase in discomfort. He leaned up against the side of the building for support.

"You need to have someone look at that." Ron retrieved his cell phone. "I'm calling an ambulance."

McGaven was just about to object, but he felt sick and decided to sit down and wait.

THIRTY-SEVEN

Tuesday 1150 hours

Katie assisted the deputies in searching the area to make sure there wasn't anyone hiding. She couldn't figure out how someone could move around the yard so efficiently. They would have to have had knowledge of the place. Once they knew how long Tim Denton had been dead, they would know how long the wrecking yard had been taken over.

Detective Hamilton had arrived and immediately checked the auto bay and the office areas. He met up with Katie.

"What were you doing here?" said Hamilton, looking at the marshal as well. There was a slight accusatory note to his voice.

"Following up on a lead. We wanted to talk to Tim Denton, well, who we thought was Tim Denton."

"I see."

"I was following up because of the connection between Trent Gaines working for Tim Denton. A neighbor of the Reys said she saw a tall older man regularly visiting the house, and it seemed likely it was Denton. Well, who we thought he was."

Hamilton kept a sour expression. "Gaines was released a couple of hours ago."

"What?"

"The judge put up a ten-thousand-dollar bail. He paid it and left."

"No," she said as complete frustration turned into anger that she was always a step behind. All the people who were persons of interest were leaving. "They're making their escapes and cleaning up any loose ends."

"It looks that way," said Hamilton.

Katie turned, looking out at the yard and the perfectly orchestrated rows. She knew they had everything they needed right in front of them.

"And that means that Emily Banks's time has run out. Her photo is on a picture collage on one of the computers in there." Katie could barely breathe. She wasn't going to let Emily die.

"John should be here anytime to process the scene," said Hamilton. "We'll go through everything. And make sure all those girls are identified and accounted for, and use any facial recognition software that's available to us. It will take some time, but don't worry, we're on it."

"Make sure all the video, computers, and all that high-tech stuff is taken." Katie turned back toward the detective. "If Tim Denton has been dead for a while—by his condition it seems at least a month—why wasn't he reported missing?"

"Denton was a widower with no children. I guess no one had missed him," said Hamilton.

Marshal West remained quiet, taking in everything. He looked to Katie for the next steps. But Katie didn't know what to say.

"Detective," said a patrol officer as he jogged up to Katie.

"Yes."

"Detective McGaven has been taken to the Pine Valley General Hospital. He was attacked at the school."

. . .

Katie broke most traffic laws to get to the hospital. West rode shotgun and seemed uncomfortable with her driving—he held on while the Jeep cut corners too tight. But the marshal didn't complain and he kept his composure until they arrived at the hospital and pulled into the parking lot.

Katie was immediately out of the car and heading into the main entrance. She didn't care about West following her or not. The only thing she cared about was her partner. She hadn't had his back and if anything happened to him, she would never forgive herself.

Katie never wanted to take advantage of the people she loved and respected. Her mind whirled with the what-ifs. She and McGaven had been in tight predicaments but always managed to come out victorious. But their luck and fighting spirit would someday end. Nothing ever stayed the same.

She hurried down the long hallway to the emergency area. Not bothering to stop for information, she looked in each room. Finally, she saw her tall partner sitting on a bed while he was having his ribs wrapped. The left side of his face was already bruising.

"Gav," she said, moving into the room. "You okay?"

"I'm fine. Just more of a bruised ego than a bruised face. I let my guard down," he said.

The nurse left the room as McGaven pulled on and began buttoning his shirt. He grimaced.

"Let me do this," she said and helped to button his shirt. "Broken ribs?"

"No, just bruised. But it still hurts like hell…"

"What happened?"

"I was leaving the school the way I entered."

"What do you mean?" she said.

"They had closed the school today as a memorial for Gabby

Rey, so there were just a few teachers, a security guard, and the maintenance guy." He stood up slowly. "I went in through the maintenance entrance."

"Did you see anyone?"

"The weird maintenance guy," he said and laughed. "And before you ask, it wasn't him who got the drop on me."

"They could've killed you."

"I don't think so. They had the opportunity... but they deliberately didn't. I can't help but think they were sending a message."

"A message?"

"Yeah, like telling us to back off—except this time it was with force instead of a written message on a Jeep." McGaven noticed then that Katie's jacket was torn and there was grease on her clothes. "What happened to you?"

"I think you're right about sending a message... because we're getting close."

McGaven examined his face in a small mirror above the sink. "Ugh... it's going to be worse tomorrow."

"You need to go home and rest."

"No way." He looked at his partner. "Are you going to tell me what happened?"

Katie told McGaven everything that had happened at Sierra Roadside Towing. Even as she recounted the events, it sounded more like a movie than reality. She looked at the doorway expecting to see West, but he wasn't in sight. Most likely he was giving her privacy to talk with her partner. McGaven also updated Katie on what he found at the school.

"We have more information to process and we need to make our next moves strategic—and make them count," she said.

McGaven was quiet, which was unusual.

"What?"

"We now have a fake Tim Denton on the loose. Trent

Gaines was released earlier. So I'd say we have our work cut out for us."

"I believe Emily is still alive," she said quietly.

McGaven sat next to his partner. "We are going to do everything we can to find her, but..."

"I don't want to hear any buts... we're going to find her—alive."

McGaven didn't argue, he squeezed Katie's hand.

"Let's go find West and get back. There's going to be a lot of evidence and information coming in and we need to be able to disseminate what's immediately important and what can wait," she said.

While Katie's gut told her that Emily was alive, her heart also told her that time was running out.

THIRTY-EIGHT

Tuesday 1425 hours

After leaving the hospital, Katie and McGaven made a few stops before getting back to their investigation command center at the sheriff's department. She took her partner to the Pine Valley Elementary School to pick up the police sedan and then she stopped to load up on food and beverages—especially lots of coffee—for their long night.

Katie pulled into the sheriff's department parking lot and cut the engine of her Jeep. She had sent her uncle a text message to ask if he could visit Cisco and feed him dinner. She didn't want to bring the dog to the police kennel—being home would be better for him than in a dog run at the department.

She grabbed several handled paper bags along with a cardboard tray of coffees. Her mind never stopped pushing scenarios. She couldn't get the image of the real Tim Denton out of her mind. The way he had been jammed into the small opening underneath the auto bay.

She saw the face of the man who had identified himself as Denton. Remembering his dark eyes that seemed to peer into your soul, it unnerved Katie now. She should have listened to her instincts and done a complete background check on him that day. There was definitely something off about the man. She could imagine him and Gaines killing and shoving the body into that small space. It would take some muscle and creativity, which those men seemed to possess.

Katie hurried to the entrance of the forensic division and made it in, balancing everything. Once inside, it was quiet. She knew John and Eva had a ton of work to document and collect from the crime scene at the wrecking yard. She moved through the division and paused at the main examination room. She was used to seeing John bent over a microscope or reading the numerous reports, but he wasn't there tonight. Opening the door to the investigation room, Katie entered.

"There she is... I'm starving," said McGaven sitting at the table with piles of paperwork in front of him.

"Nice to see you too." Katie put down the bags and drinks on a small side table.

Marshal West was on the floor in the corner going through files.

"Okay, get it while it's still warm," she said unloading hot sandwiches, soup, and a salad for her.

They mostly ate in silence. They were obviously each thinking about the cases and how much work they had ahead of them.

Katie stood at the board looking at the faces of those lost: the two families, the Reys, and now the real Tim Denton. She studied the way the scenes had been left. The family homes were cleaned up—no garbage, unnecessary blood, or finger-prints. Everything had been removed from the houses and prop-erty and appeared to have been taken with the killer or killers. Even the trash cans were empty and without any prints.

What didn't fit to Katie was the motive. Everything they had seen and discovered either pointed to a much bigger organization or one of the craftiest serial killers on record. She mentally walked through the crimes in the order they had been discovered beginning with finding Emily Banks. Why did everything point back to the little girl?

"There's something we're not seeing here," she said.

"It's not for the lack of looking," said McGaven.

"It feels like... a lot of white noise."

"Meaning?"

"Meaning that every time we run down a lead something bigger confronts us," she said.

"Diversion?" said West.

"I think someone is trying to scare us—and fear makes you not see things clearly." Katie drank some coffee and wrinkled her nose. "Sorry, this is terrible coffee—bitter."

"Doesn't matter. We're not drinking it for taste—we're drinking it to keep awake and see what the killer is trying to tell us," said McGaven.

Katie wrote as she spoke.

"The trail took us from the discovery of Emily and her murdered family, then to the murdered Sandersons and missing Tessa, then to Mr. Banks's real estate office, then Mrs. Banks's work in Gabby's classroom, Tessa's body at the foreclosed house, Gaines's home, the Rey residence, and then the Sierra Roadside Towing yard." Katie was talking more to herself than making a speech.

She took a step back. "The arrangement of the bodies and the cleanup suggests the killer wants to keep evidence to a minimum. But there's more, something much more personal. Things like this, excessive cleanliness, can stem from memories as a child. Something they witness or are taught. Perhaps one of the killer's parents instilled this type of behavior? It can sometimes manifest into obsessive compulsive tendencies. Or it's part of their learned actions reflecting as behavioral evidence at the crime scene."

"So you're saying it's possible that the killer is cleaning up as part of his behavior and not necessarily because he's trying to deceive us?" said McGaven.

She nodded. "There's something deeply rooted here in his psyche—showing in his methodology at the crime scene." Katie continued to study the board.

"There's some interesting information from the investigations into the murdered girls in Colorado," said McGaven. "It seems that the two crime scenes were similar to Tessa's: the bodies were found in a remote location after a tip-off from an anonymous caller. And the girls resembled each other in age, with blonde hair, and dressed similar. They look as if they were related, like sisters or cousins."

"It still doesn't mean that the victims are connected," she said.

"No, but it's interesting since Samantha Banks seemed to be following these particular cases," said McGaven.

"What's the connection? Why? And if they weren't in witness protection, would she still have been following it?" Katie turned to West. "You doing okay?"

He nodded. He was still eating a sandwich.

"Do people get to choose where they are relocated?" she said.

"No. But they get a choice of a few places that *we* select."

"What are the odds that they were relocated here?" Katie thought about how everything had played out. Her heart was heavy due to the fact there was still no word about Emily. Now she was anxious about getting that call—it might be a crime scene instead of a rescue.

McGaven didn't say anything.

"The place that seems to be in the middle of things is the wrecking yard. Why did the unknown man and Gaines use that location?" Katie asked. "There has to be something more..." She sent a text message to Hamilton. "We'll see what they say... if they found anything."

"I almost forgot," said McGaven.

"Forgot what?"

McGaven grimaced as he pulled his phone from his pocket. A moment later the laser printer hummed and spat out a piece of paper.

Katie's phone chimed with a text: *Nothing yet. Tech forensics is trying to decipher the computers... but nothing unusual. Will keep you updated.*

"Anything?" said McGaven as he grabbed the printer paper.

"They're still working the scene."

"The techs are from Hill Valley County, right?" said McGaven.

"They're the only one around."

McGaven gave the printout to Katie. It was a copy of the photo from the cabinet at the elementary school. "What do you think? I found this taped behind that cabinet in Gaby's classroom."

Katie studied it. What stood out to her was the man. His eyes and expression seemed grim. But the two children seemed happy. The little blonde girl drew her eye. "The little girl."

"She looks similar to Emily, right?"

"Yeah, it's like seeing her twin. But the photo looks to be at least twenty years old."

"Let me see," said West as he stood up. "Not necessarily. I think it's the clothes. They seem old. Maybe they're thrift clothes or hand-me-downs?"

McGaven nodded. "Good observation."

"I may be useful yet. Until my supervisor pulls me out."

"You itching to get back to the city?" she said.

"Actually, if you asked me two days ago, I would've said yes. But now, with everything going on, I don't mind being here." He smiled.

"Look at this guy. He had to come to Pine Valley to get some real experience," said McGaven as he chuckled.

Katie pinned the photo of the man, woman, and two children on the investigation board. She studied it for a moment.

"Aren't you a criminal profiler?" said West.

"She's awesome at it," said McGaven.

"Where's the profile for the killer?"

"The profile and behavioral evidence are important, but the problem is that it's convoluted and contaminated."

"What do you mean?"

"When there's more than one perpetrator it can complicate things," she said. "I feel we need more information, forensics, and autopsies before I can get a clearer picture of the killer."

"What do you immediately see about the Banks and Sanderson murders?" said West.

McGaven looked at his partner.

"As I said, the killer, most likely the person in charge of the rampage, is organized. In fact, obsessive would be a better description. It's clear that he orchestrated everything down to the pajamas and placements of the bodies and other items. But the feeble attempts at leaving a piece of evidence—like the pottery shard and hammer, and the phony break-in attempt—speak volumes," she said.

"What if he wanted it to look more like a crazed or insane person to throw off investigators?" said West.

"Valid point, but no." Katie went to the board. "A person who thinks things through to this extent when it comes to a murder scene has fantasized about it for some time or has performed it before. Generally, what we see has to be something important to the killer, something that feeds his fantasy."

"What happens when the fantasy isn't fed?" said West. His curiosity was evident and he seemed more at ease than he had been when he arrived. He watched Katie closely.

"That's when we will see an escalation. More frequent, more violent... and, unfortunately, more victims."

"Do you think the killer started here in Pine Valley?"

"There's no definite or direct evidence to suggest otherwise. But, from the way the crimes were committed, there's no way it's the killer's first crime," Katie said. She looked at the photograph again and struggled to imagine why Samantha Banks had this photo, and most importantly, why she'd hidden it.

"So at this point, we're looking for the ghost who impersonated Tim Denton, and Trent Gaines," said McGaven.

Katie nodded. "I'm going to search for more listings of foreclosures that could be the temporary holding areas for Emily— or any other girls. It seems to fit with the MO. As I've said before, there's someone calling all the shots and I think," she said, pointing to the photo that McGaven found, "Samantha Banks knew something."

"You want to go check out the Bankses' house to see if she had anything else?" said McGaven.

Katie nodded. "And if we missed something for Emily."

"You can't go by yourself," said McGaven.

Katie laughed. "Of course I can. You're going to stay here to rest up."

"Who can't go by themselves?" said John as he stood at the doorway.

"Hey, shouldn't you be at the wrecking yard?" said McGaven.

"My job there is officially done and Eva is finishing up. But computer forensics will be there awhile and I expect some preliminary report by noon. They are also trying to find the identities of the little girls found on the desktop computer. Some could be stock photos."

"Or on missing persons reports," Katie said.

"Either way, there may not be a way to track them all."

"Are you on overtime?" said McGaven.

"Always."

"Katie wants to go back to the Bankses' house. You game?" said McGaven.

"Sure. For an hour or two?" he said.

"About," said Katie.

"I'm game. Let me get some stuff in case we need to collect or photograph more evidence. Meet you at the car." John left the office.

"I'll be back," Katie said. "You two behave." She smiled. She knew both McGaven and West would continue to scour pages of information to not only find something new but also to connect the dots.

"We'll be here," they said.

THIRTY-NINE

Tuesday 1720 hours

Katie decided to take her Jeep in case there were any issues off the road. Basically she was more confident driving an SUV than an older police sedan. Plus any neighbor or someone passing them on the road wouldn't think the vehicle was the police. She wanted to keep a low profile.

A text message came in on her phone. It was from her uncle.

I want an update tomorrow morning.

He had attached a photo of him and Cisco sitting on her couch, her uncle smiling with his arm around the dog.

Katie laughed.

The passenger door opened. "Hey," said John. He placed a couple of briefcases on the back seat.

Katie noticed he was wearing a holster carrying his Glock. He rarely did that but it was probably a good idea considering everything that had transpired.

John got in and shut the door. "You were smiling. What's up?"

Katie showed him the photo of the sheriff and Cisco.

"That would do it." He laughed. "Maybe that could be the photo for his next campaign poster?"

"He loves Cisco and I think he looks for any reason to hang out with him," she said.

Katie drove out of the parking lot and headed for the freeway.

"Tell me," John said. "What are you really looking for?"

"What do you mean by that?"

"I've known you long enough... and I've worked with you and Gav for a while now to know when you're up to something."

Katie sighed. She didn't realize she was so transparent. "Samantha Banks was working on something that had to do with missing girls, many from Colorado. She hid some stuff at school, but I have a feeling she split things up in case one of her hiding spots was discovered at the school or at home."

"Makes sense. But she was probably also covering her tracks due to being in witness protection and for what she was researching."

"That's true. I also believe it was she who was able to get Emily out of the house and to safety."

"Where you and Cisco found her. What would have happened to Emily if you decided to take another running trail that day?"

Katie had thought the same thing and that was why she had to find the little girl. There was no other choice and she couldn't accept anything less.

Katie pulled into the circular driveway at the Banks residence. The truck and minivan were still in the driveway. It gave her chills. It looked as if the family was home doing their usual things—cooking, homework, watching television. But in truth the house was the remnant of a grisly family homicide crime scene, which was more indicative of a horror film.

"It looks really dark," said John looking around. "There should be some outside lights."

Katie had already observed how dark the place was and was deciding whether or not they should enter the location. It was still technically a crime scene as it hadn't been released yet. She opened the car door. "Let's check it out. Where are the breakers?"

"In the barn," he said.

"Okay, let's go."

John grabbed a satchel that had various tools, his digital camera, and some evidence bags. Katie kept feeling like they were the prey and the predator was close. She shook off her fears and concentrated on the barn. They opened the large doors and entered.

There was still some daylight, but Katie flipped on her flashlight. The beam filled the space and it was easy to see the electric panel. The file cabinets had been emptied and were now shoved in the corner. It made her think of Samantha and what she had discovered—she wondered if her husband had known too.

John quickly went to the panel and in a moment the lights came on.

"It looks like everything was turned off when we left. I didn't do it, but it's not unusual for one of the team to do so," said John.

"There should be a lock on the barn," said Katie.

"There should, but I don't see one."

The driveway and courtyard area were now illuminated with patio lights. Katie still kept her attention around them due to the heavily forested area. Her instincts were on high alert—but when they reached the porch her anxiety lowered and she focused on the house.

"What are you hoping to find?" John asked, taking a quick scan around the yard before entering the farmhouse.

Katie was already inside. She pulled on a pair of gloves. She stood in the middle of the living room, imagining the family spending the evening at home. "I'm not sure, but it seems that Mrs. Banks was clever in where she hid her research."

"There were filing cabinets filled with information."

"That was just the filing. I'm positive she hid the most telling, or damaging, information somewhere in the house," she said.

John looked around. "You mean like a secret cubby area."

"Something like that."

Katie looked at the bookshelf next to the dining table. There were neat stacks of paperwork. She quickly thumbed through them. They had scoured the area before and nothing seemed to be telling of what happened to the family. She stopped on piece of paper that had been dated almost two years before—before Samantha had begun working at the school. It was an announcement of a school district meeting. There were several teachers, school board members, and volunteers listed. Gabby Rey was on the list.

"Find something?" said John.

"Look at this," she said. "It seems that Samantha Banks might have gone to this meeting."

John studied it.

"And, if so, she would have met Gabby." Katie looked around. "I know there are gaps here, but it seems that the two women had met before Samantha began working at the school."

"And... we won't know the exact extent of their friendship."

Katie sighed. "We can only speculate and infer the connection and why, but my instinct says they became close and it most likely had to do with these missing children. The hidden papers in Gabby's classroom is a big indicator, along with the files in the Bankses' barn." She took a photo of the list to send to McGaven.

Katie decided to begin in the kitchen. It would be a natural place for Samantha to hide something since she would have spent quite a bit of time preparing food, making school lunches, or having a late-night snack with her husband.

Then it struck her. All the memories and feelings about Chad flooded her mind.

Katie took a breath and sucked up the negative energy, pushing on. It was the absolute worst moment to have an emotional hiccup. Her personal life was just that—personal. She ran her hand along the clean, clutter-free counters. Remembering the chip of a porcelain cup, Katie examined all around the area where she found it. There were two small cupboards that held some nice wineglasses and clear glass dessert bowls—but no porcelain cups, plates, or bowls. They were located on the other side of the kitchen.

Katie pulled the wineglasses out and set them on the counter.

"Got something?" said John as he joined her.

"I'm not sure." She got a chair from the dining table and put it next to the counter. Standing on it, Katie could see the narrow shelves better. Nothing looked out of place. She ran her fingertips on the shelf and around the corners. There was a slight raised area. "Check this out," she said and stepped down.

John peered into the narrow cabinet. He took his small flashlight and moved the beam slowly around the edges and corners. "It looks like..." He pushed the raised corner and then ran his fingers down and pushed again. There was a click.

Katie waited expectantly.

"There is something here..." He moved a small narrow strip, and revealed a very skinny cubbyhole like you might find in a roll-top desk. "Wait..." He pulled out a plain white envelope. John stepped down and put the envelope on the counter. "You want the honors?"

Katie moved closer. "It better not be a secret family recipe of some kind."

John smiled, but he too waited anxiously.

The envelope wasn't sealed. She carefully opened the flap, finding several pieces of paper inside. She pulled them out and laid them on the counter, opening them one third at a time. The paper appeared old—not antique, but it had some age attached to it. It had been opened and closed many times, leaving well-worn creases.

"It's an agreement of some kind, but it's a poor photocopy," she said. "Look at the date."

"It's from almost twenty years ago. And it seems to be about custody of children," he said.

"I think it's a portion of some sort of divorce agreement. There's no legible name, but it says two children: Melissa and Robert. But I can't read the rest." Katie thought about their suspects and the murder victims. "It doesn't identify who the parents are."

John immediately took photos of the area and the envelope. He put the folded paper and envelope into an evidence bag. "Well, your hunch paid off," he said.

"Samantha Banks seemed to like to hide things. I don't understand why she hid the photograph at the school. Anyone could have found it."

"They would have to be looking... and it wouldn't seem too likely."

Katie wasn't so sure. There were things going on with the family, besides witness protection, that would make her extra cautious. "I'm going to look around."

Katie spent the next half hour looking through the bedrooms, pulling out drawers, looking behind furniture, and anywhere else she could think of that might make a good hiding place. Nothing showed up.

She walked down the hallway and stopped in front of Emily's room. Not going in, Katie stood at the doorway. Looking at the twin bed, toys organized, clothes in the closet, she wanted to cry for the little girl. It had been too long and the killer knew they were getting close. But why would he have killed Tessa? It didn't make sense unless they were cutting their losses, like with the Reys and the wrecking yard owner.

"Everything okay?" said John.

"Just thinking about little Emily."

John didn't immediately respond. He seemed to be processing what he was going to say. "Katie, I've seen you and McGaven work so many cases. And I know none of them have been easy. You doubt your abilities, but in the end, you always find the killer."

Katie turned to John. "I know... but I don't want to lose this little girl. We could've done something differently, so it wasn't so easy for someone to take her."

"You can't dwell on what-ifs. You have to move forward and know that anything a killer does isn't your fault," he said.

Katie understood what he was saying, but that still didn't change the fact that she had to find Emily before it was too late.

"C'mon, let's finish looking around," he said.

Katie spent another fifteen minutes searching, but nothing seemed out of place. She looked in the barn again, but it had been already searched. However, she did her due diligence and checked under the filing cabinet drawers and the backs—just in case. But nothing more came to light.

Katie and John left the Bankses' residence.

"Do you mind if we stop by Sierra Roadside Towing yard?" said Katie.

John glanced at his watch. "Sure. What's up?"

"You sure?"

"Of course. I'm not letting you go alone."

"You sound like Gav," she said.

"It's only because Gav and I know you..." He smiled.

Katie couldn't help but smile. "I guess you're right. It'll be a quick trip."

FORTY

Katie drove up to the high-tech main entrance of the wrecking yard. Police tape, stay out signs, and one deputy were now at the front making sure no one would try to infiltrate the area. There was a van, an SUV, and a patrol vehicle parked.

"Looks like the computer forensic guys are still here," said John.

"What stumps me is why they chose this particular place?" she said.

"Well, it's isolated somewhat. And the owner didn't have family, so it wouldn't raise any suspicions for a while. Let's face it, the technology helps the killer find his victims more easily."

"True. That's what leads me to believe that there's someone else we haven't identified yet. Someone running everything behind the scenes. But there has to be more." Katie decided to pull in next to the other cars. "You don't think I'm overthinking this?" she said. She hated sounding like she was unsure of herself, but her time might be better spent going through the paperwork and databases.

"It's not my place to say. I'm not a detective, but everything I've seen you do gets the bad guy. So no. You're not overthinking this."

"This case has so many moving parts. Does that make sense?"

"It does. That describes forensics in a nutshell," he said.

"Something bothered me the last two times I was here. First time, when we came to talk to Gaines, I got the feeling he was looking for something when I caught up with him."

"Like what?"

"At the time, nothing seemed out of the ordinary. Now, after finding Samantha Banks's hidden places, I can't help but think there's some type of hidden space here. It would be a perfect cover—it's huge." Katie thought about it.

"And he stuffed the body of Tim Denton underneath the car bay." John opened the door. "Let's go check it out. Show me the area he was looking in."

Katie and John identified themselves to the deputy on guard and they went inside. There were security lights that the police had put up, as well as the lights around the wrecking yard. Katie retraced her steps to the aisle where she and McGaven had caught up with Gaines. She stood for a moment studying everything from all sides. It seemed the same.

"You sure this is the area?" said John.

She nodded. When she had stopped running, and lowered her gaze, she had seen Gaines's feet on the other side of the pile of metal. That was when Katie decided to backtrack and come around from the other end. Thinking about it now, it did seem a little unusual that Gaines easily gave up as soon as she approached him.

Katie recounted everything to John, and he walked the area to match her story.

"I think when I arrested him he might have been hiding something. Or looking for something," Katie said. Looking up, the towering metal jigsaw puzzle loomed over them. Katie didn't think something would be hidden up high because Gaines hadn't had time to climb up on anything.

She estimated where Gaines would have had time to leave something. "Okay," she said and stepped back. "I would estimate a fifteen square foot area. Here and here." She gestured.

John began looking closely on one side while Katie began her search on the other. They would work their way across and meet up. Then they would search the other's area to make sure nothing was missed.

Katie used her flashlight, illuminating the tight spaces under each flattened piece. Sparkles of different colors flashed whenever the light hit them. The more she searched, the more she became discouraged and thought she might be wasting time.

Katie had been looking at everything thoroughly, but she paused for a moment to regroup her examination. She watched John, who was hunched over checking every crevice, but she knew he was hitting the same wall as her.

Her motto at crime scenes was if all else fails, expand the area. So that was what Katie did. She moved farther up the aisle and something caught her eye. It was part of a red vehicle. Moving in closer, it appeared to be a car door handle. Why would there be a door handle? It would have been either dismantled or flattened when the car was crushed like a pancake.

"John?" she said.

"Found something?" he said and joined her.

"What do you make of this?"

"It looks like a car door handle." John carefully examined it. He cautiously put his hand on it and found it solid, not loose. "What do you think?"

"I think it's out of place here."

"You're right." John wrapped his fingers underneath and

pulled up. It moved upward, slowly at first, but it didn't move very far.

"There must be some type of release, or key, or something that unlocked it," she said looking around. "Or something like a puzzle box release."

"Meaning?"

"A shift, pull, or push."

John ran his hands around the area until he found two levers; they were difficult to see at first but were obvious when touched.

Katie held her breath. When they arrived, she'd questioned whether there was something more at the wrecking yard, but now she knew.

John finally released the cleverly designed levers. He put his hand on the door handle. "Ready?" he said.

"Do you really have to ask me that?"

John pulled the handle and there was a strange clicking noise as an opening appeared the size of a sedan car door. It had been disguised by the crushed parts blending seamlessly with the rest of the pile. Katie turned on the flashlight. To their surprise, there was a ladder leading into a space in the ground.

"A secret room?" she said.

"Let's find out," said John and he effortlessly climbed in and began descending. It was clear his Seal training had made him agile and strong.

Before Katie could object or wait for a plan of attack, she found herself following John down the ladder. The door had been cleverly disguised and it would have taken someone who was knowledgeable in construction, steelwork, and auto dismantling. The entrance seemed well used and maintained. She wasn't sure if that was a good thing or bad.

As they climbed down, Katie caught the distinct odor of stagnant water, like old pipes, which meant it had been connected to some form of drainage or waterways. This was common in the rural areas of Pine Valley and neighboring towns. She'd run into this type of situation with other cases. There used to be a problem with flooding, but over the years of weather, soil erosion and proper land grading helped to correct the issue.

They reached the bottom, which felt solid and level beneath their feet. Katie fanned the flashlight. The old tunnel reminded her of a bunker or deep cell of some sort. It was much colder, causing goose bumps to rise on her arms and up the back of her neck.

Suddenly a row of lights went on. "Got it," said John. He was at a breaker panel.

"What is this place?" said Katie. She knew it was for something more sinister than it appeared.

A fan switched on and blew air. It was on a timer to keep oxygen flowing.

Katie looked up and could see the opening at the top and the lights shining in the ceiling, which was about twenty feet above their heads. "Talk about a secret place out in the open."

"No one would ever find this unless they knew where to look," he said.

"People would have walked by it, workers would have piled things next to it, and it would still be hidden in plain view." Katie swung the flashlight beam in each direction. "How far do you think it goes?"

"Not sure, but it doesn't seem to empty out anywhere."

"Meaning that it has been cut off to keep this area intact," she said. Katie rolled a few scenarios in her mind. "Objectively, this place could be used as a safe room or protection from a storm," she said. "But knowing what we do, I would say that this is a holding area."

John looked at Katie. His expression was troubled.

Katie understood. It was unthinkable, but due to their professions it was more than a likely working theory.

"I don't see anything that indicates anyone was held here, but that doesn't mean they weren't. If the hatch was locked, you wouldn't be able to get out. And I doubt anyone up there could hear screams or pounding," he said.

"Can you photo-document everything?" she said.

"Of course."

Katie waited while John took shots of everything in the tunnel holding cell. He made sure to take close-ups of the breaker panel, ladder, and anything else of interest.

Then Katie and John climbed the ladder and secured the entry. John took photographs of the inventive doorway, and Katie helped him measure and document the area around it.

"Looks like your hunch paid off," said John.

"It's good and bad."

"What do you mean, bad?"

"We still don't have all the answers."

"Katie, if there's one thing that's a sure thing—you will get the answers you need."

FORTY-ONE

Tuesday 2300 hours

It was close to midnight and Katie hated the fact that the hours, minutes, seconds were counting down for Emily. She was physically and mentally exhausted. Working as long as she could at the office, she could barely keep her eyes open. She and McGaven decided they needed to go home to sleep and then meet back to begin again in the morning.

Once home, Katie kicked back on her sofa with Cisco at her side. It was the usual after a long day. She had brought home some files to look over as she had a bite to eat and some hot tea. The day was cool and she still seemed to be chilled to the bone —not sure if it was because of the weather or the cases. Moving to get more comfortable made Cisco grumble, but Katie pulled the quilt closer. She was almost going to put on a second pair of cozy socks to warm up.

Katie must've dozed for a few minutes because she woke with a start. She had thought she heard something, but Cisco slept soundly next to her. If there had been anything moving or a small noise, the dog would have alerted. She knew the sound she thought she heard was in a dream. Katie knew she would soon have dreams, or more specifically nightmares, of victims begging her to solve their cases. It was the usual, but she hadn't had any about this case—yet.

Katie moved slowly and managed to get herself free from the blanket. Cisco was still sleeping. She sat on the floor looking at the pages spread out on the coffee table. The photocopy of the numbers that were written down and stuck in Gabby's cookbook caught Katie's attention. She had memorized the nine digits: 1 7 3 9 2 1 5 4 7. Denise in the records division had tried a variation of phone numbers, Social Security numbers, and even business ID numbers, but nothing seemed to come up with anything tangible.

"What are these numbers?" she said quietly. "Gabby, why were they so important?"

There were so many secrets, clues, and hiding places that it almost made Katie's mind spin. She needed to get to bed, but she wouldn't be able to sleep if she didn't try to look up some things first.

Katie couldn't get past the bunker at the wrecking yard. It seemed to indicate that the killer, or killers, made sure they had hiding places—like with the foreclosed houses. It was a perfect way to hide for a few days or a week without anyone knowing about it. If planned strategically, a person could move from one to another easily, especially when the properties were in rural areas.

Katie opened her laptop and waited for it to warm up. She made another cup of chamomile tea and returned to the coffee table. She sat on the floor. It was uncomfortable, but it kept her awake.

She typed up several coordinates and used Sequoia County as her first searches. She had already run a few searches on foreclosures, but she'd kept them near the houses they had searched. Now she broadened the area. Most foreclosures were in rural areas that had farmland, which was sad that an entire farm or livestock ranch couldn't pay its mortgage. She began to read through the areas and marked several that were near Tessa's crime scene and the two houses where there was evidence the killer had held victims. At first, Katie couldn't make heads or tail, but then she noticed that most of the property identification numbers of the foreclosures, the PINs, began with 1 7 dash 3. Just like on Gabby's note.

"Okay, we're getting somewhere."

Most PIN numbers were fourteen and fifteen digits, so had Gabby only recorded a partial number? Then Katie wondered why the Reys had these numbers and what was important enough about them for her to write them down.

A working theory came to Katie: What if Gabby and Samantha were trying to help the missing girls? What if they were working together? It was possible. Maybe they needed to look at the situation from all angles.

Katie leaned back against the seat of the sofa. Maybe she'd been looking at everything wrong. From the most obvious perspective only. It was possible that Samantha had tracked down Gabby and then, whatever happened or how it transpired between the two, they decided to join forces.

Katie knew it was a longshot, but she remembered when she spoke to Gabby that she seemed to be holding back on possible information and was fervent about the detectives solving the murders.

One of the searches she ran completed and notified her of the results. She was able to dismiss right away several of the foreclosures listed: individual condos, mobile homes, and apartments. She reduced the list to five potential residences that would be quiet, out of more densely populated areas, and where the PIN began with the first digits of Gabby's list.

Noticing one of the apartment complexes had been vacant for more than two and half years, she brought up photos and last known listing prices. There wasn't a year listed, but it seemed old. It was within a mile and half of Gaines's residence. That gave her pause, but she didn't think it would be a good match. There was no electricity and the building structure looked extremely unstable and potentially dangerous, but she'd check it out if she had time. Looking at the photos of the twelve apartments, they were really run-down. They had been nice at one time but for whatever reason it was one of those properties that fell on hard times and no one wanted to try to remodel and fix them up again. Perhaps it would be more beneficial for a buyer to knock down the existing structure and build new ones.

Katie focused on the five homes that would be a good place to hide—specifically to hide little girls. As she viewed each property profile, a couple of them only had the exterior views, making it difficult to form an educated opinion of the interior. It was a longshot, but since they had no way of knowing the situation status of Emily, if she was still in the area, still alive, they had to cross potential properties off the list.

Out of the five homes, she decided two needed to be checked out immediately—they were in reasonable condition and isolated, set along roads with little passing traffic. The other three didn't fit the criteria so well but had to be searched anyway.

Katie was fading fast. She would begin again in the morning. As soon as she climbed into bed, she fell asleep immediately.

It was shadowy around every corner in the bunker or basement. There were no lights except for faint glimpses from outside, but she kept walking directly into the darkness. She heard the little voice saying, "Katie... Katie... I can't see you."

Katie moved faster until she was running, but the long dark corridor kept getting longer. The little girl's voice became faint—

as if farther away. She ran even faster and could barely catch her breath.

"Emily, is that you?" said Katie.

"Please... Katie... I can't see you..."

The faster and farther Katie went, the softer the little girl's voice became until she couldn't hear it anymore.

Katie stopped turning around in a three-hundred-sixty-degree direction. There was nothing but darkness... never-ending darkness.

Until she felt someone touch her...

Katie woke with a start breathing heavily and covered in perspiration. She threw the covers off her body and waited until her pulse returned to normal. She looked to see Cisco curled up in the big upholstered chair in the corner. Obviously, her restless sleep didn't disturb him.

She glanced at the clock, which read 6:10 a.m. It was still dark outside.

Katie contemplated for a moment, but decided she needed to get up and go to work. They needed to keep the investigation moving as fast as they could.

FORTY-TWO

Wednesday 0700 hours

Katie had a renewed strength and focus as she drove into the parking lot of the sheriff's department. It was barely 7 a.m. and she had wanted to get there sooner, but she'd decided to go over a few more details before going to work. In the daylight, Katie was even more convinced about Gabby's numbers and the PINs she had searched. She hoped that McGaven was feeling better and ready to go search the properties.

The department was trying to locate Trent Gaines and the unidentified older man who had played the owner of Sierra Roadside Towing. Katie's anxiety began to slowly rise. Everything seemed much more dangerous—the stakes had risen.

Katie hurried to the back entrance carrying the files. Once inside, she made her way into the forensic division. Her mind still reeled at the new evidence and the recent murders. She realized the body count was high—it was more than any of their previous investigations. The more she thought about it, the more it became almost unbearable. How could she have let this happen? It was the question that resonated in her mind as she walked down the hallway to the investigation office.

Before Katie could open the door, it opened suddenly from the other side.

McGaven stood there. "Hey, partner. I didn't figure you would be in for another hour or so," he said.

"I couldn't sleep any longer," she said.

"Looks like you worked even later," he said, motioning to the files she was carrying.

"Some."

"Anything?"

"Yes."

He raised his eyebrows. "Really?"

"How are you feeling?" she said.

"Rested and sore, but ready for duty."

She smiled. "Okay, I'll fill you in."

"Katie, Gav, you have a moment?" said John. He had come out of the forensic exam room.

"Sure," she said. "Let me put these down." Katie quickly did so and then joined McGaven and John in the examination room. She had some hope there would be something new that would help find Emily—and the killer.

John didn't go to the computers as he usually did. He waited until the detectives were ready.

"What's up?" said McGaven.

"Well, I wanted you both to be up to speed."

Katie waited. She noticed that John was more intense than usual, even more than when they were searching the Bankses' house and the bunker at the wrecking yard.

"First, the bullets that killed Gabby and Ryan Rey were from a nine-millimeter."

"Okay," said Katie.

"But... Gabby was shot first and there was gunshot residue on her husband's hands and possibly on his shirt."

Katie began thinking through the scenario. "But Ryan's injuries weren't that of a suicide."

"That's because it wasn't a suicide."

"How do you know Gabby was shot first?" said McGaven.

"She died at least an hour before her husband. The ME suggested she was dead one to two hours before her husband," said John.

"So Gabby's body lay there for more than an hour before someone shot her husband," she said. "Now we need to figure out who was there."

"Gaines or his boss," said McGaven.

"Most likely, but why did they kill Gabby?" she said. "I had theorized that Gabby and Samantha were working together. Some things didn't add up when I had met with Gabby. She seemed more scared than grieved. I think there was something she was keeping to herself."

"Interesting," said McGaven.

"The nine-millimeter bullets were from a Glock and a Smith and Wesson," said John. He went to one of the desks where there was a small stack of paperwork. "Gabby was shot with a Glock and Ryan with the Smith and Wesson."

"Okay, so that proves there was another person," she said. "Since Gabby was killed and more than an hour went by before her husband was shot... could mean there was some type of confrontation. Or the killer was cleaning up loose ends."

"And maybe, like you said, Ryan killed his wife because she was working on something... like with her friend Samantha," said John.

"She turned against him, you think? Her conscience got to her?" said McGaven.

"We don't know yet," Katie said.

John grabbed a stack of paperwork and handed it to the detectives. "Here's the preliminary report from the computer forensic team. Nothing that stands out, but I'll leave it up to the professionals."

"Thank you, John," said Katie.

Katie and McGaven went back to their office and sat down. Katie updated her partner on her theories from last night and showed him the PINs of the foreclosed properties. They discussed the probabilities and ultimately decided to look at the two properties at the top of Katie's list.

"Where's West?" she said.

"He was exhausted when he left last night. I don't expect to see him until later."

"Did he help?" she said.

"Yeah, he found some inconsistencies with phone calls to Robert Banks's real estate office." He picked up a stack of collated paperwork. "He's actually okay."

"Good. Maybe he can help us when we need information that only the feds have access to."

"Do I detect some sarcasm?"

"No, he's been fine and keeping back."

"Keeping back?"

"He's letting us do our jobs, which he should. But I'm a bit surprised about it."

"I don't know. He was really talkative last night."

"Really?"

"Yeah, I think he's intimidated by you." McGaven smiled.

"I don't think so. He came to my house—twice. Remember?"

"True. He might be a little sweet on you," he chuckled.

"Okay, tick-tock. Let's go," she said.

"I'm ready when you are." McGaven grabbed the computer forensic paperwork to read on the way.

FORTY-THREE

Wednesday 0930 hours

Katie drove toward the first foreclosed listing that was located in the mountains of Pine Valley. It was a breathtaking area where there were mostly newer homes and acreages. It wasn't unusual to have foreclosures in newer developments. Sometimes buyers bought homes with high monthly payments they couldn't afford.

McGaven was quiet as he skimmed the computer forensic report. "This is the most boring reading I've ever read," he finally said.

Katie couldn't help but laugh. "What do you mean? How bad can it be?"

McGaven looked at his partner with a sad look.

"Is there anything we can use or that points to someone?"

"Yes and no. This report is thorough, but it seems to repeat itself over and over but said in different ways. It reminds me of a boring legal brief." He frowned and continued to read.

"Here we go..." Katie knew basically what that meant. They had scoured the files and found anything that could be criminal had been erased. And she speculated that if certain files were looked at, they would immediately be automatically deleted. "Is there anything we can use?" she said again.

"I'm not sure. I have a few questions, which I'll need to ask one of these guys," he said and sighed.

Katie matched her partner's disappointment. "Should have known with all that high-tech equipment and the computer command center, it wasn't going to be amateur hour."

"But even with the best plans... there's always a weakness somewhere."

"I agree," she said. "But Emily is running out of time." Katie clenched her jaw and gripped the steering wheel harder.

McGaven studied his partner for a moment. "I know this is eating away at you, besides the personal things you're dealing with."

"I appreciate your concern, Gav, but I'm fine. I don't let it interfere with work." Katie was partially telling the truth. The fact was she thought about Chad often, and why he hadn't called her since he left was on her mind.

"I respect your privacy, but you know you can talk to me anytime. I haven't heard from him. He didn't say goodbye."

"He had a small party at the firehouse but didn't want to make it a big ordeal. Who knows... he may be back in a few months." Katie looked down. The thought stung but she wasn't really sure what was going to happen except that he was gone.

"You have me and the sheriff, and a ton of other people. We're here for you," he said.

"I know. You're the best, Gav." Katie glanced at her partner and, once more, she knew how fortunate she was to have him in her life.

She tried to shake everything off for now. They were nearing the property. The landscape turned more suburb-like, with nice, bigger-than-average homes. Many were built like large log cabins. The grounds were beautifully landscaped.

"Wow, are we in the right area?" said McGaven.

"Yes. I know these are luxury homes, but a foreclosure is a foreclosure."

Katie drove up a long drive and they saw fewer homes and individual properties. Once at the top, there was a heavy black iron gate.

"Of course there would be a gate. I didn't see it in any photographs," she said.

McGaven looked around and studied the area. "It's not lost yet. Besides, there wouldn't be an alarm set, right?"

Katie pulled to the side and parked.

She quickly got out and looked around. The first thing she noticed was they were higher than most other properties and there was a hillside that was at the front and side of property. "I think we can climb around here to get on the property."

McGaven walked back to his partner. He looked down the side she was explaining and nodded. "We can do that. It's not like a major cliff."

Katie walked up to the front gate and studied the house and immediate surrounding areas. It was a lovely home, but the weeds had overgrown the front yard. It had been empty for about a year. She wondered why no one had bought it.

"You coming?" said McGaven. "Let's do this." He began to step down the hillside to go around the fenced area. "This is easy for someone like you."

Katie joined her partner. Even though it was cool outside, she shed her jacket. She followed his example of treading carefully, one step at a time. It was surprisingly easier than she had thought.

The detectives made it around the end of the fence and found several places to enter.

"Okay, that was fun," he said stomping his shoes to get the mud off.

Katie listened for a moment; it was extremely quiet. She

went to the front door, where there was a key lockbox hanging around the door handle. It was extremely dirty and looked as if it hadn't been used in months. She peered through the windows on each side of the front door. From what she could see, it looked empty and clean.

The detectives took a quick search around the rest of the house and it appeared no one had been there. Katie didn't know if she was relieved or concerned. There were many emotions running through her mind about the case.

Once back at the car, they left the luxury location and headed to the other house.

"You know, your instincts were right. That would make a great place to hole up or hide," McGaven said.

"I agree, but it still feels like we're grasping at straws here. I know there's a lot of stuff to filter through. But..."

"But you don't want to sit and wait. You need to do something."

Katie smiled. "You know me so well."

It took another twenty minutes to get to the next foreclosed property. It was a very different neighborhood to the one they had just been in.

Katie drove up the road. "I'm not sure if this is the right area. Where's the house and driveway?"

"I think over there," he said and pointed just up ahead.

Katie parked on the side of the road. "I guess we walk in. I don't trust not running over something and damaging the police sedan."

She could tell that McGaven wasn't happy about walking into something that was basically the unknown. They both took a moment and looked around them.

"This entire area seems forgotten," McGaven said.

Katie nodded. It did give off a surreal feeling, as if they'd traveled to the past. The oak and pine trees looked different than the other areas. They seemed like they were dying with dried out leaves, spindly branches, and trunks that were thinner than usual. It was quiet. No birds nested in the nearby trees or brush. If she didn't know better, she would have thought the area was in a desert with little rain.

Katie walked to where there was once a driveway. Remnants of concrete and gravel were visible in the overgrown weeds. It looked more like a fire hazard than a neglected yard.

"How long has this been in foreclosure?" said McGaven.

"It has some complications due to the well and structural issues."

"It looks like it was the first house built in Pine Valley."

"They were unusual records. I think there were several people who owned it and then it ended up in probate. So I'm not sure why it's still sitting vacant," she said.

"It would cost a fortune to renovate."

"But the land is still worth something. They could bulldoze it and then rebuild or bring in manufactured housing..."

Katie looked around. There had once been landscaping surrounding the house, like rosebushes, ferns, and fruit trees. The house was a modest one-story, two-bedroom, one-bath home, which was fairly typical of older homes. Half of the windows were missing and replaced with plywood. The front door was missing and also replaced with plywood and various two-by-fours to secure it. The coverings didn't look recent, but also appeared to be easily moved. The house was painted a dark brown, but now was faded in areas, making it look more like an abstract painting.

Katie and McGaven moved slowly on the property, since they knew they could encounter just about anything: wildlife, squatters, or another wild dog.

Katie gave the silent gesture of each of them going the opposite way on each side of the house. McGaven nodded and went to the left and Katie went to the right. The dry weeds crunched under her boots. She made sure each step was a solid one where nothing would impede or cause injury.

Katie walked around the home, seeing more boarded-up windows, but there was an area that resembled a path. The weeds were flattened and there were footprints, not made by animals, but by sneakers.

She immediately stopped. They seemed odd and out of place. She scanned the area to see if there was anything that would indicate someone from the county for water or electricity could have entered the property, but it seemed unlikely. Katie moved forward with caution and came around to the backyard. There were construction bones of what was once a cement patio. It had been cleared and there were no weeds popping up in between the aged cracks.

As soon as she stepped onto the patio, she heard a shot.

Katie hit the ground running to get to her partner. All types of things flashed through her mind and none were positive.

As soon as she was on the other side of the house, she slowed her pace with her back against the building. Her gun was already out of the holster and she kept it out in front of her. She listened intently. The only thing she could hear was her elevated breathing. She didn't hear her partner's voice or anyone else's.

Katie inched forward. Paused. She kept slowly moving forward.

"Get on the ground now!" yelled McGaven.

Katie bolted and was almost to the front of the house when she saw McGaven targeting his gun at the building. Moving closer, she saw there was a man standing at one of the entrances, which used to be a sliding door, and he held a gun pointing at the ground.

Katie joined her partner.

"He shot at me," he said.

"No, I didn't know who you were. I didn't know you were a cop. I thought you were one of them," the man said.

"Put the gun down," said Katie.

"Do it!" yelled McGaven.

The dark-haired man in his thirties seemed conflicted. He slowly put the gun on the ground and took two steps forward.

Katie holstered her weapon. "Who are you?"

"Hugh," he said. "Um... Hugh Rodriguez." It was clear he didn't fully trust them.

"I'm Detective Scott and my partner, Detective McGaven." She studied him. "Hugh, what are you doing here?" She remembered the last name on the paperwork had been Rodriguez.

"I live here."

"This place is foreclosed."

He looked down. "I know."

Katie took a step toward him. "Hugh, you can trust us." In her gut, she knew the man had fallen on hard times, so she decided to change her approach. "We're detectives from the Pine Valley Sheriff's Department."

"My family..." His voice trailed off. "My family owned this house and property. We used to grow fruit trees on the back ten acres."

"What happened?" she said.

McGaven holstered his weapon and waited patiently. He was still shook up about being fired upon. He entered the house to look around to make sure the man's story checked out. A minute later, he came back out and shook his head to Katie, letting her know there wasn't any indication of Emily or the men.

"Just bad breaks. Life. Whatever," the man said.

"Where's your family?" she said.

"Gone. My parents are dead. My brother dead. My wife left with my daughter. Everyone is gone."

Katie watched the man's anguish in his eyes. She knew he was telling the truth. "How long have you been staying here?"

"About three months."

"How do you get food and supplies?" said McGaven.

"I have a motorcycle out back that's camouflaged under some bushes."

"Have you seen anyone around here?" she said.

Hugh looked away.

"Please tell us."

"Bad people."

"What makes you say that?" she said.

"What they do... and those little girls."

That hit Katie like a bomb. "What little girls?"

"They were young like five or six. And—"

"Did they see you?" said McGaven.

"No. I camped out back. There's a small barn. They stayed for a couple of days and then moved on."

Katie watched the man closely. He was scared, but it was clear he knew more. "Hugh, please, can you tell us what they were talking about?"

He shook his head. "No. I don't know..."

Katie had a suspicion he knew a lot more than he let on. "Hugh, I think you know."

"No, I can't—"

"Please, Hugh, we are investigating several homicides and a missing little girl," she said. "Anything you can tell us would be helpful."

Hugh walked out farther and looked around as if he was expecting someone or something. "Look, all I know is they were talking about meeting someone and that they were going to get paid. A major payday, they said."

"Do you know if it was ransom or trafficking?"

"I don't know..."

Katie retrieved her cell phone and pulled a photograph of Gaines. "Is this one of the men?"

He looked and it took him barely two seconds. "Yes, that's one of them."

"And what did the other man look like?" said McGaven.

He shrugged. "I don't know... tall... older... thin... and..."

"And what?"

"His eyes. Cold. Black."

Katie glanced at her partner.

"I'm not going to tell you what to do, but you have to realize that this is a foreclosed property and owned by the bank. It's not safe here. There are places that can help you to get back on your feet." Katie pulled one of her cards and wrote another phone number on it. "If you change your mind, please give them a call. They can help you with a place to live, a job, and some financial and legal advice for this property."

Hugh took the card. "Thank you, Detective. Both of you."

"Take care of yourself, Hugh."

The detectives walked back to their car.

"Detectives!" said Hugh, running across the front yard to meet them.

Katie turned to face him.

"I don't know if this helps or not, but they did mention someone else."

"What do you mean?" she said.

"I don't know... it's just they had someone they answered to. A boss or something. Maybe a business? That's all I know."

"Okay, thank you."

Katie and McGaven left the property and headed back to the police department.

FORTY-FOUR

Wednesday 1215 hours

Katie and McGaven entered their office with more information but no idea where to find Gaines and the other man. Katie stood in front of their investigation walls. What were they missing? They had more information, but they seemed to be following two steps behind the suspects. There was still no proof or direct evidence yet that they killed the Banks and Sanderson families, the Reys, and Tim Denton.

The words *Fishing for souls* and *You'll never find her* were at the top of the board. They had to mean something to the killer. Katie was sure it was at the crux of his perspective and mindset. The photograph of the family of four that Samantha hid was also important, but Katie didn't know how or who they were.

Katie began writing a list for the killer profile. She wasn't one hundred percent sure if she was profiling one or two people based on the behavioral evidence, victimology, and autopsy reports, which was one of the reasons she had hesitated to create a profile. But that day there was something instinctive about her decision, she wanted to put down on the board the characteristics of this killer.

> *Organized. High intelligence. Wears a mask of normalcy. Blends in?*
>
> *Knowledgeable of crime scenes. Cleaned up trash. Seems to be practicing? Testing law enforcement? Leaving clues on purpose? Dress in garbage bag? Dress hanging in Reys' closet?*
>
> *Spent considerable time planning. Staying ahead of investigation. Taunting leaving message "You'll never find her." Bragging.*
>
> *Taking advantage of foreclosed houses.*
>
> *Built a bunker. Taking over a wrecking yard—murdering owner.*
>
> *Has a vision?* **Fishing for souls?** *Symbolizing in the mind of serial killers why they hunt their victims.*
>
> *Psychological need? Fantasy? Fulfilling what has been taken? Family? The families lined up and tucked neatly in their beds? Represents order/togetherness? Control? Childhood experiences? Defining moments in his life now being played out?*
>
> *Knows how to recruit—risk involved (most likely will kill them as well). Gets rid of potential witnesses. Inevitable disagreements/Ryan Rey?*
>
> *Technologically trained?*
>
> *Why focus on little girls? Loss of someone? Abused? Abandoned? Representing perfect family?*
>
> *Need never fulfilled.*
>
> *Escalating.*
>
> *Nothing to support child trafficking.*

"I guess searching today's foreclosures has inspired you?" said McGaven.

"Something like that." She stepped back and thought about

the timeline. "Everything began with Emily in the woods and took off from there."

"Actually, it began when Robert Banks had his tires slashed. It was a setup, a means to get what he really wanted. He was doing his homework for finding out more information about the family," he said.

"Right. But it began for us with the family murders. That's where we were drawn into the investigation." She looked at the photos. "The beginning point, where we, law enforcement, were pulled into this entire killer's scenario. And I don't think the killer counted on me running that trail and finding Emily. I think he was going back to the house..."

"To do what?"

"I'm not sure. Plant more evidence to distract us. Bide time. Take files out of the barn. Clean up..." she said. "Because it would have taken more than a day or two for anyone to realize they were missing and go looking for them. I think the killer thinks and rethinks everything."

"Obsessive-compulsive overthinker?" he said.

Katie's phone chimed. She picked it up hoping it was about Emily, but it was the medical examiner's office.

"We need to go talk to Dr. Dean," she said.

Katie and McGaven stood in the hallway of the medical examiner's office. Their moods instantly dropped. It didn't matter how positive things were going, it was like the morgue sucked any happiness right out of them as soon as they entered. There were so many bodies without souls that came through the office. Sometimes Katie could feel the mood; the natural causes versus the homicides and suicides. Sadness, anger, and a feeling of wanting to flee were some of the emotions she felt.

Katie noticed there were more technicians than usual, which meant there were more bodies coming in. Most deceased were there from natural causes, medical emergencies, or accidents, but it was still disturbing. She watched the men and women move bodies and sanitize rooms, which made the disinfecting smells that much more heightened.

Since the examination rooms looked full, Katie decided they should go to Dr. Dean's office to wait. She was anxious, and was hoping for something they could run with instead of having to be reactive when something came in.

"Detectives," said Dr. Dean as he poked his head into the office. "Come this way."

Katie looked at McGaven with curiosity and then they followed the medical examiner to the first examination room, which was the largest and primarily used for teaching or a big investigation. There were two tables, one holding Gabby and the other Ryan. Seeing the couple lying side by side in death made Katie cringe and think about the Banks family lined up together.

"So, I assume John let you in on the fact that they were both shot with a nine-millimeter, but from different guns."

"Yes," she said. "A Glock, and a Smith and Wesson."

"Correct." He moved to Gabby. "Both were in good health. No drugs, either prescription or otherwise, were found in their systems. Gabby Rey was shot in the back, just once, which penetrated her heart, causing instant death." The doctor picked up her hand and turned it over. "She had written in blue ink four numbers: one, five, seven, two."

McGaven instantly wrote down the numbers. Katie thought about the small piece of paper they found in the cookbook.

"Does it mean anything to you?" said Dr. Dean.

"Maybe," she said. "Anything else?"

"No defense wounds because she was running away from the shooter."

"What about Ryan Rey?" said McGaven.

"Not much except two bullets directly in the chest, close range. That's why there are burn marks and stippling."

"His hands tested positive for GSR?"

"Yes. But, it's a bit strange."

"How?" she said.

"Well usually when someone shoots someone, there's GSR on their hands and it also transfers to the clothing like the sleeve cuff or the front of the shirt. But this was just the hands."

"I see." It was possible someone else could have shot Gabby and then shot Ryan with the other gun.

"Over here," Dr. Dean, said rolling in another gurney, "Tim Denton, fifty-seven, poor health, smoker, took pills for his heart, high blood pressure, and diabetes."

Katie looked at the man's body, which had been smashed and broken. It was difficult to look at him. His elbows, knees, and ankles had compound fractures so they could fit into the auto garage drain. The body had been going through the stages of decomposition and it was impossible to see his facial features. "How long has he been dead?"

"About three months."

"Why is he in such an advanced state of decomposition?" she said.

"Even though he was put into a small space, it was warmer in the car garage than the outdoor environment, making the decomposition process accelerate. It makes it a bit more difficult to estimate TOD." He moved around the body. "Taking in the area, temperatures, and the stage he's in, I put it at three months, give or take a few days."

"What was his cause of death?" she said.

"Well, if you see here," he said, indicating Denton's chest, "there are wounds similar to the Banks and Sanderson families across the chest."

Katie grimaced as she looked at the body. It was difficult to see the wounds due to the purplish and blackened skin, but she leaned closer and could see two long cuts similar to those that killed the families.

"He likely bled out or possibly had a heart attack. Then all these battering injuries that appear to have been done by something like a bat or a two-by-four are postmortem. It's definitely overkill, but unfortunately not something I haven't seen before. Then the joints were broken with any type of heavy tool to be able to fit into the space where you found the body."

Katie thought about the description of *overkill*. It resonated in her mind. She didn't see overkill with the families or the Reys. Was the killer escalating? Or was it done by someone else?

"The tools used were most likely found in the auto garage," said McGaven.

"I believe John has all the tools documented and they're still in the middle of testing them," said Dr. Dean.

"Is there anything else from your examination?" Katie asked.

"It's obviously officially a homicide. But there's nothing else. Everything will be emailed to you."

Katie glanced at the bodies one more time. She theorized that Mr. Rey found out what his wife was doing and killed her. Then, someone came to the house. Maybe he called them to report what had happened. But who? And why? And then the person thought Mr. Rey was a loose end and killed him.

"Katie?" said McGaven.

"There's nothing more for now. Thank you, Dr. Dean."

The detectives left.

FORTY-FIVE

Wednesday 1545 hours

Katie and McGaven grabbed a quick bite and returned to the office. After viewing the bodies at the morgue, the investigation seemed more intense than ever. The detectives entered their office again and Marshal West was waiting.

"West," said McGaven.

"Detective," said the marshal. "I like what you've added to the board. I see you're working on the killer's profile."

Katie put her things down. "It's a work in progress."

The marshal looked tired. "I've been in meetings with my boss. It looks like they're going to be ordering me back to work another case."

"Is that because the murders of the Banks family don't seem to be related to their witness protection status?" she said.

"Yeah. But they haven't pulled me yet. I want to help until then."

Katie thought about it. There was still a large amount of information to sift through.

"We have plenty to do," said McGaven. "I'm going to check

out Hugh Rodriguez's story and see if I can get more info on that property. Maybe there are wildlife cameras nearby?" He groaned as he sat down.

"You okay?" she asked, concerned about her partner.

"To quote you: I'm fine," he said and smiled.

Katie sighed. "Okay, fine." She went to the door.

"Where you off to?"

"I have a couple of questions for John. I'll be right back." Katie left the office. She stopped at the closed door of the forensic examination room. It was usually open, so she thought she might check back later.

"Don't just stand there," said John behind her. He was holding a steaming cup of coffee.

"Hi."

John stepped in front of her and opened the door. "C'mon in. I get the feeling you have something on your mind."

Katie went into the room. There were several items laid out and she saw the tools from Sierra Roadside Towing yard.

John didn't take a seat; instead, he leaned against one of the tables. "What's up?" His dark eyes seemed to watch her with curiosity.

"I'm having a difficult time with some of the evidence. My profile seems to be lacking and I'm not sure why." Katie felt vulnerable admitting she didn't have her profile in line and she hated feeling vulnerable.

"What can I do to help?"

"Can you walk me through the tools from the tow yard?"

"Of course." He walked to the items. "Is there something specific?"

"I want to understand the circumstances. The two families were killed with a plan and preciseness. But the owner of the tow yard... it was frantic and brutal... It contradicts the main profile."

"Maybe the killers are different people?"

Katie nodded. She was more interested in the behavioral evidence and the signature.

"There were a lot of smudged fingerprints all around the auto bays, and there were a number of them that belonged to Trent Gaines."

"Makes sense, he worked there," she said.

"There were two sets that we can't identify. Not in the system."

Katie was disappointed. "What about the tools?"

"The same. But, I was able to reconstruct what tools were used before and after death." John went to the area where there was an oversized wrench, handsaw, pliers, Bowie knife, and screwdriver. "From the massive head wounds, he was struck with the wrench. That rendered him unconscious, didn't necessarily kill him right away," he said and indicated the tool. "And then it was a free-for-all with the cuts and smashing. Before some of the smashes and breaking of the joint, the two slices to his chest were made."

Katie thought about the situation. It didn't match the other murder crime scenes. "Thank you."

"What else is bothering you?"

"I've discovered that the numbers that Gabby Ray wrote down and slipped in her cookbook seem to match property identification numbers."

"Shouldn't Gav be helping on this?"

"He's swamped with other lists and he's hurting from the attack the other day."

"Attack?"

"When he was leaving Pine Valley Elementary School through the maintenance area, someone got the drop on him. He has bruised ribs, not to mention a bruised face."

"Okay." John moved to his computer. "What are the numbers?"

They were burned in her mind. "One, seven, three, nine,

two, one, five, four, seven and the four digits on her hand: one, five, seven, two."

John typed in the numbers and one property popped up. "Looks like a foreclosed apartment building." He looked at the photo. "Wow, looks more like the backdrop to a horror film."

Katie looked over his shoulder. "This property came up on my initial list, but it's so rundown, looks dangerous, and there's no electricity or water running to it."

"That it does."

"I'm going to check it out," she said.

"Wait. By yourself?"

"I'll be fine. Maybe I'll bring the marshal with me just in case." Katie wasn't worried about it, but they needed to check all the foreclosures that could be a place to hide out.

"I'd go, but we're swamped here. And Eva's at a burglary."

"Don't worry about it. I wasn't expecting you to go. You're doing far more important work here." She smiled. "Thanks, John."

He gazed at her for a moment but didn't say anything.

She left and returned to her office, where McGaven and West were working on searches and paperwork.

"Okay, I'm going to check out one more foreclosed property," she said.

McGaven stood up to go and he grimaced.

"No, Gav, I'm going alone."

"I don't want you going alone," he said.

"I'll go," said West. "I agree with your partner. You shouldn't go somewhere like that alone, law enforcement officer or not."

Katie studied the marshal for a moment. "Sure. Meet you out at the car." She turned to McGaven. "We'll be fine. Be back soon. It's going to be another long day."

FORTY-SIX

Wednesday 1620 hours

The daylight was fading and clouds were rolling in. Katie programmed the sedan's GPS as Marshal West got in. They left the parking lot and headed in the direction of the foreclosed apartment complex. She wanted to make it quick so she could get back to help McGaven.

"How did you find this property?" said West.

"I did a foreclosure search, which gave quite a few properties. Then I whittled them down by trying those with PINs, including the numbers written down by Gabby Rey."

"Good find."

"Then she had four digits on her hand."

"And it's the identification number for the property we're heading to?" He seemed impressed.

"That's why I'm checking it out. Just to eliminate the property as a potential base for the killer."

"You don't think someone might be there?"

"No, but we'll be able to tell if someone has been there and hopefully there will be forensic evidence and some answers."

"And clues. I get it." He watched the scenery. "I think I've learned more from you and McGaven than in my entire, short-lived career."

Katie took the road heading to the property. Almost instantly, the road narrowed and there were fewer cars. The countryside was beautiful with low valleys and a view of the mountains in the distance. The homes and farm acreage became farther apart and the forest became denser.

"We should be there in…" Katie looked at the GPS. "About ten minutes."

"So, I was reading your killer profile. Does it really help? I mean, does it help in the investigation? It seems to me that following the clues and talking to suspects wouldn't really benefit by a vague profile," said West.

"I understand what you're saying. Most people believe that a profile is some vague, generic view of the killer."

"I didn't mean to—"

"I get it. But a working profile consists of the behavioral evidence, forensics including autopsy reports, and victimology."

West nodded as if he was beginning to understand. "Is it true serial killers have issues with their mothers?"

"Not necessarily. But it can definitely be a manifestation from childhood. Traumas. Learned traits from repeated abuse along with their toxic surroundings. There can be so many variables."

"Why do you think that? I mean, some people can have a terrible childhood, but that doesn't mean they will start killing people."

"True. We're all individuals in how we respond to certain situations. Some people can handle abuse, while others protect their psyches in other ways. If there was an equation, then we would be able to stop them before they start."

"Makes sense."

"Do the marshals use profiling?"

"I wouldn't say officially, but they do make lists like what you've done."

Katie thought about how criminal profiling could be another set of tools for them. She knew many police agencies didn't want to spend the time putting them together, even though they could give more insight into who the killer was.

Katie came to the end of the gravel dirt road. It was clear heavy rains in the past had wreaked havoc on the drive and caused deep gullies along the sides. She drove as far as she could before parking the police sedan.

"This is it. It won't take long," she said as she unhooked her seat belt. She stepped out into muggy and heavy air. She looked up and saw dark clouds.

"Looks like it's going to rain," said West.

"We have enough time to check it out before it does."

From what Katie could deduce looking at the property, in the middle of the front of the one-story apartment complex there was a circular drive with the units' parking places down each side of the building. It had most likely been attractive and inviting at one time. The location wasn't far from shops and facilities, about twenty to thirty minutes.

A rumbling sounded in the distance—thunder was accompanying the dark clouds overhead.

The overgrowth around the building was immense, making it difficult to see the car parked at the street. There was a dilapidated fence that was now lying on the ground under the weeds and encroaching forest debris.

Katie walked to the entrance, which was where tenants would pick up their mail and anything else. She assumed there would probably have been a manager on duty. There were two large pieces of plywood over the doorways, but they were loose and it was easy to enter. She noticed there wasn't trash or graffiti around the building, so it was unlikely that kids had been partying there.

She pulled back the wood and glanced to West. The marshal helped to hold the plywood as they entered.

Inside, it was how you would expect an old building to look and smell. It was musty and the walls were full of holes. Wires hung precariously. There were ceiling tiles scattered, broken on the floor.

Katie stepped carefully. She surveyed the main area but didn't see anything unusual or recent. There was no trash or footprints—nothing that would indicate anyone had been there recently. West moved to the right looking around. He kicked some of the ceiling tiles and examined the area.

"I'll check out this way," West said.

"Great. I'll go this way," she said, indicating the left wing. "We'll meet back here." Katie's hope was now dwindling as they walked through another ghost building.

Katie moved toward the wing and could see six apartment doors. The area was cleaner and she could see the old carpet. There were no leaves or debris as in the main entrance. She took a few minutes to look in each apartment—two of them were missing the front doors. The apartments she inspected were empty and looked like the hallway with the same rotting old carpeting.

She still had one apartment to search when a gunshot rang out.

Katie immediately ran out of the apartment she had been exploring. "West!" She pulled her weapon and ran down the hallway to the other wing.

"Katie!" he yelled.

Katie was relieved that he was okay. "West!"

She reached the end and saw him lying on his side with his gun next to him. Kneeling, Katie checked him out. His face was bloody and he held his arm, obviously in pain. "You okay?"

"I... someone came out and clubbed me in the head and arm..." he managed to say. "I got one shot off."

Katie looked around and saw the bullet had hit above the nearby window. "Where did they go?"

"That way," he said, indicating the door leading outside. It was still ajar. Wind whistled through the opening as thunder boomed in the distance.

"Stay right here. I'm going to call it in. You sure you're okay?" She looked at the stunned marshal trying to push himself into a sitting position.

He nodded.

Katie pushed the door open, staying close to the side of the building. She skimmed the wall with her body and continued toward the back of the property. Noticing flattened areas in the weeds, she continued with extreme caution.

She retrieved her phone but there was no signal. She pressed the emergency button to call the police but it didn't go through. She kept moving on high alert. There was a maintenance door slightly open—it gently tapped against the frame, something blocking the way.

She hadn't been a police officer as long as she had to not pay attention to that little voice in her head. Something plagued her. She couldn't quite pinpoint what it was but everything at the property seemed—out of place. The front entrance was easily accessible, no garbage strewn around, certain areas cleaned up, and it was too easy. It was like following a trail someone was creating. Pulling invisible strings. Her mind worked the scenario and the killer's behavior.

Katie stayed against the side of the apartment building and looked back to the door she had come through. The events of the investigation filed through her mind. Her gut told her it wasn't Gaines or the unknown older man orchestrating this. Something wasn't right. But who? In theory, it could be anyone who attacked West. Maybe someone was squatting there? Maybe they'd interrupted some type of criminal activity?

Katie decided to retreat and check on West. He was a relative rookie and she wanted to make sure he was safe and didn't do something rash. She slipped back in the door. West was now standing and leaning against the wall. He had his weapon out and was looking all around as if someone would appear to attack him again.

"You sure you're okay?" she said.

"Did you see anyone?"

"No, but I need to check out a maintenance area and the rest of the complex. Are you okay to back me up?" Katie hated relying on someone she didn't know well and who was fairly inexperienced, but he was all she had.

"Yeah, I'll cover you."

Before she could exit the door again, they heard a little girl crying.

Katie stopped as every nerve in her body heightened. Did she really hear what she thought she had heard? It was coming from where she had just been searching in the other wing.

"This way," she said. Her mind swirled. Could it be Emily or some other little girl? She moved as fast as she could, pausing only where there was a window or doorway to an apartment.

Fishing for souls...

Katie had cleared everything except the last apartment, which was larger than the previous ones. She stopped at the door. Using hand signals she directed West to stay on the left and she would enter and stay right. She glanced to the marshal, who now seemed relaxed. The behavior seemed odd to her.

She had been trying so hard to figure out who the killer was... he wasn't like one of the hired thugs. He was different and most of her profile told a story about him... She thought about the hooks again. Something about them had stayed with her. They seemed to be a symbol. Something that had made such a lasting impression that it catapulted the killer into a frenzy of trying to make things right again.

Katie kicked the door wide open. Directing her gun out in front of her, she took short steps, and was ready for anything. Her mind flashed back to one of her tours in the Army when she and Cisco led her unit into unknown danger. She moved with swift efficiency and control as her military experience surfaced.

Emily sat in the corner of the main room wearing a dirty dress and still clutching her teddy bear. Her blonde curls were ratted and filthy. Her bright blue eyes told an entire story. You could almost see everything she had been through just by looking into her eyes.

Katie's adrenalin flooded her system, causing a violent jolt to her body. She gasped and felt lightheaded as she saw the little girl—she was apprehensive that Emily was merely in her imagination.

Standing in the middle of the room was a tall man with darting black eyes, unrelenting, as he smiled at Katie. She recognized him immediately as the man who had identified himself as Tim Denton, owner of Sequoia Towing.

"Drop your weapon!" she yelled. "Do it now!"

The man smiled and glanced to West and back to Katie.

"Drop your weapon!" she repeated.

The man moved forward two steps.

Two quick shots blasted him in the chest and he crumpled to the floor.

Katie turned toward the marshal. "What are you doing?" By killing the man, she wouldn't be able to squeeze him for information about the murders or other little girls.

And in that instant everything tumbled into place with the force of a wrecking ball. Katie knew. Imagining a child who had been berated, expected to do things beyond their capability, and seeing a family dysfunction that helped to create a serial killer persona. Abuse. Watching horrible things against a family member—specifically a sister. She kept her gun steady, turning slowly to face West. His expression had changed, he appeared much older, hardened, and his face seemed to have morphed into an entirely different person.

"You," she managed to say.

FORTY-SEVEN

Wednesday 1845 hours

McGaven worked diligently, going through files and paperwork, glancing at the time, and expecting Katie to be back any moment. He thought about calling her, but he knew that would annoy her.

The office phone rang.

"Detective McGaven."

"You and Detective Scott need to come up the sheriff's office," said the sheriff's administrative assistant.

"Scott is out in the field and won't be back for about forty-five minutes."

"Then you need to come up."

"Okay, I'm on my way," he said.

McGaven dropped everything and went upstairs. He wondered what was up, but he was sure it had to do with the cases. Maybe it was about Emily. And if they were being summoned to Sheriff Scott's office, it wasn't good news.

McGaven stood at the assistant's desk.

"Go on in, Detective," she said.

McGaven took a breath and straightened his shirt before opening the door. He saw the sheriff talking with a tall man in his forties who had a badge and gun holstered. He looked official and he had a very serious expression on his face.

"Sir," said McGaven as he stood across the desk.

"Detective McGaven, meet Marshal Kyle West. There were other cases that stopped him from getting here any sooner," said the sheriff.

McGaven didn't say anything at first. He was stunned, looking at the man.

"Detective?" said Scott.

"I... Sir, Marshal West is already here."

The man standing with the sheriff shifted his weight and looked confused. "I'm sorry, Detective, but I'm Marshal West and I've just arrived."

"Sheriff, a man came a week ago identifying himself as Marshal West and has been working with us."

"What? Where is he?"

"He's with Katie and they went to a foreclosed location to check it out."

The sheriff picked up the phone. "Commander, we need to get officers, SWAT, and anyone else ready to be deployed at a foreclosure location. I'll have details momentarily." He hung up the phone. "How is this possible?" said Scott. He was clearly angry but kept his composed demeanor.

"He had identification and we didn't question it. There was no need to," he said feeling sick to his stomach. In a heartbeat he realized everything this meant. "That means Katie is with the killer. And he's been cleaning up his loose ends..."

McGaven hurried back downstairs to get the exact location to forward to the sheriff. His mind went in so many directions. They had been giving the killer all the investigative information. He knew everything. He'd been smart enough to keep out of the way of Katie and McGaven's superiors, and then come back when the sheriff wouldn't be around to ask questions.

McGaven forwarded the address information, the property layout and building condition to the sheriff.

John poked his head in. "Hey, did Katie get back yet?" He saw the expression on the detective's face. "What's wrong?"

"Marshal West is an imposter. The real one just arrived and is with the sheriff."

"What?"

"So Katie is with the killer at that remote location."

"What can I do?" said John.

The sheriff appeared and walked into the detectives' office. "This is what I want you to do." He gave McGaven some keys. "I want you to get Cisco and follow everyone up to that property."

"And?" said McGaven.

"Based on Katie's reports of how the killer hides children and leaves dead people behind, we may need Cisco to find Katie, and anyone else." The sheriff took a step closer to McGaven. "And if we can't find Katie, you are going to work Cisco. Understand? We're losing daylight."

"Yes, sir." McGaven didn't know how he was going to work the dog, but Cisco would know how to find Katie after the search command. McGaven took the keys.

"I'll meet you up there," the sheriff said before he left.

"Hey, I'll cover you if you need it," said John.

"C'mon, let's go."

FORTY-EIGHT

Wednesday 1845 hours

Katie stood in the middle of the rundown apartment staring at the man she'd thought was Marshal West. Her memory recalled the first visit to her house. He even looked different now, his posture and expression, and he didn't look like the young man who had knocked on her door in the middle of the night. Her heart pounded. Her mouth felt dry. The adrenalin was still pumping, making her hand tremble. She watched as the killer took his aim from Katie and turned it to Emily. Katie knew she could kill him but couldn't guarantee that Emily wouldn't be killed or hurt during the shooting.

"What's wrong, Detective? Calculating the risk assessment and don't like the odds?"

Katie gritted her teeth and couldn't stop wanting to kill him where he stood.

"Ah, Detective, I've had plenty of time to study you, see how you approach things. It's quite intriguing, perhaps even inspiring. I've been in your house. I've read your reports and I've seen your profile on the killer."

"Put down your gun and we can walk out of here," she said. "You still have a chance of life behind bars."

He laughed. "Oh, *we* are going to walk out of here, but you are going somewhere else."

Katie remembered the photograph of the family found at the school. "So what happened to your sister?"

"Here we go. You want to stall so you can figure out how to get out of this predicament. It's not going to work. I know you."

"Your dad was a mean, even brutal man," she said, watching the killer's reaction. Even though it was slight, she knew she'd hit on something inside him. "You and your sister were both abused. Maybe your mom couldn't protect you anymore—or maybe her cold and strict attitude left you alone and afraid."

"Don't speak about my mom. You don't know anything. You're very intelligent and have some intuition, but you don't know anything about me. I've seen unspeakable things. Abuse. No little girl should have to go through that—it's better that they die now, innocent, than with pain and suffering and with no chance at a regular life. But I make the decisions now—who dies and who lives!" He took a step toward her and stood in front of her gun. "Put it down or I'll shoot the girl." He stared hard at Katie. "Don't test me, Detective. I've had lots of practice. All kinds of information is so easy to come by now. My research led me to your town through website chat rooms. It's amazing how desperate people will give out personal information. Mrs. Banks had a lot more than she should have... She didn't have the stomach... she was getting too close."

Katie knew he was telling the truth—he would kill Emily. "This isn't about money or trafficking. This is about your fantasy. Don't give me that poor 'pitiful me' story." She didn't lower her weapon. "It's about setting things right. I have news for you: it'll never be set right."

"You don't know anything. I'm making a difference, and sometimes, innocence is lost and must die to make room for the others. Colorado was a perfect place to complete my mission. But when I found the Banks family—it was sheer genius and some luck of getting what I wanted. I was going to make sure that those little girls didn't suffer like my sister. I researched the witness protection and everything about it, including the marshals."

Katie knew she was striking some chord with him and he was trying to cover with the trafficking story angle early on at her house. He seemed lucid but she had the distinct impression that he fought with delusions. "You really think you're going to find your sister? Or make things right by making others pay for what she went through?"

The man fired the gun toward the ceiling.

Emily began crying again.

"Stop!" said Katie.

"No more of this nonsense." His eyes dilated and looked black, almost demonic in appearance.

"You know that's not your sister." She tried to trigger him.

"Of course, but she will join her if you don't do what I say," he said, but his voice sounded strained. "Put your gun down."

Katie held firm and wouldn't lower her gun.

He smiled and fired directly at her.

FORTY-NINE

Wednesday 1925 hours

It didn't take long for McGaven to catch up with the tactical unit and police vehicles heading toward the apartment complex. He'd redlined his truck.

"We're going to get there in time," said John. "Katie can handle herself."

McGaven was focused but worried about his partner. These cases had been extra taxing and his partner had also been dealing with the loss of Chad. He worried she might find Emily's body and what that would do to her.

John tried Katie's phone again. No answer.

"She's not going to answer," said McGaven.

"The signal is sketchy out there."

It didn't matter to McGaven. He knew every second counted.

"Hey," said John.

"I'm okay."

"I know these cases have been heavy and they seem to keep on coming."

"That's an understatement," said McGaven. He pressed the gas harder.

Cisco gave a bark from the back seat.

"Is there something else going on?"

McGaven hesitated and wasn't sure if Katie would want her private business shared.

"What is it?" said John. "Is everything all right with Katie?"

McGaven sighed. "Chad called it quits. He's moving to LA. I think he's already gone."

John sighed. "They were the last couple I would ever see break up." He looked out the window. "I'm sorry to hear that. She didn't say anything when we went to the tow yard."

"She wouldn't. She's that way. Stoic. Figuring out her problems. That's what Katie does."

"And she can handle herself. And remember, we don't know if there's anything wrong."

McGaven glanced at John. "We don't know everything is okay."

The radio crackled. "ETA ten minutes," said the SWAT commander.

FIFTY

Wednesday 2000 hours

The hot searing pain ripped through Katie's arm, knocking her off her feet. She lay on the filthy floor writhing in pain. Her ears still rang from the shot. Her gun had dropped from her hand when she fell, bouncing across the room. She rolled to her side to get it but saw the killer had grabbed it.

"I bet you didn't profile that I'd shoot you," he sneered. "Get up!" The killer went to Emily and seized her arm and began dragging her.

The little girl screamed out in pain. "No... no... no..." she cried.

"Stop!" Katie tried to stand and wavered. Blood covered her arm and was dripping down from her fingers. She felt light-headed and unsteady.

"Get up," he said. "It's just a scratch. If I wanted to kill you, you would be dead."

Katie got her bearings. She put her right hand on her left upper arm. It had bled quite a bit, but it was clear that the bullet had gone through the outside of her arm and hadn't hit anything life-threatening. She pushed the discomfort aside and continued to stay alert to when the killer made a mistake or hesitated so she could make her move.

"Go," he ordered.

Katie went out of the apartment and headed down the hallway to the main entrance. He pushed her toward the outside door again, Emily in tow. Katie let her arm dangle in the hope her blood would make a trail. The killer didn't notice what she was doing. Perhaps she would be dead shortly and it wouldn't matter anymore. Once outside, it was dark and the air was cooler and not humid as it was earlier. It felt good against her face.

"Where? Are you just going to kill us here?" she said.

"Detective. Shame on you. I'm not going to kill you." He smiled. "I can't tell you how much fun I've been having watching and waiting. I can blend in anywhere. I've been closer than you think."

She stopped at the maintenance door. It was a foot that was stopping the door from shutting all the way.

"Move the body," he said. "Do it."

Katie opened the door wider and felt faint. She saw the beaten body was that of Trent Gaines. By the looks of him, he had been dead for a while—at least a day. She looked at the killer and then at Emily. The little girl looked weak and scared. Her eyes drilled into Katie's soul.

Katie took Gaines by his ankles and dragged him from the maintenance area. Pain shot up her arm, making her breath heavy.

"Keep going," he said. "Around back. There's a deep ravine. Dump him."

Katie's arm burned with the extreme pain one would expect, and it made her weak. Dragging the body was difficult in the darkness. She could smell the precipitation in the air, which gave her some strength.

"Hurry up."

Katie got Gaines close to the ravine and pushed him over the edge. She stood her ground, wondering if the killer was going to push her down there as well.

"Go," the killer ordered.

"So what's your name?" she said breathless.

He laughed. "Just call me James."

"Okay, James," she said and had a feeling that was indeed his real name.

"I know you think you know me, what drives me, and what my endgame is... but you don't know anything."

"Then tell me."

"That would make a great conversation. Give me your cell phone."

Katie reluctantly retrieved it. She had engaged the tracker app.

James slapped it out of her hand. The phone clattered on the cement. He stomped it and then walked away.

"It *would* make a good conversation. Why don't you tell me?" she said. Katie thought he had some narcissism in his behavioral makeup, so he liked to talk about himself, but he would never take responsibility for what he had done.

"It's wasting time. Move."

"All this time. Why don't you enlighten me?" She ran several scenarios in her mind, but her condition and having Emily with them made everything impossible. "Don't tell me you're afraid."

James's expression changed. His face softened and he appeared as it did when Katie had first met him. It was as if he'd returned to his childhood. "You have no idea and your brief profile didn't even scratch the surface."

Katie remained quiet. She wanted him to talk.

"My life was almost unbearable. My dad never stood up for us. It was my mother who ruled. Her idea of parenting was to

keep us locked up when we weren't cleaning to her exact speci-
fications. I spent most of my youth locked in a room adjacent to
the garage that was filled with old fishing gear. Every kind of
hook and lure hung on the wall. I stared at them for hours imagining all kinds of things and what I was going to do once... I
hated it... almost as much as I hated her... and the family
dynamics." He suddenly stopped talking, realizing he had said
too much. He stared at Katie.

At first, Katie thought he might let them go, but she realized
then it wouldn't fulfill his fantasy and illusion.

"So what you're saying is that your parents were mean and
abusive."

"I'm done talking." James directed her to the maintenance
room.

"Why kill the entire family?"

"To prevent them from existing or bringing more children
into the world."

Katie didn't know what he was going to do next. There
hadn't been any hesitation she could use and her weakened arm
would be a drawback. She didn't want to put Emily's life in any
more danger than it already was.

"Open the door wide."

Katie slowly did what he asked. It was a small room with
electrical panels, old phone lines, and plumbing.

"What do you want?" she said.

"I want what's mine," he said. "I want what I was supposed
to have but was never allowed to be a kid and have a *real*
family."

Fishing for souls...

James pointed down. "Pull it up."

Katie saw there was a trapdoor, most likely used to run
wiring or pipes for the complex.

"Pull it up!"

Katie wrapped her fingers around the lever and used her

body strength to open the hatch. She peered downward. It was difficult to see in the dim lighting, but she saw it was about the size of an average storm shelter. But this one didn't have air pumped in and it was reinforced with metal. After a while, you wouldn't be able to breathe and no one would hear you. It was a dark metal tomb.

Extreme fatigue washed over Katie, causing a weakness in her arms and legs. She had lost more blood than she had first anticipated. Her vision began to blur and she thought she would faint. She wavered and felt extremely unsteady.

"Bye, Detective. What a pity, I really like you. But you're too smart and I can't have you spoiling everything. You're a liability now."

James knocked Katie into the underground maintenance compartment. She hit the floor hard and came in and out of consciousness, her pain waking her intermittently. She heard Emily cry as James dropped her into the hole as well.

James leaned down. "Goodbye, Detective Katie Scott." He slammed the hatch shut, securing it—and then stepped outside and closed the maintenance door.

There was silence.

FIFTY-ONE

McGaven drove up to the apartment complex behind all the police emergency vehicles. Emergency lights were flashing through the heavy mist, giving a dreamlike quality to the location. It hit McGaven hard. The reality of seeing the forgotten property, Katie's empty car, and the isolation of everything in front of him caused extreme anxiety. He didn't feel his own discomfort of his injuries anymore. It was all about finding Katie —safe.

"Let's go," he said getting out of the truck.

Cisco whined and wanted to go.

"Stay, Cisco. We'll be back for you."

McGaven and John headed to the commander and the sheriff.

"All right, everyone, we need to search everything and lock this place down," said the sheriff. "Break up in teams. We don't know what we're dealing with yet. Keep in mind there could be traps and that Katie could be here. There's a rogue person who identified himself as Marshal West, but he is an imposter. He's considered armed and extremely dangerous. Got it?"

"On it, sir," said the tactical teams and first responders.

The commander quickly organized the teams and the locations. "Move out!"

Everyone spread out to search the building, apartments, and nearby property area.

McGaven looked at the sheriff.

"Just wait until it's cleared," said the sheriff. His face was grim. "Let's get some lights out here!"

The radio buzzed with activity. "Clear! Clear here! Apartments one through six clear!" and it continued for the next several minutes. "Apartment one has one body. Gunshot."

McGaven, John, and Sheriff Scott froze.

"Identify," said the sheriff.

"Male, forties to fifties."

"Copy that." Relief washed over him.

More emergency vehicles arrived from the fire department and ambulance.

"Katie is here somewhere and she's alive," said McGaven.

"Katie is a survivor," said John.

They waited until the teams began emerging from the property and it was declared clear.

The sheriff looked at McGaven. "You and Cisco find Katie no matter where she is."

McGaven nodded and ran back to the truck to get Cisco.

"Hey, buddy," said McGaven petting the large black shepherd. "You have to find your mama—no matter where she is." He wasn't going to get emotional, but it was close.

The dog whined and thumped his tail against the seats.

McGaven fitted the dog with a search harness and led him out of the truck. "We can do this."

"I've got your backs," said John as he checked his weapon; he wore the stern look of a soldier going into battle.

They walked toward the building through the misty night, the lights shining down highlighting their outlines. Then the two men and the dog disappeared to the left side of the building.

FIFTY-TWO

Wednesday 2200 hours

Katie stirred. She opened her eyes, but it was pitch dark, making her feel like she was on a precipice hanging over an abyss. The pain was excruciating. Her head ached from the front to the back. She felt a wetness on her arms and knew it was blood. She pushed herself up in a sitting position—pain shot down her arm and back. Her mind was foggy, but all the events of the cases came rushing back to her. How could she have not known West wasn't who he said he was?

There was a weak murmuring in the darkness.

Katie gasped. "Emily? I'm right here, honey."

"Katie..." she said weakly.

It struck a chord with Katie that she remembered her name. "I'm right here." She slowly moved toward where she thought the little girl was, keeping her hands out until she touched her. Pulling her close, she hugged the little girl in the darkness, and whispered, "It's okay... we're going to be okay..."

Katie rocked the little one until she stopped crying. "Okay," said Katie. "Stay right here. I'm going to see what I can find.

Okay?" When Katie let go of the little girl, she began to weep. "I'm right here..."

She crawled first, before she tried to stand up. She felt the area around them and could ascertain that the room was approximately six feet by eight feet. She touched heavy pipes that must've been channeled into the rest of the building. With her fingertips, she could feel the metal that lined the room. When she reached the end, which led into the nearby apartments, there was a gap. She worked her fingers and then her hands to try and make a hole. After a few minutes, she found what seemed to be drywall. It was a very small hole. She put her nose up to it to see if there was any air coming in—but she couldn't detect any.

Sitting back in the darkness, Katie feared they would run out of oxygen before anyone came looking for them. It wasn't a perfectly airtight room, but it was such a low amount of ventilation it was still a danger. Katie already felt weaker. She kept going over all the time she had spent with James, and when he came to her house. He was trying to get a feel for the investigation. He was profiling *her*. She assumed he had also been watching them when he was supposedly off talking to his superiors.

Katie slowly stood up to see if she could reach the hatch. On the very tips of her toes, her fingertips touched the square entrance. She ran her hand around the perimeter, and could feel some air.

She had to stop and rest. The darkness and low oxygen made her senses unsteady, including her balance. She took a step and kicked something. Reaching down clumsily, her hand touched a thin metal rod. As her hands examined it, she realized it was one of those metal bars used to turn water meters on and off.

Taking a moment, Katie slowly and steadily inhaled and exhaled as deeply as she could to ramp up a burst of energy.

Her head felt funny, but she maintained focus. She took up the metal bar and managed to tap it against the opening. It didn't make as much noise as she thought it would and she had no idea if anyone could hear it. But she kept tapping until she had to rest again.

Her arm throbbed and grew in pain, she was breathless, and her body was exhausted.

Katie sat down, hugging Emily to take a break—she fought her tiredness but lost the battle and passed out.

FIFTY-THREE

McGaven gave Cisco the search command, but the dog already had the scent he was supposed to search even without the word. The wind began to blow, along with heavier rainfall. It was cool outside, but he felt his hands sweat holding the dog lead.

John took a wide trail away from McGaven and Cisco, he searched and viewed the property through the weeds to see if there was anything out of place. He had McGaven's back.

McGaven watched Cisco and gave him more leash from six feet to eight feet ahead. The dog went into the search mode with his senses focused on the ground and air. His ears were always straight and front. His body was taut and ready—his focus was unsurpassed.

McGaven relaxed a bit as it was clear Cisco knew what to do.

They went around the building and entered from a doorway that had been removed during the police search. They entered the large hallway and moved into the first apartment where there was a dead body. McGaven recognized the man that had been identifying himself as Tim Denton. Looking around the room, he could tell something went down. There were firearm casings and bullets wedged into the upper walls and ceiling.

"Was there a gun battle?" said John scrutinizing the area as well.

"I don't know."

John bent down and observed blood droplets. "These are fresh and didn't come from that guy."

"Katie?"

"Don't know. If it was, where is she?" said John.

Cisco let out a strange howl and became agitated.

"What's up, Cisco?" said McGaven.

Cisco lowered his nose and led them out into the hallway following a direct line leading away from the other apartments.

McGaven stopped, but Cisco clearly wanted to go.

John kneeled down again. "More blood. Recent."

"Let's go," said McGaven.

Cisco tensed, but his nose never wavered from side to side, or upward, he kept it down and led the men toward the opposite side of the building. Once at the door, Cisco scratched furiously at the frame. The dog began panting incessantly.

John opened the door and Cisco bolted out and led them down the side of the complex before stopping at another door. He barked several times.

John opened the door and held it back with a nearby rock. He looked inside with his gun drawn and a flashlight sweeping the area. There was nothing inside. "Clear."

McGaven tried to lead Cisco away, but the dog wouldn't leave. He pulled on the leash, bit at it, and began barking.

"Cisco."

But the dog wouldn't leave the area.

McGaven didn't know what else to do so he let him move

into the maintenance room. Cisco ran from corner to corner in a frenzy, jumping up, spinning around, but he still didn't alert.

"What's going on?" said McGaven. He thought he might have done something wrong.

John walked into the room looking closely at the walls and corners. He didn't see anything unusual or any blood. He turned to McGaven and shook his head. "I don't know. Maybe Katie was here?"

Cisco slowed down and funneled his scent pattern to the bottom of the room. He sat down and stared at the floor—not budging. His wolf eyes became intense, he panted, and after a few moments barked, looking at the floor and then back to McGaven.

"What is it, boy?"

The dog began scratching at the floor in a fury. His large size seemed to become even larger as he became more intense.

"What's that?" said McGaven.

John looked around them and then bent down to the floor where he could see edges to a trapdoor with a broken lock. He tried to move it, but it wouldn't budge. "It's an opening to a service entrance to where utilities come through. There's something down here."

McGaven spoke into his radio. "On the east side of the building. We need to open a metal door—now!"

In less than two minutes, two SWAT officers ran up with various breaking tools.

"There," said McGaven. "Get it open. Be careful. We don't know if anyone is in there or if it's a trap." He pulled Cisco back.

They watched as the two men worked the opening, having to use a cutting torch. The flame ignited as they cut through, breaching the entrance, the lighting becoming a strange orange color. Once done, the officers tossed the metal square to the side. The strong burnt smell permeated the air around them as the smoke settled.

One of the officers leaned down into the hole, directing a flashlight. "We have two victims. Not moving"

"Is it Katie?"

The officer nodded. "And a child."

"Get her out." McGaven gave Cisco's leash to John and pushed his way to see. "Katie! Katie!" She sat in the corner with a little girl on her lap. They were both unresponsive. "We need paramedics now!" said McGaven into the radio.

One of the SWAT officers lowered himself into the room. Within seconds, he handed up a blonde little girl. She looked like a rag doll and didn't wake as they laid her down gently.

Two paramedics ran to the area carrying gear. Immediately they began to work on Emily with oxygen and CPR.

McGaven and John were helpless as all they could do was watch and wait.

Then Katie was brought up. She, too, was limp and lifeless. The second SWAT officer picked her up and carried her a few feet away from the maintenance door and laid her down. They immediately began CPR. She was covered in blood and it was difficult to determine where it originated and what kind of injury she had.

Cisco began barking and pulling on the leash.

Emily was conscious and began crying. They wrapped her in a blanket. One of the paramedics held her, walking back and forth, until she stopped sobbing.

McGaven and John watched as they worked on Katie. They couldn't get a heartbeat. They kept breathing for her and hitting her with the defibrillator.

"Katie," whispered McGaven. Everything they had investigated together rushed into his mind. He knew she was selfless and wanted to make things better for everyone else, but the thought of losing her like this... She had saved Emily but had sacrificed her own life.

McGaven looked up and saw Sheriff Scott running toward them.

With every jolt, Katie's body didn't respond.

The sheriff watched and didn't say a word. He looked and saw Emily, but the sorrow in his eyes was indescribable.

They waited.

"Got her!" said one of the paramedics.

Finally Katie's heartbeat began again and became strong and steady. She opened her eyes and saw the crowd around her. "What's going on?" she whispered. Her chest hurt like there was a semi-truck sitting on it and her arm burned. It took a moment for her to be present as she tried to calm the intense pain.

Sheriff Scott and McGaven ran to her.

Katie sat up and the world spun a bit before it settled down again. "I'm okay. Where's Emily?"

"She's fine and being checked out before going to the hospital," said the sheriff. He lowered his authoritative attitude and hugged his niece. "I can't imagine what I'd do if I lost you. I love you so much," he whispered in her ear.

"I love you too," she said, holding back the tears. "Did you get him? Tell me you got him."

The sheriff hesitated. "No, we've searched the area and nothing."

Katie stood up and wavered a bit. "Gaines is in the back down the ravine. He told me his name is James and we have his identification on security cameras... we should be able—"

"You've done enough... leave the rest to us," said the sheriff.

"And you need to be checked out," said McGaven as he put his arm around her waist and guided her toward the ambulance.

"It's nothing. Just a graze," she said.

"A graze?"

"The bullet grazed me."

"You'll have a cool scar."

She stopped. "Thanks, Gav." She hugged him.

"I'm your partner. I've always got your back."

John and Cisco joined them.

"Cisco," she said petting the dog.

"We might not have found you if it wasn't for Cisco," said John.

"Oh, Cisco, you're the smartest dog."

The sleek black dog stayed in step with her.

Katie sat down in the ambulance as they checked her blood pressure and tended to her arm and head wound. She watched McGaven put Cisco in his truck. The SWAT officers, police officers, and other emergency personnel were speaking with the commander and Sheriff Scott. She couldn't stop going over what James had told her.

I've been having fun watching and waiting. I can blend in anywhere. I've been closer than you think.

Katie's energy spiked. Her vision cleared, but her bruised chest definitely restricted deep breaths. She watched McGaven and John walk back to the apartment building. Everyone was busy working the area and coming up with a plan.

Katie looked around in the blackness surrounding the old apartments wondering if they would catch James—or would he just disappear as quickly as he had appeared. She thought she saw an outline of a man moving in the darkness. She knew what she had to do and there was no time to waste. McGaven or the team weren't anywhere near her.

Katie left the ambulance and moved to McGaven's truck. She opened the passenger door unnoticed, then opened the glove box. She knew he carried a backup weapon. She snatched it along with a sweatshirt.

Then she made her move and disappeared into the darkness.

McGaven looked around. "Hey, where's Katie?" He walked around searching for his partner.

"What's wrong?" said John.

"Katie's gone."

"What do you mean, gone?"

"Gone."

"Where?"

McGaven ran to his truck and checked his glove box. "I knew it!"

"What?"

"She's gone after him and she took my backup gun."

FIFTY-FOUR

Thursday 0155 hours

Katie knew James was close. He had to be, it was what drove him, watching, waiting; he wouldn't be able to stop his need to know what was happening as he imagined he was in control. He had been successful so far at getting rid of loose ends, so his arrogance and obsessiveness wouldn't let him not watch the police. Even though his delusions of what really happened as a child versus what he had created since contributed to making him into the predator today, it still didn't stop Katie.

Katie moved with renewed strength, her eyes adjusting to the darkness. Her gun was her guide, like that of a divining rod. She was now the hunter and she liked the feeling—being in control. It would be only a matter of time before the police and McGaven were on her trail and then James could slip away forever. That wasn't going to happen on her watch.

She moved with the stealth of a jungle cat and kept up her pace. Looking for the best vantage point to see as large a range of the scene as possible, she moved to that area. It was just short of a longshot, but she wouldn't have another chance once they left the property. She wouldn't stop hunting him until she physically couldn't or if she was dragged away—either way, she was going to find him.

Katie stopped. There was a slight sound in the bushes. It was minor, but still it sounded. It could have been a footstep or a change of position, but it was there.

There it was again.

Katie moved toward it, one step at a time. And then she saw it, the outline of a crouching figure. It moved back and forth and then settled again. It reminded her of a wild animal waiting for the right time to pounce on its prey.

It was just as she'd thought. James couldn't stay away; he was obsessive and compulsive. He needed to see what happened. He knew it was only a matter of time before the police came looking for her, but he also wanted to see them pull her dead body from the maintenance room, watching the pain and anguish of her fellow officers.

Katie moved closer. She was so close she could almost see the color of his eyes. He seemed to be fixated on the police, ambulance, and the sheriff.

Taking inch-long footsteps, she moved in right next to him. Katie placed the gun against his side.

"Don't move." Her voice was steady.

"Detective, you do continue to surprise me." Again, he wasn't taking responsibility that he had been predictable.

"You're coming with me now."

He stood up straight as she kept careful aim on him.

"Not so fast. Easy. And go."

"I have to say you've more than exceeded my expectations. You are something special." He turned to face her. "And that's why it's such a pity I have to kill you."

"Your talk and ego aren't going to save you now. You're a killer. You kill families. Children. You need to be put down like a rabid animal," she said. "Move."

He looked down. "Looks like you're bleeding again. I definitely should have killed you."

"You know you're never going to find your sister or have peace killing those girls. You can't destroy them all and their families... You have no peace... and never will—"

Before Katie could get the last word out, James's arm moved like a cobra and released a knife that hit her right arm. She screamed out and was caught off balance.

James was on top of her, tearing at her injuries and trying to get to her throat. It was like he was a wild animal.

Katie could barely keep herself from being torn apart. She grappled for her gun but couldn't find it. She fought with everything she could, but her strength dwindled quickly.

She thought she heard a dog barking.

Katie tried to keep his strong hands from grabbing her throat and slashing at her face, but he managed to dig his fingers in. His expression seemed to change into an almost demon-like persona. It was what a serial killer battles with every day inside their mind.

The dog barked louder and approached. Crashing footsteps closing the gap.

Katie suddenly realized it was Cisco. She could hear his heavy paws clear the weeds and low-lying brush.

Within seconds, the black dog hit James and dragged him away from Katie. Cisco kept biting to get a better grip. He violently shook the man's shoulder and arm.

James screamed out in pain.

The sound pierced Katie's soul. She got to her feet and spotted her gun, picked it up. "Cisco, *aus.*"

The dog instantly let go of James and returned to Katie's side.

James took his gun from his waistband, aimed it at the dog.

"No!" Katie took the shot and fired.

The bullet hit James directly in the chest, downing him in

the weeds. She ran up to him, he twitched once more, and then stayed still. His eyes fixated and then the life drained away.

"Katie! Katie!"

McGaven and John raced to her.

"You okay?" said John.

"Yeah. Cisco saved my life," she said breathlessly.

"I didn't want to send him into a dangerous situation, but I didn't have any other choice," said McGaven. "He knew exactly where you were and we might not have been able to get to you... in time..."

Katie felt weak again. "Sorry for another crime scene..."

"Let's get you out of here," said McGaven.

John stayed with the body, securing the area. McGaven helped Katie to get back to the apartment complex.

Police personnel swarmed the area.

FIFTY-FIVE

Tuesday 0930 hours

Katie was working on her laptop from her couch at home keeping up on new cases as well as reading some of the news articles about James and his victims. She was on a week leave by orders from the sheriff. Her ribs were still sore and she was also recovering from a sprained ankle. With her wrapped ankle propped up on the couch, she tried to keep herself busy until she was okayed to return to work.

Cisco was snoozing next to her, curled up, and didn't seem to have a care in the world.

The quiet time was interrupted by a knock at the door.

Cisco leaped up and began barking, but his tail wagged in anticipation of someone he knew.

A key was inserted into the lock and the door opened.

"Good morning," said Sheriff Scott. "I'm glad to see that you're actually taking care of yourself." He walked in followed by McGaven.

"Hey partner," he said.

Katie sat up on the couch as her uncle and partner took turns petting Cisco.

"What's happening?" she said.

"I wanted to tell you in person some of the updates of the case."

Katie was completely at attention.

"James was really James Paul Young, age thirty," began the sheriff. "He was originally from Colorado Springs, Colorado. And as best as we can piece everything together, he began his kidnapping and killing spree about eight years ago. His family is deceased. He did have a sister that was kidnapped and murdered—her body was found four days later."

"And, he was crafty," said McGaven. "He knew that he couldn't accomplish everything he wanted alone—so he found people that were easy to manipulate. And, they would be the perfect fall guys if something went wrong."

Katie thought about that night and everything James had said to her. His belief about these little girls and what he wanted to gain by killing them. "He kept Emily alive longer than the others."

"Probably because he wanted to get closer to you," said the sheriff.

Katie wasn't so sure, but it eased her mind that Emily survived. "Did you get an ID on the man claiming to be Tim Denton?"

"A felon by the name of Christopher Connor. In and out of prison his entire life, he was also wanted for felonies across three states." The sheriff sat down next to his niece. "And, the *real* US Marshals along with local and state agencies have assisted with stopping this multi-jurisdictional gang of killers—because of you Katie." He hugged her.

"That's my partner," said McGaven.

Cisco gave a quick bark.

Katie was relieved that this wouldn't continue, but her heart was still heavy that so many people and children had to die before they could stop them.

"Everything okay?" asked the sheriff.

"I'm fine," she said. "Thank you for the update."

He looked at her closely but didn't push. "Good news, you'll be back on duty in a few days."

"That's great. Cisco and I are getting a bit stir-crazy here."

Katie's heart was also heavy that Chad was gone, and it was going to take more than a week, or month, to heal.

"We're going to let you rest. So stay off that ankle too." The sheriff stood up to leave.

"Denise and I will drop off dinner tonight after work. Is that okay?" said McGaven.

"Of course. I may be recovering here, but I still have my appetite." She smiled.

Sheriff Scott and McGaven left.

It wasn't until she heard the vehicle pull away that Katie felt alone—again.

FIFTY-SIX

Two Weeks Later...

Katie received an early text message from the sheriff requesting she bring Cisco to the K9 kennels at the sheriff's department. He said they might need the assistance of her and Cisco today.

Katie thought nothing of it as she loaded up her Jeep and Cisco. She drove into town and pulled into the training area for the Pine Valley Sheriff's Department where the K9 kennels were located and noticed there were more cars there than usual. She figured there was a training event. Sometimes the department would host other K9 teams from various departments to come and train.

She drove around to the back and saw McGaven's truck. Katie parked and got out. She hooked up Cisco. Her arms were still bandaged but getting better every day. Cisco seemed extra energetic and his tailed wagged.

Looking around, she thought it was strange there was no one wandering around, nor any K9 units she could see. She glanced at McGaven's truck, but nothing gave her an indication of what was going on.

McGaven walked out of the building. He smiled.

"Hey, what's up?" she said, noticing her partner seemed upbeat.

"Just thought I'd meet you and Cisco here this morning," he said.

"What's up?" she asked again.

"Nothing." He kept walking.

Katie was confused.

"But... you need to see this," he said.

Katie and Cisco followed him. Instead of going inside like they usually did, they walked around the side of the building. McGaven kept moving at a fast pace; Katie and Cisco jogged behind him to keep up.

"Gav, what's going on?"

As soon as they reached the other side, which was generally used as a large training area with agility equipment, Katie saw a crowd of police officers, K9 units, and various other people waiting, including John. At the front of the group were Sheriff Scott and two lieutenants, who were dressed officially in department uniforms.

Katie stopped. To say she was surprised was an understatement.

Cisco gave two barks to let everyone know of his pleasure to see them.

On one side, there were more than a dozen K9 units from various departments standing side by side. It was a spectacular image of dogs and handlers at full attention.

"What is going on?" she said. "What did I miss?"

Several officers laughed.

"Detective Katie Scott and K9 Cisco, this is your day," said McGaven.

Katie walked up to her uncle. "What's all this for?"

Sheriff Scott smiled but kept his authoritative manner of being the sheriff as he spoke to the crowd. "Today, based on the works of excellence of Detective Scott and K9 Cisco working as a team, I'm going to swear in Cisco as an honorary member of the Pine Valley Sheriff's Department."

There were cheers and hollers from the crowd.

"That's my partner," said McGaven as he gave a whistle.

Katie was stunned, which was unusual. She really didn't know what to say. But then she realized this was her family and they supported one another. There would be no more feeling alone because as she looked around she saw what it meant to be appreciated, loved, and respected. It was family. It was her family.

Cisco gave a couple of spins as if he knew what was going to happen.

Katie took a breath, stood up straight with Cisco at her left side, and waited. Her heart pounded, not in fear or anxiety, but pride that she and Cisco had served in the military saving lives of her fellow soldiers. And now she felt honored once again that she and Cisco had been involved in homicide investigations making a difference.

"We are here today to celebrate the exemplary achievement of Detective Katie Scott and Cisco," the sheriff said. "Not only is Cisco a military veteran that saved countless lives, but he would sacrifice his own safety for his handler without question. He would lay down his life for us without asking for anything in return—except our love and companionship. He would gladly take a bullet for us, take down a bad guy, locate a missing child, or find crucial missing evidence in a cold case. That is the true significance and heroism of a police K9."

Katie kept back the tears, remembering how Cisco had first found and protected Emily on the Bramble Trail.

Cisco seemed to know the sheriff was talking about him and his intensity proved it. He sat up straight, appearing even taller as his black coat glistened. His ears were at attention and he never averted his eyes.

"His service and volunteerism for this department has been nothing but exemplary. So today, as we honor K9 Cisco, I hereby deputize him with my powers as the sheriff of Pine Valley, California." The sheriff moved forward to attach a special K9 badge onto Cisco's collar. Kneeling down, he said, "Do you solemnly swear to uphold the laws, constitution, and to protect the Pine Valley Sheriff's Department and the citizens of our Sequoia County?"

A lieutenant handed the sheriff a Bible. He then lowered it and Cisco put his large paw on it and gave a loud bark. The crowd cheered. Katie couldn't help but tear up, but she remained standing tall. Even though Cisco wouldn't be a full-time police dog, he would still be involved in searches.

"Congratulations, K9 Cisco and handler Detective Katie Scott."

The sheriff extended his hand to Katie and she shook it, but then she leaned in to give her uncle a hug.

"Thank you, Uncle Wayne," she whispered in his ear. Katie turned to the crowd. "I don't know what to say. Cisco and I are in shock, but excited and honored. Well I'm not sure if Cisco is surprised because he probably already knew you were here," she said. "But thank you all so much for being here and supporting us. It means more than you will ever know. We are family."

The crowd clapped and took turns congratulating both Katie and Cisco. There were lots of laughs and positive words. There were deputies that Katie hadn't seen in a while that took the time to come to Cisco's swearing-in. Celebrations and acknowledgements had a way of bringing people together.

McGaven and John waited until most had spoken to the K9 team, before approaching them.

"You knew, didn't you?" Katie said to McGaven.

"Well..." he said.

"You did," she said smiling.

McGaven pet Cisco. "What can I say? I really *can* keep a secret—even from *you*."

"This was really nice and unexpected," she said.

"Is that a tear I see?" he said.

She wiped her face. "It's been overwhelming."

"Congratulations, Katie," said John. He moved in and gave her a hug. "And you too... Cisco the Great." He smiled. "See you both later at the lab." He left the area.

McGaven raised his eyebrows at the display of affection from their forensics head.

Denise moved forward to the group. "Congratulations, Katie... and handsome Cisco." She squeezed McGaven's arm, giving him a quick smile. "See you both later. There are more reports on your desk." She joined the crowd of people heading back to the department.

Katie and Cisco walked to the kennels.

Sergeant Blake Hardy met them. "Great to see you both get the recognition you deserve."

"Thank you."

"We would love to see you both out in training more."

"I know Cisco would absolutely love that. We'll be out soon."

Katie put Cisco in a large indoor-outdoor kennel run and removed his leash. She kneeled down and ran her hands along his neck. "You are the best. I'll be back later and the sheriff will probably give you a break soon." She smiled, still petting him.

As Katie left the kennels she saw McGaven had waited for her.

"You didn't have to wait," she said.

"Don't get used to it. But since it's your day."

"It's Cisco's day," she said and smiled. "Thanks, Gav."

"For what?"

"For being the best partner ever."

FIFTY-SEVEN

Early morning...

Katie with Cisco at her side walked through the cemetery and stopped at the Sandersons' family plot. She stood over Tessa's tombstone, now joining her family with an angel figurine guarding her. She was unable to save this little girl, but she was able to save Emily. It would have to be enough.

A flurry of emotions flooded through her. They were conflicting and difficult, but it was something she had to live with. She still had bandages and stitches to remind her of what happened at the apartment complex, but she had closure of catching a killer. The exterior wounds were only temporary, but the internal ones would take longer to heal.

Katie sat down. She took a moment of silence for the family, then she relayed a prayer.

"Katie!" said a little voice.

She saw Emily running toward her as her blonde curls bounced. A tall dark-haired woman was accompanying her, which she presumed to be her aunt. The little girl ran up to Katie and hugged her tight.

"Katie. I love you."

Katie choked up a bit. "I love you too, Emily."

The little girl then pet Cisco, who had been her protector on that fateful day. The dog loved every minute of it.

"Hi, your partner said you would be here," said the woman. "I hope you don't mind. We're on our way out of town now and Emily wanted to say goodbye."

"I'm glad to see you." Katie hugged the little girl again. "Emily, I want you to be happy. You will always have a guardian angel looking out for you."

"Bye, Katie. Bye, Cisco."

Katie watched Emily and her aunt walk away. Her feelings were full—not just of sadness but with joy. She got up. "C'mon, Cisco."

Katie and Cisco left the cemetery walking back to the Jeep. It was a satisfying day. She knew her life was never going to be the same. But that was okay. She lived by her life motto. If you couldn't help someone, save a life, or make a difference—life wasn't worth living.

A LETTER FROM JENNIFER CHASE

I want to say a huge thank you for choosing to read *Count Their Graves*. If you did enjoy it, and want to keep up to date with all my latest releases, just sign up at the following link. Your email address will never be shared and you can unsubscribe at any time.

www.bookouture.com/jennifer-chase

This has continued to be a special project and series for me. Forensics, K9 training, and criminal profiling has been something that I've studied considerably and to be able to incorporate it into a crime fiction novel has been a thrilling experience for me. It has been a truly wonderful experience to continue to bring this series to life.

One of my favorite activities, outside of writing, has been dog training. I'm a dog lover, if you couldn't tell by reading this book, and I loved creating a supporting canine character, Cisco, to partner with my cold-case police detective. I hope you enjoyed it as well.

I hope you loved *Count Their Graves* and if you did, I would be very grateful if you could write a review. I'd love to hear what you think, and it makes such a difference helping new readers to discover one of my books for the first time.

I love hearing from my readers—you can get in touch on my Facebook page, through social media or my website.

Thank you,

Jennifer Chase

KEEP IN TOUCH WITH JENNIFER

www.authorjenniferchase.com

facebook.com/AuthorJenniferChase
x.com/JChaseNovelist
instagram.com/jenchaseauthor

ACKNOWLEDGMENTS

I'm grateful to all my law enforcement, police detectives, deputies, police K9 teams, forensic units, forensic anthropologists, and first-responder friends—there's too many to list. Your friendships have meant so much to me over the years. It has opened a whole new writing world filled with inspiration for future stories for Detective Katie Scott and K9 Cisco. I wouldn't be able to bring my crime fiction stories to life if it wasn't for all of you. Thank you for your service and dedication to keep us safe.

A very special thank you to A.N.R. for your Navy military service and for allowing me into the world of military working dog training. Thank you for your unwavering support, training, and friendship. I have learned so much with my own hands-on experience about what it takes for K9 training and scent detection work. It has helped to bring alive the K9 searches in my books.

Writing this series continues to be a truly amazing experience for me. I would like to thank my publisher Bookouture for the incredible opportunity, and the fantastic staff for continuing to help me to bring this book and the entire Detective Katie Scott series to life.

Thank you, Kim, Sarah, and Noelle for your relentless promotion for us authors. A thank you to my absolutely brilliant editor Jessie and the amazing editorial team—your unwavering support has helped me to work harder to write more endless adventures for Detective Katie Scott and K9 Cisco.

PUBLISHING TEAM

Turning a manuscript into a book requires the efforts of many people. The publishing team at Bookouture would like to acknowledge everyone who contributed to this publication.

Audio
Alba Proko
Sinead O'Connor
Melissa Tran

Commercial
Lauren Morrissette
Hannah Richmond
Imogen Allport

Cover design
Head Design Ltd

Data and analysis
Mark Alder
Mohamed Bussuri

Editorial
Jessie Botterill
Ria Clare

Made in the USA
Monee, IL
27 August 2024